WIFE OF
MOON

**Center Point
Large Print**

**This Large Print Book carries the
Seal of Approval of N.A.V.H.**

WIFE OF MOON

MARGARET COEL

CENTER POINT PUBLISHING
THORNDIKE, MAINE

This is for
Aileen, Sam, Liam, and Eleanor

This Center Point Large Print edition
is published in the year 2005 by arrangement with
The Berkley Publishing Group, a division
of Penguin Group (USA) Inc.

Copyright © 2004 by Margaret Coel.

The text of this Large Print edition is unabridged. In other
aspects, this book may vary from the original edition. Printed in
Thailand. Set in 16-point Times New Roman type.

ISBN 1-58547-533-5

Library of Congress Cataloging-in-Publication Data

Coel, Margaret, 1937-
    Wife of moon / Margaret Coel.--Center Point large print ed.
        p. cm.
    ISBN 1-58547-533-5 (lib. bdg. : alk. paper)
    1. Curtis, Edward S., 1868-1952--Exhibitions--Fiction. 2. O'Malley, John (Fictitious
character)--Fiction. 3. Holden, Vicky (Fictitious character)--Fiction. 4. Wind River Indian
Reservation (Wyo.)--Fiction. 5. Photography--Exhibitions--Fiction. 6. Arapaho Indians--Fiction.
7. Women lawyers--Fiction. 8. Indian women--Fiction. 9. Wyoming--Fiction. 10. Clergy--
Fiction. 11. Large type books. I. Title.

PS3553.O347W54 2004b
813'.54--dc22   2004014868

ACKNOWLEDGMENTS

My heartfelt thanks to Elizabeth Happy, archivist, Dayton Library, Regis University Denver, for guiding me into the world of Edward S. Curtis; and to Eric Paddock, curator of photography at the Colorado Historical Society, Denver, for guiding me through the technical nuances of early photography. My thanks, also, to Ed McAuslan, Fremont County Coroner, Riverton; Paul Swenson, special agent, FBI, Lander; Richard Ortiz, Riverton; Fred Walker, firearms expert, and Sherrie Wolff, PhD., international political consultant, Boulder; Rob Kresge, former CIA agent, and Anthony Short, S.J., former pastor of St. Stephens Mission;

And to Bob and Marianne Kapoun and Christopher Webster, Santa Fe, New Mexico; Luther Wilson, director of the University of New Mexico Press; and Ann Pruitt, Boulder Public Library, reference department;

And to my husband, George, and my daughter, Kristin Henderson, and to my good friends who read versions of this story and offered suggestions that could not be ignored: Virginia Sutter, PhD., and Jim Sutter, members of the Arapaho tribe; Beverly, Sheila, and Mike Carrigan; Sybil Downing and Jim Lewis;

And especially to Karen Gilleland.

Ho'hou'!

Bi'gushish—the moon, literally "night sun," from *bi'ga,* night, and *hishi'sh,* sun, or celestial luminary.
—Arapaho glossary, in *The Ghost-Dance Religion and the Sioux Outbreak of 1890,* by James Mooney

There was a camp circle along the river. One night when Moon was shining brightly, as were also all the stars, there were young women sitting outside enjoying the night breeze. One of them said that she wished very much that she could marry Moon. Of course Moon heard the remark and immediately began to consider the course of events were he to marry a human being.
—*Traditions of the Arapaho,* George A. Dorsey and Alfred L. Kroeber

1

October 1907

THE THREE WARRIORS sat their ponies against a glass-blue sky broken only by the mare's tail cloud streaming overhead. The October sun turned the wild grasses and underbrush gold and vermilion and sent tongues of fire leaping off the silver spheres that decorated the harnesses. As the warriors started down the slope, brown puffs of dust rose around them. The sun illuminated the white and blue stripes painted on the flanks of the ponies, marking them as war ponies. The warriors were painted, too. Red, white, and yellow stripes ran across brown naked chests and arms. White paint smeared their faces so that their eyes were like charcoal smudges behind white masks. They wore brown buckskin trousers fringed down the sides. Black hair hung long and straight over their shoulders, secured by headbands that each held a single eagle feather. The warriors reined in and stared down at the village.

Village! Jesse White Owl wanted to laugh out loud. A couple dozen canvas [tipis] dragged out of sheds where they'd been folded away for thirty years. The grandmothers had to show people how to erect the tipis because no one else remembered. Still it had taken all day when, in the Old Time, the grandmothers had set up an entire village while the warriors unsaddled the ponies.

"It must be a traditional Arapaho village," Edward S. Curtis had said three days ago when Jesse guided him to Black Mountain, which the photographer had pronounced "the perfect location." They'd dismounted and trudged across the flats at the foot of the slope, the photographer talking out loud—talking to himself, Jesse thought, picturing in his mind the images that he would capture. Curtis was a tall man, half a head taller than Jesse, with a thin frame and arms and legs that moved at angles. He had yellow hair and a yellow beard that jutted from the front of his chin. His eyes looked like pieces of blue glass caught in his pink face, reflecting the images all around him. He wore dark trousers, a white shirt with a black string tie looped at the opened collar, and a light-colored slouch hat that threw a band of shadow across his forehead.

"We'll set up the village here." The photographer had taken off his hat and waved toward the clumps of sagebrush and wild grasses. Then he'd swung around. "I'll set the camera on the tripod over there and take pictures of people in the village going about everyday chores, not knowing the enemy is coming."

"They would know," Jesse had told the white man. "The guards would spot the enemy and warn the chiefs. The women and children would be sent from the village. When the enemy rode toward the village, the men would be ready."

The photographer had waved his hat toward the mountain, as if he hadn't heard. "First a picture of the warriors riding down-slope, then pictures of the village, and then the attack." He'd set his hat back on his head and squinted into the sunlight, as if the images had already etched themselves in his eyes. "The pictures will document an attack on a peaceful village. Everyone will be shooting blanks, but the noise will sound like an actual attack."

"There are no more villages," Jesse had told the photographer. "The people have lived on the Wind River Reservation for many years." In wood boxes, he'd been thinking, except for one elder who refused to live in a log cabin. Human beings weren't meant to live in boxes made from trees, he said. So he lived in a buffalo-hide tipi. At night, he led his pony into the box.

Jesse had pushed on, explaining that Arapahos lived like white people now. Farmers. He had his own allotment—one hundred and sixty acres of rocks, brush, and hard, dry earth. He'd plowed the earth the way the agricultural instructor at Fort Washakie had said, planted hay, and sold the crop in Casper, with enough left over to feed his horses over the winter. Sometimes he caught on with the freighters who drove wagon teams to Casper and brought back goods for the Mercantile Store in Arapaho.

Last week, when he'd brought in a wagon load of flour, salt, sugar, and coffee to the store, he'd seen Curtis for the first time, talking to a group of Arapahos, showing around the paper images he'd made of other tribes. He wanted to make images of Arapahos, too, he said. He'd pay anyone willing to pose for him. And he needed an assistant, an Arapaho who could speak English, somebody willing to learn how to make images.

There was a time when Jesse would have been reluctant to speak up. It was impolite to put yourself forward. But after six years at St. Francis Mission School, he'd absorbed the white ways along with the language, and he'd stepped over to the porch and said, "I can help you, sir."

Now the photographer waved his hat toward the warriors paused halfway up the slope. They nudged the ponies forward out of the half-shadow and into the light, and the photographer turned his attention to the village.

It was as quiet as one of the images the photographer made on paper, Jesse thought. Not like a village in the Old Time, filled with shouts and laughter and the

10

sounds of horses neighing in the corral. This was like a village of ghosts. The men wore skin shirts and trousers handed down from the ancestors and brought out of storage from time to time for ceremonies. The women had on deerskin dresses, their brown arms flashing through the fringe on the sleeves, and beaded moccasins that poked past the fringe around the skirts. Their hair was in braids wrapped with red and yellow cloth that hung down the fronts of their dresses.

Most of the women hovered near the kettles slung over campfires, pink and blue flames licking the metal. Two women were scraping hides stretched between poles set upright in the earth—kettles holding nothing but water and hides scraped years ago.

The men looked out of place, out of time. Sitting cross-legged on blankets, chipping stones into arrow heads, bending willow branches into bows. A woman was combing the long, black hair of one of the men. "Gonna get my hair braided and wrapped in red cloth," he'd told the photographer, "just like the warriors used to do." Jesse figured the man wanted to make sure he'd look handsome in the pictures.

Curtis was approaching Bashful Woman's tipi now, and Jesse made himself look away. He did not want to taste again the bitterness that welled in his throat each time he saw Bashful and Carston Evans—the white man driving a team of horses into Arapaho, Bashful on the wagon bench beside him, the child clutched to her.

Jesse had opened a box of glass plates when, out of the corner of his eye, he saw Bashful dash past the photographer. He looked around, unable to ignore her any

11

longer. His heart felt like a fist of lead in his chest. The child ran ahead on short, wobbly legs, trailing a toy that clinked over the ground. Bashful scooped up the child—kicking and laughing—and nuzzled her face against the small chest.

The photographer ran forward, gesturing with his hat, his voice bursting like pellets from a shotgun. *No white toys in the village.*

Jesse walked over. "My people were traders," he said to Curtis. "There were many things made by white people in the villages."

But the white man waved away the explanation. The images would show the village that existed in his mind.

Bashful pried the toy from the child's hand and gave it to the photographer. With back straight and head high, like the image of the woman that Jesse carried in his heart, the proud and beautiful daughter of Chief Sharp Nose, Bashful walked back to the tipi, dropped onto the blanket next to her husband, and cuddled the child in her lap. Carston Evans did not lift his eyes to her. His gaze remained on the rifle in his hands.

Yesterday, Evans had ridden into the photographer's camp just west of the village, dust swirling behind him. He'd reined in next to the supply wagon where Jesse had been organizing the bottles of chemicals and boxes of paper. Wanting the portrait of Bashful and the child that Curtis had made the day before, Jesse thought.

He said, "The photographer's in the tent still developing his images."

"Tell him we'll be in the village for the attack he's orchestrating."

12

"No white men in the Arapaho village."

The white man had laughed at that. "White traders were always around. Took themselves Indian squaws."

Jesse had hooked both hands in his belt to keep from pulling the man off his mount and smashing his face. So Bashful was a squaw, not an honored wife, the daughter of a chief.

"We'll be there. Bashful and the girl and me," the white man said, turning the horse.

The photographer was examining the Premo now. He ran a finger over the top of the bellows, then ducked under the black focusing cloth, his back curved into the camera. He looked like he had a wooden box for a head, the black lens for a single eye. He was framing the image he wanted and focusing on a spot one-third of the distance from the camera to the warriors, the farthest point in the picture, just as he'd taught Jesse. Then he would stop the lens down and adjust the shutter speed so that he could capture images of the warriors attacking the village.

"Give the signal," Curtis said, emerging from under the black cloth.

Jesse stepped back to the supply wagon and took out the Winchester 73. Earlier he'd loaded ten cartridges in the rifle, each cartridge a blank filled with black powder and wads of cardboard. Pointing the muzzle to the sky, he pulled the trigger and fired. The loud report stopped up his ears for a moment. In a half second, other shots sounded from the bluff, the reverberations lost in the yells and shouts of the warriors as they galloped toward the village.

The photographer pushed the plunger to make the image.

"Stop!" he yelled, and Jesse shot off another blank, then set the rifle on the ground. Out of the corner of his eyes, he saw the warriors rein in the ponies as he turned to the camera. He inserted the dark slide into the holder next to the exposed plate, then removed the holder. Working as fast and as carefully as he could, he handed the photographer one of the other holders that he'd also loaded earlier. Curtis pushed the holder into the slot behind the lens and pulled out the dark slide. Jesse picked up the rifle and fired again.

The warriors broke into a gallop, bearing down on the village like a whirlwind that churned up the earth around the horses' hooves, howling into the volley of gunshots and the puffs of gray smoke that rose over the village. Curtis snapped the image.

"Stop!"

Jesse pulled the trigger again, but the noise of the gunshot was lost in the wall of noise falling all around. The warriors were galloping through the village as if they had entered another time and become the images the photographer intended to capture—the enemy attacking, compelled to go on and on until the village was reduced to ashes with bodies strewn about and the wounded clawing their way around the dead.

It was as if the people had also entered into that other time, as if they could sense the destruction crashing over them. Men ran toward the warriors, throwing up their palms in the sign of peace, trying to stop the attack. Other men pushed women and children into the tipis before dropping onto one knee, pointing rifles, spears, and bows and arrows in the direction of the warriors galloping past. Gunshots exploded in the air.

"Wonderful, wonderful," the photographer shouted.

Jesse removed the exposed plate holders and handed Curtis other holders with new plates, all the time fighting back the urge to pick up the rifle, run to the village, and kill the enemy. They were firing blanks, he kept telling himself. It wasn't the true thing, only an image—*wahsahk,* shadows of the old world being captured on the glass plates.

The photographer emerged from under the focusing cloth. "Success," he shouted. "I have caught everything." He clapped his hands overhead, as if the sound would puncture the wailing and screaming, the rifle fire still bursting into the air. "Enough," he shouted. Then he started toward the village, waving his hat overhead.

Jesse went after him. It was then that he saw the crowd flowing like water toward Bashful's tipi. He lunged around the photographer and broke into a run, darting through the waves of people, the images of shock and fear on their faces printing themselves in his mind. He was barely aware of the silence that was flooding the village, as if a river had jumped its banks and was inundating the earth.

He pushed past Carston Evans and stopped. He felt as if a bullet had slammed into his chest. Bashful lay on her side on the blanket, the child crawling close to her, grabbing at her with small brown hands, as if she were only resting after a busy day tending to her child and caring for her home. That was the truth Jesse wanted to see, not the truth that his eyes took in. In her back was a small hole, no bigger around than a marble. But in her chest was a hole the size of a fist. The ground around the blanket was running red with her blood. The thin wail of the child cut like a knife into the silence.

Jesse dropped to his knees and stroked Bashful's silky black hair.

"They killed her," Evans shouted above him. "They killed my wife."

2

A CHILL HAD settled over the evening, and moonlight shimmered in the frost that covered the grounds of St. Francis Mission on the Wind River Reservation. The moon was almost full, bright and low in the metallic sky pressing down over the earth. Most of the buildings around Circle Drive—the small, white church with the steeple gleaming in the moonlight, the yellow stucco administration building, the two-story, red-brick residence—merged into the shadows of the cottonwoods that sheltered the grounds. But light glowed in the oblong windows of the two-story, gray stone building that had once been the mission school but was now the Arapaho Museum.

Father John Aloysius O'Malley, the Jesuit pastor of the mission, zipped up his jacket and plunged across the grounds. He was a tall man, almost six-feet-four inches, and at forty-eight still retained the look of the athlete he'd been when he pitched for Boston College. He'd inherited the red hair, blue eyes, and quick smile that ran

16

through his Irish family, and despite the freckles on his face and the laugh lines at the corners of his eyes, he had the strong features—high, intelligent forehead and solid chin—of a handsome man, although he'd never thought of himself as handsome. Even though he spent a few minutes looking at himself in the mirror every morning when he shaved, it had been years since he'd actually seen himself.

He dipped his face into the collar of his jacket against the icy air that reminded him of Boston and home, a long way from the reservation that had been home for the past eight years. It could be a hard winter, he thought, the first frost coming so early, casting a silvery sheen over the brush and shrubs that had turned golden red with autumn. It was the second Monday in October, the Moon of Falling Leaves, according to the Arapaho way of marking the passing time.

The meeting in Eagle Hall behind the administration building had ended twenty minutes ago, but he'd stayed on until the members of the planning committee had shrugged into bulky jackets and, one by one, filed out into the pale gray light of evening, coaxed a line of old pickups and sedans into life, and bumped around Circle Drive toward Seventeen-Mile Road. By then, Father Damien Henley, the new assistant priest, had already left.

Past the museum windows, Father John could see the blurred figures moving about in the gallery. Normal closing time was eight o'clock, but the Edward S. Curtis exhibit on the Plains Indians that opened two weeks ago had brought in a steady stream of visitors who seemed

17

to lose themselves in the century-old photographs of Arapahos, Cheyennes, Piegan, Crow, and Sioux. He veered left, taking a shortcut through the frost-stiffened wild grasses in the center of the mission. Christine Nelson, the new curator, might need help closing up tonight.

He bounded up the steps to the porch that extended across the front of the stone building. The floorboards creaked under his boots. The moment he let himself through the oversized wooden door, he heard the voices buzzing like an electric current from the gallery on the left. He glanced through the doorway of what had once been a classroom. A group of Arapahos—students, he guessed, by the notebooks clutched in their hands and the earnest way they bent their heads in discussion—clustered around a middle-aged white man who looked like a professor, with tortoise-shell glasses and a mass of gray, curly hair that dipped over his forehead like a fur cap and, in back, was caught in a pony tail. One of the girls looked familiar—the shiny, black hair that hung down her back, the narrow, pretty face with prominent cheekbones. And it had been a while since he'd seen Hiram Blue Feather and Roy Glick. Three years ago, they'd been skinny kids playing for the Eagles, the baseball team he'd started his first summer at St. Francis. With Hiram on the pitcher's mound and Roy behind the plate, the Eagles had brought home the district championship.

Arranged along the walls were the black-and-white Curtis photographs that glowed with tones of pink and gold under the overhead fluorescent lights. Large portraits of elders and grandmothers with weary eyes and wrinkled faces; women holding young children and staring out across the plains; men in breechcloths, eagle-feathers poking from headbands, lined up like schoolboys in front of a small building. In one photograph, a woman walked out of the trees carrying a load of kindling wood, unaware of the camera that had stopped the moment in time. None of the photographs were originals from the portfolios that Curtis had produced almost a hundred years ago, Christine had explained. But they were excellent copies made from the original copper plates.

A couple of the students had wandered over to the far wall where the nine photographs that Curtis had taken of Arapahos were displayed. Fewer images than the photographer had made of other plains tribes, as if he hadn't spent much time on the reservation. And the photographs were smaller than the large photogravure images that Curtis had selected for his portfolios, no more than seven by nine inches. Still they were beautiful. A youth in a feathered headdress and long, bone necklace that looked too heavy for his thin chest. A young woman with the innocence of a girl still about her, in a heavy robe that shimmered like black velvet, looking away from the camera, as if she were looking into the future. An elder with gray hair parted in the middle and lines burrowed into his brow, and another elder in a plaid shirt and black trousers, seated on the ground, legs folded, smoking a long pipe. A haunting image of a woman seated on the ground in front of a tipi, cradling a child in her lap, sunshine beginning to fall over them, as if they were about to emerge from the shadow.

Set apart from the group of Arapaho photographs was a photograph of the log cabin at Black Mountain where Curtis had stayed while he was working on the reservation. On one side of the cabin stood a conical-shaped tent, like a tipi, where Curtis took photographs of individuals, Christine said. The photographer could adjust the flap to create the exact amount of light and shadows that he wanted to play over the faces. Next to the photographic tent was the small, box-like tent where Curtis developed the glass plate negatives.

Standing a short distance from the tents, one elbow propped against the railing that ran around the porch at the front of the cabin, was a fine-looking Arapaho dressed in a white shirt and light, canvas trousers, probably in his twenties, Father John guessed, with black hair cut short and a smile playing at the corners of his mouth. Next to the photograph was the small plaque with the title, "Home and Studio at Wind River. My assistant Jesse White Owl."

But it was the photograph in the center of the wall that drew Father John's attention each time he came to the museum. Three warriors riding down a mountainside, rifles and feathered headdresses silhouetted against the clear, open sky. A small village below, canvas tipis shining in the sunlight. A normal day, people in the village going about their chores. Women cooking and scraping hides; men standing about, visiting with one another. One man was having his hair combed by a woman who bent over him, her back curved in gentleness. Another man was cleaning his rifle. The photograph was titled, "Before the Attack."

The group of students had clustered in front of the photograph, everyone talking at once, voices low and intense, the gray pony tail nodding, encouraging. The girl with shiny black hair reached out and swept her hand across the image of the warriors, as if she might wipe them out of the picture and protect the village.

"We can all agree that the photograph is powerful." The woman's voice behind him was tight with exasperation.

Father John looked around. Christine Nelson stood outside the office on the other side of the entry, arms folded across the front of her navy-blue turtleneck sweater. She was small and fine-boned, probably in her late thirties, and attractive in a brittle kind of way. She had dark, straight-cut hair that hung to her shoulders and framed a pale, oval face whose most distinguishing features were the light, watchful eyes and the red-tinged lips drawn into a tight line. She had on slacks that matched her sweater and diamond earrings that flickered through her hair when she moved her head.

Six weeks ago, after the former curator left for a position in Cheyenne, he'd placed ads in newspapers across Wyoming: Curator, Arapaho Museum, St. Francis Mission. Anyone could read between the lines: low-paying job on Indian reservation. Christine Nelson had been the only applicant, and he could hardly believe his good luck. The woman was eminently qualified: Two years at the Field Museum in Chicago, internships at the Louvre in Paris and the Museo Nacional de Anthropología in Mexico City.

"I'm ready for a change," she'd announced. A low-pressure position in an out-of-the-way place was exactly what she'd been looking for. He'd hired her on the spot, and not long after, he'd started to feel as if he'd conjured up a whirlwind. The woman arrived at the museum early and left late, always running, running. He'd seen her cream-colored Range Rover parked in front of the museum in the evenings and on weekends. It was as if the old stone building couldn't contain the energy in the small figure. Within two weeks, she'd arranged for a gallery in Denver to loan the Curtis photographs for a special exhibit.

"Maybe you can get them to stop yammering, agree that the photographs are magnificent, and get out of here," she said as he walked toward her. "They can argue all they want in class. I was about to throw them out. Care to do the honors?" She pulled back the cuff of her sweater and glanced at a gold-banded watch. "I have an appointment in twenty minutes."

"I'll be glad to close up," Father John said.

"In that case, I'll be on my way." The woman checked her watch again, then swung into the office and plucked a briefcase from the desk. After grabbing a coat from somewhere behind the door, she emerged into the entry, grasping the coat and briefcase against her chest. "They're all yours," she said, throwing a look of irritation toward the gallery before she let herself outside. A gust of cold air blew through the entry as the door whooshed shut.

"Hey, Father!"

Father John turned back to the gallery. Hiram was beckoning him forward. "Settle a debate for us. What do you say?" The young man lifted one hand toward the village. "You think Curtis staged the photograph? Created his own little village? Enacted the attack?"

"Like he was directing a movie in nineteen-o-seven." This from the girl with long, shiny hair.

Father John started toward the students, aware of the thud of his boots on the old wood floor and the eyes fastened on him. For a moment, he felt like the American history teacher he'd once been in a Jesuit prep school, student eyes following him as he paced the front of the class, searching for the logical answer to a question, the answer that seemed to make the most sense out of the past.

He stopped next to Hiram and studied the photo. "The Indian battles were over and the villages were gone by the late 1890s, when Curtis began taking photographs," he said. "Curtis wanted to document Indian traditions, so he created scenes that he thought depicted traditional life."

"A legitimate documentary technique." The man with the gray pony tail looked from one student to the other, then turned to Father John and thrust out a mitt-sized hand with a grip of steel. "Don Cannon, Father. I teach the film class at Central Wyoming College." He shifted his gaze to the students clustered in front of the photograph. "True, Curtis paid Indians to stage scenes, such as mock battles. After all, he worked in the pictorial style popular at the time. But let's not lose sight of the

23

man's artistry. Keep in mind that he used a Premo camera. Very advanced technology then, with its reversible back capable of either horizontal or vertical shots. Exposure time was as fast as one-one-hundredth of a second, so he could shoot pictures as fast as his assistant could hand him new plates to load into the camera. Still primitive technology by our standards. Nevertheless, Curtis managed to get images with so much clarity and detail that the scenes might be taking place before our eyes, which gives them a power that's almost magical," he said. "When we look at them, it's as if we are transported into the past."

"I don't call it a legitimate technique," the girl said.

"How else could Curtis have photographed an enemy attack?" Hiram locked eyes with Roy, and both young men nodded.

The girl's chin jutted forward. "Curtis could have admitted that he staged the scenes. Like rolling the credits at the end of a film. Then we'd know what we're seeing. But he presents the photograph as if enemy warriors were about to attack an actual village."

"What do the rest of you think about Miriam's point?" Cannon asked.

Ah, Miriam Redshield, Father John thought. Eunice Redshield's granddaughter. The small girl with black braids—how long ago?—squirming in the front pew next to her grandmother at the ten o'clock Sunday Mass.

The others were shaking their heads in unison, like soldiers in a drill. "Hiram's right," Roy said. "Curtis recreated the scene, like a documentary. He wanted us

24

to experience what it was like in the village before enemy warriors attacked and people died."

"But that's not what happened." Miriam's face tightened, and for a moment, Father John thought she might burst into tears. "It was the warriors who died."

She had everyone's attention now.

"Obviously, some of the enemy would die in an attack," Cannon said.

"All of them died." Miriam lifted her chin and stared at the warriors riding down slope, zigzags of paint crossing their faces and naked chests like streaks of lightning. She seemed transfixed, as if the photograph had yielded some meaning to her that had eluded everyone else.

"What are you saying?" Father John asked.

The girl kept her gaze on the photograph. "Grandmother said the warriors were killed." The girl tapped the glass over the image of the warrior on the right, a forelock of black hair bunched over his forehead, black eyes narrowed in determination, the faintest mark of dimples in his cheeks. "He was her grandfather. He was called Thunder."

"Your grandmother identified one of the warriors?" This was good news. Father John felt a familiar surge of excitement, the same feeling that used to come over him when he was doing research in some archives and stumbled upon an obscure fact—the key to the puzzle that made everything else fall into place.

"Does your grandmother have a photograph of Thunder?" he asked the girl.

She shrugged. "That's what the curator asked her. All

grandmother said was, 'I guess I know my own grand-father.' "

The other students had started talking all at once, and Cannon put up a fleshy hand to quiet them. "I'm not following," he said. "Why would anyone have died if the scene was staged?"

The girl remained silent for a long moment, her gaze still fastened to the photograph. Finally she said, "Grandmother told me that after Curtis came, the warriors in the photo all died, and it was real hard on the families. That's what her father told her."

It was several minutes before the group began drifting down the gallery, reluctance in the way they moved toward the entry, as if the photographs still exerted an invisible pull, drawing them back to the past. Father John followed them out and told them to come back any time. "You can count on that," Cannon said as Father John closed the door.

He walked back into the gallery and snapped off the overhead lights. The photographs shone in the glow of moonlight filtering through the windows. He could almost sense the fear pulsing through the village, the shock and panic as the warriors galloped toward the tipis, shouting, firing rifles overhead.

"Thunder," he said out loud, the sound of his voice coming back in the stillness of the empty room. "What happened that day, Thunder?"

3

A COLUMN OF light filtered from the kitchen down the hallway and into the entry of the residence. Walks-On, the golden retriever that Father John had found in a ditch a few years ago, came clicking along the wood floor. Father John hung his jacket over the coat tree and patted the dog's soft, furry head. In a second, the dog had bounded back to the kitchen and stationed himself in front of the door, wagging his tail. Father John went after him and let him outside. Even the gust of cold air didn't erase the aroma of stale coffee hanging over the room. He watched the dog make his way across the snow-slicked back porch and down the wooden steps. It still amazed him that Walks-On didn't seem to know he was missing a hind leg. He had three good legs, and that was good enough. There was a lesson in that, Father John thought.

He poured himself a mug of coffee, then rummaged through the refrigerator for the half-full carton of milk, which he stirred into the thick, black liquid until it turned the color of caramel. From the front of the house came the thud of footsteps on the stairs, the scrape of boots coming down the hall. He glanced around as Father Damien Henley walked into the kitchen.

"Coffee?" Father John gestured with his mug toward the glass container. This new assistant might work out, he'd allowed himself to think. Might even stay at St. Francis longer than a few months. He'd been here six weeks, arriving with a computer and several cartons of

27

books after the last assistant had left to take a position in the economics department at Marquette University. The Wind River Reservation and the Arapahos—the history and the culture—all seemed fascinating to Father Damien, who possessed an unlimited store of ideas on how to make St. Francis Mission work better. He also possessed an unlimited store of energy, not unlike Christine Nelson, Father John thought. New ideas. An infusion of new energy. He supposed that was good.

"Leftover from dinner? I'll pass, thank you." The other priest wrinkled his nose. He was a thin, wiry man, half a foot shorter and at least seven or eight years younger, which made him about forty, Father John guessed. The other priest had blond hair that was starting to thin, exposing little strips of pink scalp; a narrow face marked with light-colored, energetic eyes that seemed to take in everything at a glance; and a jaw set in determination.

Father John took his mug over to the table and dropped down onto a straight-backed chair. "Have a seat," he said, sensing that the other priest had something on his mind. He was struck with the irony in the way life unfolded. He, a third-generation Irishman from Boston, raised in a walk-up flat over his uncle's saloon a couple of blocks off of Commonwealth Avenue, who'd pitched his way through Boston College and somehow—by the grace of God—had been called to be a priest. A Jesuit.

Across the table was Damien Henley, III, son of the CEO of a communications conglomerate, whose ancestors had probably arrived on the Mayflower, raised on an estate somewhere on Long Island. A Princeton graduate also called to be a priest. A Jesuit. Not long ago he'd asked the man what his father had thought of his decision. Damien had shrugged his shoulders and rolled his eyes, mimicking his father, as though the decision was just another phase that Damien would outgrow, like a bad case of acne. But you can't outgrow the calling, Damien had said. It gets louder and louder until it drowns out everything else, and after all, Dad was a businessman, a realist, and Damien had been accepted into the Society of Jesus. That had made the decision almost acceptable. My son, the Jesuit, he could tell his golf buddies at the club.

"Just got off the phone with Dad," Damien was saying. "He had zero trouble getting past Senator Evans's staff. Chatted with the senator himself this afternoon." He paused, allowing the unspoken importance of his father to settle between them.

Father John took another draw of coffee. The milk made it barely drinkable. Lately the news had been filled with speculation about whether Wyoming's senator, Jaime Evans, intended to run for president. Local newspapers could hardly contain the glee at the prospect of a local man in the Oval Office. There had been a series of articles on the Evans family and the ranch north of the reservation that they'd run for a hundred years. Not long after the senator's grandfather, Carston Evans, had started the ranch, he'd gotten wealthy on the oil seeping into the pasture. One article had quoted the senator telling about how his grandfather had ordered the ranch hands to shovel out the black, gooey mess and clean up the fields, and how somebody had finally figured out what the black, gooey mess was.

"It's all set," Damien said. "The senator will be at the mission next Tuesday. The day before, he'll be in Cheyenne, where he plans to announce that he's running for president from the capitol steps. Tuesday morning, he'll go to Fort Washakie and give a speech on the importance of extracting methane gas from the coal beds on the reservation. Plans to appeal to everyone's sense of patriotism. You know, the importance of developing our own natural resources. There's sure to be a big crowd. Drilling for methane gas would mean jobs on the rez. Of course he'll be taking on T.J. Painted Horse and the rest of the Arapaho Business Council and their demands for additional environmental impact studies. It'll be controversial, but that's what attracts the media."

The other priest sat back and stared at the ceiling, his face breaking into a slow grin, as if he were picturing the controversy. He pushed himself to his feet. "Maybe I'll have some coffee after all," he said.

There was the sound of coffee sloshing into a mug, glass clanking against the counter, then Damien was back in his chair. "T.J. and Savi Crowthorpe are working with the senator's campaign staff on his visit to the rez," he said. "I went to the tribal offices and asked them to request that the senator put in an appearance at the mission. They passed on the request, but the senator's people nixed the idea. Well, that's changed now."

"How'd your father manage it?"

"You kidding?" Damien took a sip of coffee and grimaced. "Campaign contributions, John. It's all about money and . . ." The man broke into a wide grin. "Dad controls a lot of air time, a fact that wasn't lost on the senator's campaign staff. Think about it, John. There'll be reporters and TV cameras following the senator around. We'll give them a tour of the mission. Show them our programs—AA, parenting classes, literacy and adult education, the teenage club. We'll fill up the classrooms at Eagle Hall so it'll look like the actual classes and meetings. We'll give the senator a tour of the Curtis exhibit. Monday evening we'll be on the TV in about twenty million homes. And who knows how many newspapers will run the story?"

The man leaned into the table until the edge creased the front of his blue shirt. He looked up again, as if the scene were playing out on the ceiling. "You can bet that the senator's campaign will use the television clips to bolster his image as a candidate concerned about minorities. Helps to emphasize the importance of the new jobs that drilling for methane gas will bring. There'll be a steady stream of donations flowing into the mission. We can build a new community center, remodel the church, finance more programs. Hire professionals, John. Social workers, psychologists to help people . . ."

"That's our job," Father John said.

"Absolutely." Damien took another sip of coffee. Another grimace. "We'll have time to concentrate on the spiritual aspects. Let the professionals handle the rest. We can have a first-class museum on the Plains

31

Indians with more exhibits from outside. Offer good exhibits, and the crowds will come. We can pay Christine the kind of salary she deserves."

"Whoa!" Father John put up one hand. "The donations haven't arrived yet."

"Oh, but they will, John." The other priest pushed his mug into the middle of the table, got up, and started for the door. He turned back. "You have to have a little faith," he said.

Father John drained the last of his coffee, his eyes on the man making his way down the hallway, confidence in the set of his shoulders, the way he gripped the knob on the banister and pulled himself around. Confidence in the rhythmic tap of his boots on the stairs.

After a moment, Father John got to his feet, rinsed out both mugs, and let in Walks-On, who darted past, shaking cold air out of his coat. The dog folded himself onto the rug in the corner, and Father John patted the animal's head. Then he flipped off the light and started down the hall. Moonlight washed over the walls and floor, creating patterns of shadow and light that spilled into the study at the front of the old house. He sat down at his desk, turned on the lamp, and pulled a stack of envelopes toward him. Bills to pay, thank-you notes to write to people who had sent checks—unfamiliar names from towns he'd never heard of. The little miracles. He laughed. He had faith all right. Faith in the little miracles that arrived when he least expected them, when he most needed them.

He opened the bill from the telephone company, surprised at the uneasiness tugging at him. Even the changes Father Damien had suggested to the planning committee this evening had made him uneasy. New community center. Remodel the church. He tried to shrug off the feeling, but it clung to him, like a leach fastened onto his skin. Maybe he'd been at St. Francis too long. Eight years altogether—six as pastor, longer than he'd ever been in one place as a priest. Maybe the Arapahos needed a new pastor, someone with new ideas and exuberance. Someone like Damien.

Ah, there it was, the real cause of the uneasy feeling. Not that he might have to leave St. Francis, but that it might be best for the mission if he did.

He tossed the telephone bill onto a stack of bills-to-pay-immediately, next to the stack of bills-to-pay-as-soon-as-possible, and tried to swallow back the old longing. A thumbnail of whiskey, no more than a table-spoon, and the unease, the uncertainty, would be banished. There was courage in whiskey. "God help me," he said out loud.

He jabbed the letter opener into another envelope, tossed another bill onto the second stack. Out of the corner of his eye, he saw the yellow headlight flash through the window. An engine hummed outside. He got up and went to the front door. A Wind River Police officer was coming up the sidewalk, moonlight laying like snow on the shoulders of his dark jacket.

"Sorry to bother you, Father," the officer said as he came up the steps to the concrete stoop. "Chief Banner sent me to notify you."

Father John moved back into the hallway and motioned the man inside.

Stopping in the doorway, the officer removed his hat. His face was round and red with cold, his eyes squinted into slits above the fleshy cheeks. He might have been Cheyenne or Crow, Father John thought, assigned to the Wind River Reservation by the Bureau of Indian Affairs.

"What's happened?" he asked.

"We got a body at T.J. Painted Horse's place. Looks like suicide. Chief's already there, along with the FBI agent. Chief said you'd want to come over, most likely."

"I'm on my way." Father John reached around the door and pulled his jacket off the coat tree. Then he followed the officer out into the moonlight.

4

A BODY AT the home of T.J. Painted Horse. Father John pressed down on the accelerator and stared at the silvery asphalt rolling into the headlights of the Toyota pickup. The rear tires yawed and squealed around a curve.

Suicide.

It was hard to imagine. T.J. was one of the leading men on the reservation. He had been on the tribal council—the business council, the Arapahos called it—for four or five years, and before that, he'd represented Fremont County in the state legislature. Everyone knew T.J. and his wife, Denise. She taught third grade at Fort Washakie school, and she came to Mass almost every Sunday. Sometimes T.J. came with her.

Ahead, a single yellow light gradually separated into two headlights, coming closer. He let up on the gas pedal, blinded for a half-second as the headlights swept past. Then the moon came into view again, hanging in the sky outside the passenger window, bathing the open spaces that stretched around him in a pale, gray light.

Leading man. Father John couldn't get the words out of his mind. He gripped the steering wheel hard. Leading men made enemies, and T.J. had spoken out against drilling for methane gas in the coal beds on the eastern edge of the reservation. He'd gone to Cheyenne to try to convince the state legislature to oppose the drilling. He'd made a trip to Washington, D.C., to convince the Bureau of Indian Affairs. When the plans continued to move forward, with the support of Senator Jaime Evans, T.J. had gone to the newspapers. There had been a rash of articles about the necessity of more environmental studies, and the BIA had finally agreed to consider another environmental impact study. But people on the rez were waiting for the jobs and for the per capita payments they'd get from the royalties, people who could have gotten tired of T.J. Painted Horse holding everything up.

Dear Lord, Father John thought. Suppose it wasn't suicide. Suppose someone had decided to stop T.J. permanently.

Father John made a right onto Ethete Road. Another mile and he could make out the dense block of a house against the gray sky, light shimmering in the windows. Getting closer now. It might have been a party. Vehicles parked in front, dark figures milling about. A party interrupted by the police, red, blue, and yellow lights whirling on top of the cruisers.

He turned into the yard and corrected for another skid on the wood planks laid over the barrow ditch. He slid to a stop behind one of the cruisers and got out into the cold. The coroner's SUV stood a few feet away. A couple of police officers stepped over the yellow police tape forming a barrier across the front of the house and came toward him, gloved fists clenched. Circles and stripes of colored lights whirled over their faces and dark uniforms.

"Chief Banner and the fed are inside, Father," one of the officers said.

Father John nodded. "Okay if I go in?"

"They're talking to T.J. in the kitchen, but I can take you to the bedroom . . ."

"T.J.?" Father John heard the relief in his voice sliding toward a new kind of horror. That meant . . .

"Coroner's in the bedroom with Denise's body," the officer said.

Father John jammed both hands into his jacket pockets, vaguely aware of the cold prickling his face. "What happened here?" His voice sounded low and hollow.

"We'll have to wait on the coroner's report." The other officer moved in closer. "You want the unofficial version? Looks like the woman put a nine-millimeter semi-automatic pistol to her head two or three hours ago and pulled the trigger. She's on the floor where T.J. says he found her when he got home from the office. You wanna say some prayers?"

Father John followed the officers into the small, tidy living room with sofa and chairs arranged around a TV, books lined up in the bookcase against the far wall, and on the table in front of the sofa, a briefcase that looked as if it had been dropped by accident, knocking the porcelain knickknacks askew. A murmur of conversation flowed through the archway from the kitchen in back.

As he headed into the hallway, he caught sight of the three men at the kitchen table—Chief Banner at one end, Ted Gianelli, the local FBI agent, at the other. T.J. sat between them, shoulders hunched, eyes locked on his hands clasped on the table. The man was in his forties, Father John guessed, with black hair combed back, curling over the collar of his tan shirt, and the profile of one of the leading men in the old photographs: hooked nose and prominent cheekbones, the handsome face frozen in sadness, as if he'd failed his people somehow and the enemy had invaded the village.

The officers were waiting halfway down the hall. Father John walked past them into the bedroom jammed with uniformed officers and several men in blue jeans and heavy jackets that hung open. Lying on her side next to the bed was Denise Painted Horse, dressed in black slacks and a light blue sweater, the color of the morning sky. She still had on her shoes, black and a little scuffed. For a crazy instant, he felt as if he'd blundered into the bedroom of a woman who'd decided to lie down on the floor and take a nap. She might awaken at any moment and find him staring at her shoes. Or the small, black pistol a few feet from her curled fingers.

A man in a dark leather jacket was darting about, snapping photographs. Two other men hovered in the corner, heads bent toward the notepad that one was holding. Down on one knee, close to the body, was Tom Enslow, the county coroner, gray-haired, with muscular shoulders beneath his flannel shirt, balancing a notepad on a blue-jean-clad thigh.

Enslow leaned over Denise's head a moment, then peeled backward and jotted something in the notepad. It was then that Father John saw the dark, sticky mass in the black hair behind Denise's right ear. Little red tentacles reached from beneath her head into the gray carpet, like grasping, bloody fingers. He looked away, aware for the first time of the faint smell of blood. Folded over the back of a chair in the corner was a white quilt with a blue-and-yellow star in the center, like the star quilts he'd seen in Arapaho homes across the rez. Draped over the armrest was a flimsy, pink robe that Denise might have tossed there at some point in an ordinary day.

"There you are, Father." Enslow pushed to his feet. "We're about finished here. You want to bless her before we put her in the body bag?" There was a weary, off-key note in the man's tone, as though the job would never be normal, never routine.

Father John walked over to Denise. He felt the muscles tighten in his stomach, his mouth go dry. The woman's eyes were open, locked in shock and fear. She looked sunken in death, smaller than he'd remembered, and more vulnerable, her skin almost pale, like plastic. She'd been beautiful. Lively and intelligent, quick to express an opinion. Every fall—usually on a day flooded with sunshine with leaves shimmering red in the cottonwoods—Denise brought her students on an outing to the mission. A yellow school bus full of kids shouting and laughing, snapping the jackets they'd untied from their waists at one another. They'd head down the dirt road between the church and the administration building, he and Denise walking in front, the kids shouting behind. Past the guest house and into the stand of cottonwoods along the banks of the Little Wind River. It was here, Denise would tell the students, waving both hands toward the cool expanse of shade, that the people had camped when they first came to the reservation. Chief Black Coal and Chief Sharp Nose themselves had chosen this sacred place. The kids would become quiet, wide black eyes taking in the trees and underbrush dappled with sunlight, the river rippling over the rocks. In those moments, he could almost sense Denise's love for Arapaho history taking root in the kids.

"Tell us about the church," she'd say, turning to him as they walked back, and the kids would circle around as he told about how the Arapahos had built the church themselves and painted the walls in Arapaho symbols. At that point, the kids usually started telling him about the symbols: red and blue geometric lines for the roads in life, blue circles for the sacred center, white tipis for the people, brown V-shapes for the buffalo.

Ah, Denise. He made the sign of the cross over the still body. What kind of darkness had engulfed you? "Loving and merciful God," he said, "please accept this beautiful woman that you created into your presence, forgive her sins whatever they may be, and let her share in the everlasting joy and peace that is yours alone. Amen."

The chorus of amen's startled him, breaking as they did into the silence. Father John nodded to the coroner, who was already unfolding a large, gray plastic bag, then stepped past the other men and went back down the hall. Chief Banner stood in the middle of the living room, talking to two officers, a serious, subdued tone. Then, dismissing the officers with an impatient wave, he turned toward Father John. He might have been a chief in the Old Time, Father John thought, or one of the warriors in the Curtis photographs, with black hair; high, thick cheekbones; and the humped nose of the Arapaho. A stocky man, medium height with broad chest, wide shoulders, and big hands that hung beneath the cuffs of his navy-blue uniform shirt. A thin silver wedding ring was embedded in a fleshy finger. The man had headed up the Wind River law enforcement as long as Father John had been on the reservation. "God help me, I love the job," he'd once told him. "I want to get the bad asses out of here."

"You saw her?" Banner asked.

Father John nodded. "How's T.J.?"

"Pretty broken up." The chief gestured with his head toward the kitchen. Through the archway, Father John could see T.J. still at the table, face dropped into his hands.

"Gianelli's been talking to him." There was resignation in Banner's voice. Unexplained deaths on the reservation fell within the FBI's jurisdiction, even probable suicides, which put Gianelli in charge, a fact that, Father John knew, rankled the chief.

"T.J. claims he was working late tonight on council business," Banner went on, nodding toward the kitchen. "Came home about nine, found the front door unlocked. Not unusual. You know how Arapahos are." He shrugged. "People wanna come in and help themselves to your stuff, well, they must need it real bad. T.J. says he was surprised to see Denise's car out front because she was supposed to be at the college in Casper for a teacher's workshop today and tomorrow. He walked back to the bedroom, and that's when he found her."

Gesturing again toward the kitchen, he said, "Go on in. Man's gonna need all the consolation he can get."

The minute Father John stepped through the archway, he could see that T.J. was sobbing silently, chest heaving, shoulders shaking. He walked over and put one hand on the man's back. "I'm sorry, T.J.," he said.

At the far end of the narrow kitchen, Gianelli was leaning over the counter, writing something in a notepad. He had on blue jeans and a leather vest that hung open over a blue shirt with the sleeves rolled up over thick forearms. He glanced around and gave Father John a half-nod. There was a flicker of weariness in the man's eyes.

T.J. shuddered beneath his hand, then flattened his own hands on the table and looked up, eyes blinking in the light. Moisture glistened on his narrow, brown face. He seemed older than a man in his forties, with lines at the corners of his eyes and the collar of his tan shirt standing out around his thin neck. "There's no call for Denise to shoot herself," he said. "Why'd she do it, Father?"

Father John pushed a chair over with his boot and sat down next to the man. "Try to believe that God hasn't forgotten you, T.J. He'll help you through this."

"God!" A low, guttural sound, like a death rattle. "Why'd God let her do it? I never gave her any cause to turn on me like that."

Father John stopped himself from asking what he meant. T.J. was in shock. He recognized the symptoms—the vacant stare, the twitching hands.

"You'll bury her?" T.J. said, as if this was something he couldn't handle, the mundane tasks that lay ahead.

"Of course."

"She'd want a traditional ceremony, too. She'd want to be painted."

"I'll talk to the elders. We'll work it out." The elders would place the sacred red paint on Denise's face, so the ancestors would recognize her and take her into the spirit world. Without the paint, her spirit would wander the earth, lost and alone, frantic for eternity.

"The drums. She'd want the drums, and singers. She loved the old ways." T.J. gave a little smile. "She was a traditional. We gotta bury her within three days." A look of urgency crossed the man's face. "That's the Arapaho Way."

Father John patted the man's arm, trying to reassure him, despite the warning look that Gianelli shot across the kitchen. There would be no burial until the coroner issued his report and released the body.

"Oh, T.J.!" A woman's voice wailed from the living room.

Father John glanced around. Vera Wilson, T.J.'s sister—small and determined-looking in a puffy green jacket, black hair tightly curled around her face—rushed into the kitchen and dove around the table. She threw both arms around T.J.'s shoulders and cradled his head against her chest.

"Oh, my God." She was shouting. "It can't be true. Tell me it isn't true," she went on, hardly drawing a breath. "What the hell was Denise thinking? Are you okay?"

"Look," Gianelli said, moving a couple of feet along the counter. "We don't know the cause of death yet. Denise may have taken her own life, but the coroner could find another cause."

"Another cause?" Vera let go of her brother and turned to Father John. "What's he saying, Father? Murder? He's saying Denise could've been murdered?"

"It could have been an accident," Gianelli said.

Vera grabbed hold of T.J.'s shoulders again. "You're coming home with me," she said. "I'm going to look after you." Then, facing Gianelli, "I'm taking my brother home. Anything else you want to talk to him about, you can call his lawyer. Who you want for a lawyer, T.J.?" She leaned sideways, bringing her face close to her brother's.

"Lawyer?" T.J. shifted around and stared at the woman. "Why would I need a lawyer?"

"You're entitled to a lawyer," Gianelli said. "I'll want to talk to you again tomorrow."

T.J. was quiet a moment. "I guess I can call Vicky Holden," he said finally.

"That's settled then." Vera sucked in a breath, as if she'd been prepared to do battle and had found the battlefield deserted. "Come on." She took T.J.'s arm, urging him to his feet.

The man started to sway as he got up, and Father John jumped up and took hold of his other arm to steady him. "I'll help you out," he said.

They walked through the living room—two guards propping up the condemned man, Father John thought. An officer draped a coat over T.J.'s shoulders at the door, and they worked their way out onto the stoop and across the yard to the light-colored pickup next to the coroner's van.

Father John handed the man into the passenger seat while Vera ran around the front and crawled in behind the wheel. "I'll come by tomorrow," he told T.J. over the noise of the engine catching and growling. Then he shut the door and waited until the pickup had crossed the barrow ditch and turned left onto the road, headlights blinking in the moonlight.

He was heading around the other vehicles toward the pickup when he saw Gianelli walking toward him. "What do you think, John? Any trouble that you know of between T.J. and Denise?"

"What are you saying? You think that T.J. . . . ?" Father John glanced out at the road. The taillights on Vera's pickup glowed like tiny red coals in the distance. It wasn't possible, he told himself, but something else was ringing in his head: *Anything was possible.*

"We haven't found a note," the fed was saying. "She wasn't depressed or taking medications, according to

T.J. People don't up and shoot themselves without some reason."

Father John locked eyes again with the man. "I've never heard of trouble between them. You think Denise was murdered?"

The agent didn't say anything, and in the silence settling between them, Father John had the answer. "Look, Ted," he pressed on. "T.J.'s done everything he can to prevent drilling for methane gas on the reservation. He's made enemies. Maybe somebody came looking for him."

"Maybe." Gianelli didn't sound convinced. "There won't be any funeral until I get the coroner's report and the investigation is closed." He turned abruptly and headed back to the house.

Father John stared after the man. The wind had come up, giving the air a sharper bite. After a moment, he walked over and got into his pickup. He backed away from the other vehicles, then shot forward across the yard and onto the road. Ahead, the red taillights were swallowed by the night.

5

VICKY HOLDEN EASED the Jeep next to the curb in front of the brick bungalow that was now her office a few blocks off Main Street in Lander. A sheen of frost covered the blocklike sign in the front yard, so that all that was visible was her name and the meaningless words: ney at aw. She pulled the briefcase and black bag from the passenger seat, crossed the ice-tipped grass, and brushed at the sign until the words were clear: Attorney at Law. Cold specks of moisture prickled her wrists and sifted down into her gloves as she hurried up the steps to the porch and let herself inside.

Annie Bosey, the secretary she'd hired a month ago, sat at the desk across from the brick fireplace in what had once been a narrow living room. The phone was pressed between the woman's ear and shoulder; her fingers shuffled a stack of papers.

Vicky gave the woman a nod and opened the French doors to her private office in the converted dining room with white paneling halfway up the walls and a wide window that framed the frost-lined juniper in the backyard. She dropped the briefcase and bag onto the desk and shrugged out of her coat, catching a glimpse of herself in the glass door as she did so: shoulder-length black hair, still tinged with moisture, falling to her shoulders; oval-shaped face with the high cheekbones; the little crook near the top of her nose; and the eyes of her people—so dark they were almost black. She'd turn forty-five this year, and the admiring looks she still got from men never ceased to take her by surprise.

Vicky combed her fingers through her hair, then tossed it back and walked over to the desk, aware of Annie's voice hurrying to end the call. Twenty-five years old, divorced with two kids, a GED, and a résumé of low-paying jobs, Annie had shown up at her front door hours after the last secretary had given notice. Vicky hadn't even put an ad in the Gazette. "Heard you need a secretary," Annie had said. Of course, she'd heard. The moccasin telegraph flashed news across the rez faster than the Internet.

The outer office had gone quiet, and Vicky realized that Annie was standing between the French doors, bracing herself on the knobs, her mouth a round O, as if she were trying to catch her breath.

"What is it?" Vicky took the chair at her desk.

"It's so terrible about Denise Painted Horse."

Vicky felt a familiar hollow space opening inside her. She was the last to hear the gossip, it seemed. When she was married to Ben Holden and living on the rez, the gossip always raced to her house. That was a lifetime ago. She'd divorced Ben, left the kids—Lucas and Susan—with her mother and gone to Denver. When she came home ten years later, she was a lawyer—*ho:x'iwu:ne'n*—a woman who thought she could make herself a chief, the grandmothers said.

"You heard, didn't you?"

"Why don't you tell me."

"Denise shot herself last night. She's dead, Vicky."

Vicky lifted herself to her feet. She'd known Denise and T.J. all her life. She and T.J. had been in the same class at St. Francis School. Denise was a few years behind, but after she and T.J. were married, they'd been like family. They knew why she'd had to leave Ben. They'd understood, even though she'd never put it into words. One summer, at a powwow, T.J. had pulled her aside and, the tip of his finger tracing the bruise on her cheek, said, "How long you going to put up with it, Vicky?" It had helped her find the strength to leave.

And it was T.J., she was certain, who had tried to get the business council to hire her to file a request with the

47

BIA for a new environmental impact study on the proposed methane drilling. Afterward, when the Gazette
had reported that a firm in Cheyenne would be advising
the tribe, T.J. had called. "Damn it, Vicky." He spat the
words down the line. "You were best for the job. The
council has gotta start trusting our own people. So what
if you're a woman?"

"Where's T.J.?" Vicky was at the coat tree, pulling on
her coat, barely aware of having walked across the
office.

"Over at Vera's. He's been calling all morning."

"Better reschedule today's appointments," Vicky said,
scooping her bag off the desk and starting back across
the office.

"Want me to call T.J. and tell him you're on the way?"

"He knows I'll come." Vicky pulled the front door
shut behind her.

FROST TRACED THE reservation, like white moss clinging
to the brown prairie and outlining the stalks of wild
grass and clumps of brush that flamed gold and vermil-
lion in the October sun as far as Vicky could see. The
wind had picked up, knocking at the sides of the Jeep
and sending little clouds of dust swirling across
Highway 287. She squinted against the glare of the sun
on the windshield and tried to wrap her mind around the
impossible.

Impossible that Denise Painted Horse was dead!
When was it that she'd run into Denise at the grocery
store? Last week? Vicky had been hurrying down the
aisle, pulling items into her cart, when she'd heard a

familiar voice calling her name. She glanced around and saw Denise coming at a run behind a half-filled cart.

"I've been meaning to call you, Vicky." Denise had thrown a nervous glance behind her. There was no one else in the aisle. "I have to talk to you."

"What is it?" Vicky had asked.

"Not here." Another glance along the aisle. "I'll call you."

She'd never called.

Vicky felt herself squinting now against the moisture welling behind her eyes. She should have called Denise. Why hadn't she called? Chances were that Denise had some legal question. Something about her job at Fort Washakie School, or about one of the field days she was always planning for her students—her kids, she called them. They'd wanted a family, she and T.J., but it hadn't worked out, Denise had once confided. T.J. had thrown his energies into politics, and she'd thrown her energies into her students and her passion for teaching them about the Old Time, so that they'd know their own history, she said, and be proud.

Once—ah, Vicky could picture her at the powwow, watching the dancers coming into the arena—she said that she wished she'd lived in the Old Time, when Sharp Nose was chief, and the people lived free on the plains.

"Why?" Vicky remembered asking. "You'd like butchering buffalo? Traipsing across the plains looking for wild vegetables and berries? Cooking all the meals and looking after the children and putting up the tipis and taking them down when the village moved? The women did all the work and catered to the men."

"So what's different?" Denise had thrown her head back and laughed.

Vicky heard herself laugh out loud at the memory. The sound hung in the air like a cry above the thump of the tires over a patch of icy asphalt.

She took a right past Fort Washakie School where Denise had taught, and drove toward Ethete. Another fifteen minutes on a graveled road, and the Jeep was churning across the bare dirt yard that wrapped around a small, brown house, the sun glinting on the sloped roof and flashing off the metal bumpers of the pickups and sedans parked in front. T.J. was the only one in the yard, coatless, sunken into himself in the cold, his light-colored shirt flattened against his chest in the wind as he paced up and down, puffing on the cigarette cupped in one hand. He looked in her direction and flicked the cigarette onto the ground.

Vicky parked behind a sedan and threaded her way around the other vehicles toward the man. He stood about six feet tall, a wirey build beneath his shirt and dark trousers, black hair pushed back behind his ears, dark eyes rimmed with exhaustion. Still, he was handsome, she thought. Still the handsome man she'd known all her life.

"Thanks for coming, Vicky," he said, pulling her into his arms. His shirt was damp with perspiration and cold. The odors of sweat, tobacco, and whiskey drifted over her.

"I'm so sorry," she said, stepping back. His eyes were dark slits beneath the sharp ledge of his forehead, and a

50

tuft of hair stood out, as if he'd been pulling at it. She took another step back from the sour, whiskey breath that made her stomach lurch with the memory of Ben. It was not a memory she wanted.

"You're going to catch cold out here," she said. "Why don't we go inside?"

He shook his head. "It's my fault, Vicky. All my fault. I killed her."

"What are you saying?"

The man looked out across the yard and the plains, silent and cold, flowing into the sky. "She did it 'cause of me," he said.

Vicky set one hand on the man's arm. "You're not making sense, T.J. You've had a horrible shock. You should get some rest. Let's go inside."

Vicky tried to steer the man toward the stoop, but T.J. yanked his arm free. "All the relatives showed up to help me grieve. Where the hell am I gonna rest? I need air, need to walk around, need to get . . ." His voice trailed off.

Sober, she thought.

"Fed's on the way over. Maybe he's got the coroner's report. Wants to interview me again. Christ, he asked me enough questions last night."

Vicky felt a jab of discomfort. Last night's interview should have been sufficient for a suicide. If he had the coroner's report, Gianelli should be able to close the investigation, unless . . .

Unless there was something unusual in the report. Even the shadow of a doubt about whether Denise had committed suicide, and the fed would be taking a very close look at Denise's husband. Vicky studied the man in front of her a moment. He was in no condition for a formal interview, especially if Gianelli was investigating a suspicious death.

She dug her cell out of her bag. "I'm calling Gianelli," she said, tapping the keys. "We'll postpone the interview. You can come to my apartment, shower, get something to eat and a few hours' sleep."

There was an instant when she thought he wouldn't go along. Then he nodded.

Two rings, and Gianelli was on the line. "It's Vicky," she said. She'd dealt with the FBI agent on numerous cases over the last five years. Homicides, kidnappings, fraud, embezzlement—all the crimes that the federal government considered "major" fell into the fed's jurisdiction.

"I'm with T.J.," she hurried on, turning away from the dark, smudged eyes of the man beside her. "He needs some rest before he talks to you again. I'll bring him to your office this afternoon."

"So, you'll be with him?" There was something unsettling in the question, as if T.J. was going to need an attorney.

"He's a friend, Ted."

"See you at three," Gianelli said.

Vicky pushed the END key and looked back at T.J. "Do you have any fresh clothes?"

The man nodded. "I keep some things here. Sometimes I stay with Vera." He shrugged off any impulse he might have had to explain. "I want you for my lawyer, Vicky. I can pay . . ."

Vicky put up the palm of one hand. "Wait in the Jeep. I'll get your things," she said, starting across the hard-packed dirt for the front stoop.

From inside came the dull, staccato rip of voices. She rapped on the door, then stepped into a square living room filled with people. The faint odors of coffee and hot grease floated like a cloud over the room. Grand-mothers clustered together around the sofa and uphol-stered chairs, elders on the straight-backed kitchen chairs pushed against one wall. Everywhere she looked—T.J.'s and Denise's relatives. In the far corner was Max Oldman, Denise's great-uncle, which made him her great-grandfather, in the Arapaho Way. Through the doorway to the kitchen, she could see Vera talking to a group of women.

Vicky pushed back the impulse to cut through the crowd and go directly to Vera. It was the white way. She started across the room, greeting the grandmothers, holding roughened, blue-veined hands in her own. Nod-ding. Nodding. Yes, Denise had been a good woman, a traditional. In the compliments paid to the dead woman, she could sense the lingering disapproval of herself, a woman who had stepped ahead of the men.

The elders were next, gray-haired, with furrowed faces and black, distracted eyes that might have been staring into another time, watching other scenes unfold. Max took hold of her hand, squeezing it hard, and she heard herself saying the empty words: so sorry, so ter-rible.

"Denise kept the Old Time alive for the kids." Max shook his head. He had black hair, threaded with gray and caught in two braids that dropped down the front of his denim shirt. He was probably in his eighties, frail and bent with gnarled hands that extended past the wide silver bracelets at his thin wrists. Still there was a strength in the man that Vicky could feel with the certainty that she felt her own heartbeat. In the Old Time, Max Oldman would have been a chief.

"Denise was all the time coming around," he said, "wanting to know about Sharp Nose and what he did for the people. Now who's gonna help the kids learn how the ancestors worked hard so the future generations could be happy? Denise thought a lot about the past. T.J., all he thinks about is the here and now. You gonna help T.J.?" The elder looked up at her, searching her eyes. For the briefest instant, Vicky thought she'd detected a note of disapproval in the elder's question. She pushed the idea away.

"I'll do my best." She smiled at the old man. It had been the elders who had seen that, when she became an attorney, she'd received power—magical gifts was how they looked at it—to help the people. She'd always had the feeling that, despite the grandmothers' disapproval of the fact that she had left her husband and made herself into a lawyer, the elders were on her side.

It was another few moments before Vicky could excuse herself and head into the kitchen. Vera was waiting for her.

"T.J. said you'd come soon as you heard the news." The woman had the same sleep-starved look that Vicky had seen in T.J. Exhaustion lay in the sloped shoulders and fluttering hands. "Some bastards brought a bottle over last night. They was drinking outside, T.J., too. Hasn't had a drink in . . ." She glanced at the ceiling. "Fifteen years. I don't blame him none. He's going through hell. That woman, she had no right to put him through that kind of hell."

Quiet descended over the kitchen, and Vicky could feel the eyes of the other women turning toward them. She took Vera's hand. The woman was trembling. "I'm going to take T.J. to my place to rest," she said, her voice low. "I'll take him to Gianelli this afternoon. Will you get his things?"

Vera drew in a long breath. The trembling seemed to recede into whatever recess it had erupted from. "Wait here." She withdrew her hand and headed into the living room.

"Want some coffee?" one of the women asked. The others had turned back to the counters, cutting casseroles and cakes, stacking paper plates and Styrofoam cups. Another woman was at the stove, turning chunks of fry bread in a pan. Drops of grease spattered the adjacent counter.

"No, thanks," Vicky said. Vera stood in the doorway, holding out a canvas bag that bulged at the sides. A plaid wool jacket was folded on top.

"Try not to worry about T.J.," Vicky said, taking the bag and jacket. The load was heavy in her arms. She slipped past the woman and made her way through the knots of people to the front door.

T.J. was asleep, she thought, opening the passenger door. Then she realized that he was awake, eyes closed, staring at some image on the back of his eyelids, clasping and unclasping his hands. The inside of the Jeep was like a freezer. She set the jacket on his lap, then shut the door.

He was pushing his arms into the sleeves as she got in behind the steering wheel and tossed the canvas bag over the front seat. The stale smell of whiskey hung in the space between them.

"What else does the fed want from me?" T.J. asked, a plaintive note in his voice that made her heart go out to the man.

The Jeep plowed over the barrow ditch and out onto the road before Vicky glanced over, struggling to ignore the uneasy feeling that clung to her like the odor of whiskey. "Maybe you'd better tell me what you told Gianelli last night."

It was a moment before T.J. said anything. The rhythm of his breathing—in and out, in and out—was like a soft drumbeat punctuating the sound of tires crunching gravel. "Told him how I came home from the office and found her," he said finally.

"What time was that?"

"Late, Vicky. I don't walk around looking at the clock."

Vicky glanced over again. Shades of wariness and distrust were working through the man's expression. "No one is accusing you of anything," she said.

"Around nine," he said after a few seconds. "Maybe nine-fifteen. Council meeting ran late. Some of the councilmen are starting to think that maybe we shouldn't go against Senator Evans on the methane drilling, since he might be the next president. Maybe we oughtta withdraw the request for more studies that we sent the BIA."

Vicky stopped herself from commenting. This wasn't her business. Surely the law firm in Cheyenne would discourage the council from backing away.

"Found her in the bedroom," T.J. pushed on. "Blood all over the floor. God, I knew she was dead, but she still had her eyes open. I started screaming. I don't even remember calling 911, but I must've, because pretty soon the police were pounding on the door. Then the fed showed up and started asking me all kinds of questions. Father John came over."

John O'Malley. She'd been working at putting the man out of her mind. No more phone calls with some lame excuse about how somebody was doing, just to hear his voice. They'd worked together on a lot of cases since she'd come back to the area five years ago—DUIs, divorces, drunk and disorderlies, drug possessions, and homicides—more homicides than she wanted to remember. He would've been one of the first people called last night, and he would've gone. She wondered if her people realized the enormous space that John O'Malley filled on the rez, like the space he had filled in her life, and the enormous emptiness that he would leave behind should he ever go away.

"What kinds of questions?" She had to force her thoughts back. They were heading south now on 287 behind a truck that spit gravel off the bed. Brown dust flecked the windshield like mosquitoes. Vicky turned on the wipers and tried to focus on the road past the spray of water and the gradual appearance of a clear half-circle of glass.

T.J. sucked in a breath, then he said, "'Who'd the gun belong to? Where'd Denise get it?' How the hell do I know? Denise hated guns, never would touch them. 'Was she depressed? On drugs? Drinking?' Christ. Denise never took a drink in her life. She was the one put up with me when I was drinking. Last night . . ." He hesitated. Out of the corner of her eye, Vicky could see him jabbing his fingers into his hair. "I'm not proud . . ."

"I know, T.J." The odor of whiskey was still there, encapsulated in the Jeep, permeating the seat and dashboard. She followed the truck around the curve into Lander, staying back a couple of car lengths from gravel still rolling like marbles over the asphalt. Down Main Street several blocks, then right, left. She pulled into the empty space in front of the blocklike apartment building. Usually she ran up the stairs to the second floor, but T.J. was shaking now, unsteady on his feet, lurching as they walked up the sidewalk. Inside the entry, she punched the elevator button and waited until the yellow light came on and the doors parted. She guided T.J. inside, where he slumped against the back railing. After the elevator rocked to a stop, she took the man's arm and led him down the hall to her door at the far end.

"There's lunchmeat and fruit in the fridge." she said, showing him into the living room. "Bread in the drawer." She waved at the small kitchen and led him down the hall. The bath on the left, the cabinet with clean towels. The bedroom on the right. A white terry cloth robe on the closet door, an array of cosmetics spread over the dresser top, books stacked on the bedside table. She found a wool blanket in the closet and set it on the bed. "You can put this over you," she said.

His arms were around her, pulling her into him, his mouth moving over her face, the odor of whiskey like a blanket suffocating her. "Stay with me, Vicky," he whispered. "I need you to stay with me. I never needed anything more in my whole life."

"Stop it, T.J." Vicky managed to get her fists between them and push at his chest. He leaned away, and she pushed again as hard as she could until he was staggering backward, arms flapping at his side. He crashed into the foot of the bed and flopped down on his back.

"I'll be out front at a quarter to three," she managed, her breath caught in her chest. "For Godsakes, T.J., pull yourself together."

6

FATHER JOHN HEARD the phone ringing as he bounded up the concrete steps to the administration building. He yanked open the heavy wood door and sprinted across the entry to his office on the right. Before he could pick up, the ringing stopped. From down the hall came the voice of Father Damien, filled with the authority of an executive in his father's company. Father John tossed his jacket over the coat tree. The conversation seemed one-sided, Damien's voice occasionally punctuating the quiet.

"Very good." He was breaking off. "We'll see you later."

Father John sat down at his desk and started working his way through the papers and folders spilling across the top, aware of the clack of boots coming down the hall. He looked up as Damien executed a sharp turn and came through the door.

"It's all set." The other priest laced his fingers together and cracked his knuckles.

"Senator Evans's campaign manager—name is Martin Quinn—will be here this afternoon to assess the mission."

"Assess the mission?" Father John pulled over a stack of phone messages that he intended to follow up on: Visit Ben Little Elk at Riverton Memorial, arrange the baptism date for Lucy Monroe's grandson, stop by Dora Willow's place to see how the old woman was getting along. And he wanted to drive over to Vera's and check on T.J.

"Quinn wants to see the grounds," Damien said, an edge of impatience in his voice. "They may want to build a platform . . ."

"What?" The other priest had his full attention now.

"For the senator to speak from. Quinn intends to invite the mayors from Lander and Riverton, county commissioners, a few judges. You know, local VIPs lining up behind local man's bid for the presidency. It'll make a terrific photo-op."

"What about the Arapahos and the programs at the mission?"

The other priest cracked his knuckles again. "There'll

60

be Indians around the platform. The senator will be speaking to them, encouraging them to avail themselves of the AA meetings, GED classes, after-school tutoring. Don't worry, John. It'll be all about the mission and the people."

"It'll be all about the senator."

"Trust me, John, it'll work out for everyone's . . ."

The front door banged shut, and Damien stepped back. Catherine Bizzel burst past him into the office. She was out of breath, her chest rising and falling beneath the fronts of the green jacket that she gripped together. Her face was flushed.

"What is it?" Father John asked.

"You see all the cars at the museum?" Stout and square-shouldered, in her fifties, with short, tightly curled gray hair and narrow eyes that looked like slits in her round, puffy face, Catherine was married to Leonard, the mission caretaker, for longer than Father John had been at St. Francis. Last summer, Father John hired the woman to work part-time, helping to arrange meetings and line up volunteers for the programs. He'd had to create a space for her out of a storage closet across the hall, which was barely large enough for a desk and chair.

Yes, he told her. He'd seen the cars on his way over from the residence. Since the Curtis exhibit opened, cars had been parked out front every day. Locals, tourists—probably a couple of hundred people had visited the museum.

"Well, a lot of people are hanging around, waiting for the museum to open." Catherine let go of her jacket, scratched at one sleeve, and stared at her watch. "Supposed to open twenty minutes ago. Where's the curator? She's here early most mornings."

True, Father John thought. He said, "Something might have come up." He fished a key out of the desk drawer, walked over, and handed the key to the woman. "Would you mind looking after the museum until Christine gets in?"

"I got my own work to do today," she said, wrapping puffy fingers around the key. "I gotta get the storeroom organized."

"I appreciate it, Catherine," he said, ushering the woman into the hall. If the storeroom had ever been organized, it was long before anyone at the mission could remember.

"A reluctant recruit." Father Damien was shaking his head and smiling. "Wonder what's holding up Christine?"

Father John stepped back to the desk and picked up the phone with one hand while riffling through the cards in the Rolodex with the other. He punched in Christine's number and stared at the papers on his desk, listening to the buzzing of a phone somewhere in Riverton. Seven, eight rings, and he hung up. "She must be on her way," he said.

IT WAS ALMOST noon when Father John parked the pickup at the edge of the other vehicles in front of Vera's house. The sun was warm on his face, and what was left of the morning frost had turned into moisture that glistened like diamonds flung across the gold and orange brush. The front door stood open and he stepped inside, making his way through the crowded living room, visiting with the grandmothers and elders as he went. T.J. was nowhere around. The house was hot and stuffy, reeking with the odors of coffee and perspiration. And grief, he thought. Grief had its own distinct odor. He'd gotten so that he could detect the smell of grief the moment he stepped into a house of mourning.

Vera was on the far side of the room near the hallway, shoulders rigid with anxiety, eyes rimmed in red. He tried to hurry over, but someone handed him a mug of coffee and someone else plucked at his sleeve and wanted to know when Denise's funeral would be held. He'd tried to explain: As soon as the coroner released the body. That had started a new round of questions— didn't white people understand that the body had to be buried within three days? Didn't they know that Denise's spirit was waiting to go to the ancestors? He promised to do his best to try to explain to the coroner and to Gianelli, even though he'd explained dozens of times in the past.

"How's T.J.?" he asked, when he finally got to Vera.

"He's a mess, Father." The woman let her gaze flicker across the room. "Never seen him in such a state. Started drinking last night, so he can get through this."

Father John closed his eyes and kneaded his fingers into his forehead. He used to tell himself that it was easy to slip backward, but he'd been wrong. It was hard to slip backward. It took something horrible, the plates of the earth shifting beneath your feet. Easy was going along, guarding against the opportunity and the excuse

63

to take a drink, conquering one easy temptation after another, thinking you were safe. It was in the hard time when all the resolutions and AA meetings and firm intentions gave way to the thirst.

"He's a good man." Vera was staring across the room, as if T.J. might materialize on the sofa with the grand-mothers. "He wants to be strong for others, but with Denise up and shooting herself . . ." She shook her head. "It's more than any man can take."

"Where is he?"

"Fed's been breathing down his neck. Why can't he leave T.J. alone? Let him get on with burying his wife. Vicky came and got him."

Father John looked away, giving himself a moment for the dull ache that always came at the mention of her name to subside. It had been two months since he'd seen Vicky Holden. He'd put her out of his mind, he'd thought, and yet, there she was again, like a picture in an album that he'd come upon unexpectedly.

"Vicky will make certain T.J.'s okay," he said.

A ROW OF dark clouds—a promise of snow—had begun piling up over the mountains and drifting across the sky as Father John turned into Circle Drive. Still, a pale sun-shine speckled the grounds between the stripes of shadow. He spotted his assistant with two men in black topcoats over in front of the vehicles parked at the museum. Damien flapping an arm toward the open field in the center of Circle Drive, the other men rolling their heads from side to side.

The pickup lurched to a stop a few feet away and

Father John got out. "Here's the pastor now," Damien said.

"Ah, Father O'Malley." A stocky man, about six feet tall, came forward, extending a beefy hand. He was still in his thirties—light-brown hair combed tight against his scalp, a round face flushed with cold that made him look as if he'd just jogged a couple of miles around a track.

"Paul Russell, with Senator Evans's campaign." His grip was like an iron clamp. "Meet Martin Quinn, Wyoming campaign manager."

Father John shook hands with the other man, who had at least twenty years on Russell and a quiet authority about him. He was shorter, not more than five-and-a-half-feet tall, with a thin, muscular build and long, pock-marked face bisected by narrow, wire-framed glasses. Behind the glasses were eyes like gray steel nuggets. "Looks like we'll have the senator here about an hour after Fort Washakie."

"We'll put the platform there." Damien took a couple steps forward and jabbed one fist toward the edge of the field. "That'll allow plenty of room to set up the communication systems and folding chairs. Television cameras will be in front, but people will still be able to see the senator and the local dignitaries up on the platform." He shot a glance at the other men. "Demonstrate the senator's wide appeal to the people here."

"We'll want a big crowd of Indians in the front." Quinn turned to Father John. "I trust you can get them here."

"Hold on a minute." Father John held up one hand.

"Platform? Communication systems? What are we talking about? A political rally?"

"The campaign staff will provide the necessary equipment, Father. You and Father Damien here"—Quinn gave a brief nod toward the other priest—"will supply the Indians."

"We can't hogtie people and bring them to the mission."

"Hogtie?" What passed for a smile came into Russell's florid face. "We're aware this isn't a hundred years ago, Father."

Quinn straightened his shoulders and rocked upward on the balls of his feet, so that for an instant he seemed taller. He cleared his throat—a low, rough noise like that of an engine trying to kick over. "Senator Evans supports the right of the people here to benefit from the resources on their land." A campaign speech, Father John thought. The man might have been reading from a teleprompter.

"The senator wants to see jobs created on the reservation by opening the coal beds to drilling. We have to develop the nation's natural energy resources. I'm sure you can make the Arapahos understand that, as president, Senator Evans will support Indians' benefiting from the resources on reservations."

The man turned to Father Damien. "We'll be in touch," he said, then he started toward a green SUV. Russell followed, arms swinging at his sides like a bulky black bird trying to get aloft.

Father Damien took a couple steps after them, then turned back. Father John felt the man's hand clamp like

66

a vise on his shoulder. "Don't worry, John," he said. "Quinn will make sure that the senator mentions the programs here at the mission. The senator supports private programs, the kind where underprivileged people learn how to help themselves. It's part of his agenda."

The SUV burst past, tires spitting out gravel as the vehicle headed toward Seventeen-Mile Road. "Spoke with Dad this morning," Damien went on. "He pledged to match the donations that come in. We should be able to start building the new community center in the next few months. And we can spruce up the old place." Taking his hand away, he made a slow turn toward the mission buildings, as if he could already see the results.

Father John followed his assistant's gaze. The museum could use a coat of paint, the residence a new roof. The roof would probably leak with the first snow—a slow stream of water dripping into the upstairs bathroom. The church needed refurbishing, and the administration building—where would they start? The old building hadn't been touched in years. Maybe the donations would flow in. In any case, Damien was the first assistant in a long time who'd taken an interest in the mission. He was different. The man could be here for a while.

Which meant . . .

Father John pushed the thought away. He didn't want to follow it to the logical conclusion: With a man like Damien in place, the provincial would no doubt find another assignment for Father John.

"I asked Leonard to pick things up a bit." Damien nodded at the pile of branches broken in the wind two weeks ago. "Touch up the paint on the porch." A nod toward the museum as a couple came through the door, crossed the porch, and headed for a sedan. "TV cameras are sure to zero in on the museum, with the Curtis exhibit. Dad says it's important that the mission not look too rundown. People like to be on the side of winners." He laughed at this, his eyes on the sedan following the SUV's tracks around Circle Drive.

For the first time, Father John noticed that the curator's Range Rover wasn't parked at the far end of the porch where she usually left it.

"Did Christine come in?" he asked.

"Never showed up. Tried calling her house. No answer. Catherine's been fuming about having to watch the museum."

"Maybe Catherine's heard something," Father John said. He gave the other priest a wave, then darted between two SUVs and bounded up the steps.

Inside, knots of people were moving about the gallery, peering at the photographs. In the mixture of daylight filtering through the windows and the fluorescent lights washing down from above, the figures in the photographs took on a sharper cast—the three warriors on the far wall looked darker, more menacing; the people in the village more unsuspecting and vulnerable.

The door to the office was half-ajar, forming a narrow frame around the figure of Catherine seated behind the desk, thumbing through the magazine spread in front of her.

"Any word from Christine?" Father John pushed the door open.

"Nothing." The woman slapped the magazine closed, gripped the armrests, and pushed herself to her feet. "She oughtta take the time to call, if she isn't gonna show up. People been coming and going, asking a lot of questions about Curtis and the photographs that I don't know how to answer. Think she's gonna show up tomorrow?"

"Do you have Christine's number?" Father John picked up the phone at the edge of the desk and waited while the woman fumbled under the magazine, then handed him a notepad with a phone number on top and a series of black doodles impressed in the margins. He could imagine her dialing the number, listening to the ringing and jabbing the pen at the paper, the little circles and squares becoming darker and more jagged as the morning gave way to afternoon.

Now he punched in the number. "Come on," he said under his breath, but the ringing went on. He replaced the phone and scoured the papers on the side of the desk with his eyes, looking for a calendar or day timer that might explain the curator's absence. A conference she'd forgotten to mention, a family get-together she couldn't miss.

Then he remembered. Last night, Christine had taken her briefcase. Any day timer that she kept was probably with her.

"You can close the museum as soon as the visitors leave," he told the woman who had dropped back onto the chair. Gratitude and relief flashed in the brown eyes, as if he'd released her from a long, hard imprisonment.

He retraced his steps through the entry and held the

door for three women who were talking about the photographs—the realism, the amazing beauty. "You feel like the warriors are about to ride into the gallery," one of the women said. The others laughed.

Father John followed them down the steps and made a straight line for the pickup.

7

CHRISTINE NELSON LIVED on the north side of Riverton in a neighborhood of squat, flat-roofed duplexes with a FOR RENT, FURNISHED sign in one window and oily blue patches on the asphalt at the curb. Father John slowed past the occasional parked vehicle, looking for the address that he'd gotten from the curator's file in his office—engine running outside, pickup bucking like a corralled stallion. The units all looked the same, with green-painted siding and small windows flanking the front doors recessed from small, concrete stoops.

He spotted the numbers next to the door at the end unit, where dried stalks lifted out of a red planter at the corner of the stoop. There was no sign of the woman's Range Rover.

Father John pulled into the curb and started up a narrow sidewalk that divided a square of brown-spotted lawn. He stopped. The front door stood open a couple of inches.

He stepped onto the stoop and rapped on the hinged edge of the door. "Christine?" he called.

Silence, apart from the breeze knocking at the gutter.

He pushed at the door and stepped inside. Papers

crackled under his boots. Papers everywhere—strewn across the green carpet, spilling over the sofa and chair. Foam poked out of long slashes in the cushions tossed about. A table lamp lay shattered in the center of the room, and, over in a corner, the carpet had been yanked away and dropped back on itself in a mute triangle. The atmosphere was suffused with a sense of spent desperation.

Father John stood still a moment, listening for the sound of life. There was nothing but the sounds of his own breathing—rapid, shallow intakes of air. He headed into the kitchen, picking his way through papers and shards of glass. Whoever had done this hadn't stopped in the living room. Cabinet doors were flung open, broken dishes and glasses littered the countertops and vinyl floor. Boxes cut open, cereal tossed about. The refrigerator door hung into the room, drawers pulled out, shelves swept clean. A rectangle of white light shone over the carton of milk that had spilled across the floor, running into a broken jar that oozed red jam.

He swung around, his heart thudding in his ears, and crossed the living room to a short hallway. A pair of closed doors faced each other. He opened the door on the right into the same chaos: mattress pulled to the floor, dresser drawers upended with a few silky pieces of women's underwear spilling out, closet doors ajar, a couple of blouses and pairs of slacks pulled off the hangers and trailing into the room.

Christine Nelson was nowhere.

He crossed the hall and reached for the knob on the

other door, his hand numb with reluctance. He opened the door into the bathroom. Towel bars ripped from the walls, broken bottles scattered over the heap of towels on the black and white vinyl floor. Tiny pieces of glass winked in the pool of reddish liquid inside the door. Stooping down, he dipped a finger in the liquid and brought it to his nose. Lotion that smelled of roses.

He'd wiped his finger on a corner of a towel and made a half-turn into the hall when he heard the noise, like the noise of rustling leaves. Then, footsteps, tentative and carefully placed across the littered floor of the living room.

Father John moved along the plastered wall toward the noise, a single thought filling his mind, pushing out every other possibility. Whoever had ransacked the house had returned to take a harder look. What was next? Pull up the carpet, rip out the floors, take down the wallboard?

The footsteps had stopped moving, and Father John also stopped, his shoulder pressed against the rough plaster. He kept his breathing shallow and quiet, another thought crowding into his mind now. Whoever had ransacked the house could have gotten more information and knew where to find whatever he was looking for. Father John curled his hands into fists—whoever was in the living room could have gotten the information from Christine.

He started inching forward again, his breath tight in his chest. The footsteps had also started moving—receding, as if the person had sensed the presence of someone else in the house. The intruder would return,

Father John was certain. The violent search—the torn and crushed pieces of Christine Nelson's life—attested to the fact that he would return. It didn't matter. All that mattered was that the person about to vanish knew where Christine was.

"Hey!" Father John shouted as he burst around the corner into the living room.

A woman whirled about. Her mouth hung open a moment, gulping in air. Then she started to scream. She backed into the door, hands flailing behind her for the knob, the screaming moving toward hysteria.

Father John uncurled his fists and lifted his hands, palms outward. "I'm sorry." He had to shout over the wail of her voice. "I didn't mean to frighten you."

The woman threw both hands over her mouth, as if to stifle the noise erupting of its own will. Then she reached around and yanked at the door, moving along the edge until she was in the opening, a step away from the outdoors and freedom.

"I'm Father O'Malley from St. Francis." He tried to keep his voice calm. "I'm looking for Christine."

The woman leaned against the door for support, and, for a instant, he thought she might slide to the floor. She had large eyes that shone with fear. He guessed that she was in her thirties. A slight build beneath the baggy red sweatshirt that dropped over the top of her blue jeans and reddish-blond hair pulled back into a knot with long ends that stuck out like feathers.

"Are you a friend?" he asked.

She stared at the littered floor, then lifted her eyes to his a moment. "Jana Harris," she said, tossing her head toward the outdoors. "I live next door."

"Christine didn't come to work today."

"I figured as much," she said.

He waited, and finally the woman explained: She and Christine left for work at the same time every morning. It was always a tossup as to who drove away first, but this morning, Christine wasn't there. Neither was her Range Rover. She figured Christine must've left early, but later she'd got to thinking about it. You could set your clock by when Christine walked out of the door every morning. Maybe something had happened. So she'd called the museum and someone else had answered, not Christine. The minute she'd gotten home, she'd come over to check.

Jana Harris threw another glance around the room. "Last night when I was watching TV," she went on, "I heard a noise, like somebody sideswiping a car. I looked outside. There was an SUV parked across the street, but nobody was around. I didn't think any more about it."

"What time was that?" Father John asked.

She shrugged. "The news just ended. Must've been about ten-thirty."

Father John kept his eyes on the woman propped against the door, the upended cushions and piles of debris blurring around him. Christine had driven out of the mission grounds about eight-thirty on her way to a meeting. She could have gotten home by ten-thirty and walked in on a burglary, except that this was no burglary and . . . What was it that gnawed at him? The sparseness of the place, the worn furniture and bare walls. Nothing but shredded newspapers, as if Christine had not intended to stay long. Whoever had ransacked the place had conducted a determined, angry search.

And when he'd left, he could have taken Christine with him.

"I'm going to call the police," Father John said, starting for the door, his boots crunching the shards of glass. The woman backed outside, and he brushed past her and cut a diagonal across the yard to the pickup. He opened the passenger door and pulled the cell phone out of the glove compartment. Another couple of minutes, and he was talking to a female operator at the Riverton Police Department. He should remain at the house, the woman said. A patrol officer was on the way.

Father John tossed the phone onto the seat and walked back to the woman sitting on the front stoop, head pitched forward, arms clasped around her knees. He sat down beside her on the cold concrete.

"Just when everything was coming together for her." Jana Harris turned sideways, studying him a moment. "Christine was excited about the Curtis exhibit. Said people were coming from all over to see the photographs. She'd already started working on another project . . ."

This was new. Christine hadn't mentioned bringing in another exhibit. Usually the museum showed Arapaho artifacts—beaded clothing and moccasins, necklaces and belts, eagle-feathered headdresses, bows and arrows and quivers, a tipi once owned by Chief Sharp Nose. The collections kept growing. The Curtis exhibit was the first exhibit from outside.

"What kind of project?" he asked.

"You don't know? You're her boss."

"The boss only thinks he knows everything."

"I thought you were some kind of ogre, making her work every evening."

"She was working on the project in the evenings?" That explained Christine's Range Rover parked outside the museum after closing time.

"What else?" Jana was clasping and unclasping her hands between her knees. "Christine never told me what it was, but she was obsessed, I can tell you that. I said to her, Christine, you gotta get out more. I know a fun bar. We can go have a couple drinks, meet some cowboys. Nothing like a few laughs to take your mind off work, but she didn't want any part of it. Work, work, work. That's all she wanted."

Father John watched the white police cruiser slide alongside the curb. Blue lettering on the doors read RIVERTON POLICE. The driver's door swung open. Father John got to his feet as an officer in a dark-blue uniform, trousers, and jacket, crawled out, slammed the door shut, and started up the sidewalk. The brim of his hat shaded a round, boyish face.

"Father O'Malley?" he asked.

Father John nodded, and the officer turned his attention to Jana Harris. "And you are?"

Out of the corner of his eye, Father John saw the woman start to get up, swaying to one side. He reached down, took her arm, and guided her upward as she gave the officer her name and, nodding toward the next stoop, said that she lived next door. Father John realized that she was shivering beside him.

"What's going on?" The officer locked eyes with Father John.

"We came to check on Christine Nelson, the woman who lives here," he said, gesturing with his head toward the door. Then he explained that Christine had been the curator at the museum at St. Francis for the past month, that she'd left the mission last night to attend a meeting and hadn't come to work today. The house had been ransacked.

"Wait here," the officer said, sliding past the half-opened door. Several moments passed. From inside the house came the muffled noise of boots on carpet, the rattle of paper and the crackle of glass. Cold permeated the air, and fingers of blue shadows had started to spread over the yard. From down the block came the sound of a motor coughing into life, and somewhere nearby, a cat was meowing.

A quiet, normal neighborhood, he thought, trying to push away the images crowding into his mind. He didn't want to think of Christine coming home last night in the dark, blundering in on someone ripping her house apart.

"Looks like somebody got mad as hell," the officer said, shouldering his way past the door and onto the stoop. "Any idea who the lady was going to meet?"

Father John said that he had no idea.

The officer faced Jana. "Were you home last night?"

When she nodded, he pushed on. "Hear any noise? Any screams?"

"What?" The woman's head bounced back. She blinked up at the boyish face. "Screams? No, no screaming."

It was odd, Father John thought, the sense of relief that flowed over him. No screams, and he hadn't seen any sign of blood in the house. That gave him hope. Christine could have gotten away. *Dear Lord, let that be true.*

"Nothing but a car revving up on the street," Jana said.

"What kind of car?" The officer had extracted a notepad and pen from inside his jacket. He cupped the pad in his hand and began scribbling.

"I don't know. Big car, SUV of some kind." Jana hunched her shoulders and dipped her chin into the folds of her sweatshirt. "It wasn't Christine's."

"What kind of vehicle does the woman drive?"

"Range Rover," Father John said. "Light-tan color."

"Car belong to her?"

"I assume so," Father John said. It hadn't occurred to him that Christine might be driving someone else's car.

"License?"

Father John glanced away, trying to picture the license plate. He'd walked past the vehicle dozens of times. "The license was from Teton County. Number twenty-two on the plate," he said.

"Recall any other numbers?

Jana Harris was shaking her head.

Father John closed his eyes. *God, what were the numbers.* "Seven," he said, the first number coming into view. "Three. Four." The rest was a blur.

"Range Rover," the officer said, still scribbling. "Teton County, seven, three, four. It's a start." He looked up from the notepad. "Christine Nelson ever failed to show up for work before?"

Father John shook his head. "She is very dependable."

"I'm freezing to death," Jana said, hunching her shoulders and dipping her chin further into the folds of her sweatshirt. "Can we go to my house and talk?"

"Lead the way." The officer reached back and pulled the door shut as Jana started across the lawn, her shoes snapping against the dried leaves scattered about.

Father John started after the woman, the officer behind him, so close he could feel the warmth of the man's breath on his neck.

"I'm gonna call in the investigator on duty," he said. "He'll want to know everything that you know about Christine Nelson."

Odd, Father John thought. The woman had worked for him for a month now, and he knew nothing at all about her.

8

October 1907

JESSE WHITE OWL leaned over the fire, cupped the cedar smoke in his hands, and brought them to his face—the healing, cleansing cedar smoke. It would bring the spirit of Bashful Woman to the ancestors, the elders said, and Jesse believed that was true, even though he wished for nothing more than her spirit to come walking toward him through the junipers. A selfish wish. He closed his eyes against his selfishness and weakness. She should go to the sky world now and dwell with the ancestors, her spirit light and free and peaceful, and not return simply because a man who walked the earth loved her.

"Go in peace, Bashful, "he said, staring over at the flowers that spilled across the hump of dirt covering her grave, trying to inhale the sacred smoke into his own spirit.

Carston Evans, the white man, had said, "My wife will have a proper Christian funeral at the mission. She will be buried on the mission grounds."

It was then that Stands-Alone, the son of Chief Sharp Nose, said, "My sister is Arapaho. She shall be buried with the ancestors."

In the end, they had compromised. Stands-Alone said, "We will go to the church first, and then we will take her into the mountains and place her in the earth where other relatives are buried."

"After the funeral"—Jesse could still see the contempt in the way the white man spit out the words—"do whatever you Indians want."

Jesse had gone with Stands-Alone to the burial place, walking into the hills that lifted out of Fort Washakie and merged into the high slopes of the Wind River Range. Walking in the silence of grief, the shovel light on Jesse's shoulder.

"Her grave will be here," Stands-Alone said. Nearby were the mounds of other graves. Junipers and lodgepoles all around and through the branches, the clear blue sky from which their people had come. Her spirit would return to the sky.

"Hi'3eti," Jesse said. It is good.

He had dug deep into the earth so that the wild beasts

would not disturb her body. Later, after the priests had shaken their holy water over the pine box in which she lay, he and Stands-Alone and his son, Thomas, had lifted the box onto the wagon and brought her to the grave, a line of wagons and people on horseback trailing behind, everyone walking in silence and respect. The clip of hooves and the loud squeal of the wagon wheels dissolved into the sounds of the wind. Before they'd lowered the box into the ground, Stands-Alone had opened the lid. She had looked beautiful, Jesse thought. A fine piece of beaded deerskin covered the wound that had opened her heart. All of her belongings had been carefully wrapped in bundles and laid in the grave with her. The drumming began, and the women started singing. *A'nea'thibiwa'hana, thi'aya'ne, thi'aya'ne'*— the place where crying begins, the mound, the mound.

It was then that the holy old men had approached, lifting pans with burning cedar so that the smoke would float over her body. They had painted her face with the sacred red paint that marked her as one of the people so that the ancestors would recognize her. Not until the ceremony was finished did they lower the box into the earth. Jesse had shoveled in the dirt, and one by one people had approached and laid flowers on the grave until the mound was bursting with pink and white wild roses and the red of Indian paintbrush.

That had been four days ago. He had stayed with her since.

Now Jesse sat back on his heels and raised his face to the sky. He winced at the images coming to him, bringing a lesson he was supposed to learn. Images of the day he had first seen Carston Evans on the porch at the Arapaho Mercantile Company, his face shining like the moon in the brown faces milling about. It was sale day, and families pulled up in wagons loaded with bales of alfalfa and burlap bags stuffed with the surplus oats that the ranchers didn't need for the cattle and horses. Usually the white man who owned the store, John Cooper Burnet, checked the amount of alfalfa and oats. But that day, the new white man went from wagon to wagon, making little black marks in a ledgerbook and passing out the yellow chits that were the same as money in the store.

When he reached the front of the line, Jesse jumped down and followed the white man around the wagon, glancing over the man's shoulder to make certain that he wrote down the correct number of bales and burlap bags. He'd never had to worry about Burnet, but this white man was a stranger dropped into their midst. He didn't trust strangers.

"Where's Big Eyes?" Jesse asked, using the name everyone called Burnet.

"Gone to Omaha to buy merchandise." The white man had stopped putting down his numbers and looked Jesse straight in the eye, as bold as a she-bear. "Hired me to help out for a couple weeks. Carston Evans, the name. Move along." He pressed a handful of yellow chits into Jesse's hand and nodded toward the warehouse behind them.

Jesse had climbed back onto the wagon seat when he saw Bashful. The moment was as clear in his mind as a recurring dream. He looked for her on sales days, watching for the slightest change in her expression, the little adjustment in the way she held her head, which meant that she would try to slip away from Auntie Sara and meet him alone behind the store for a few moments. She was always chaperoned by Auntie Sara. Ever since Sharp Nose died, her brother had looked after her in the traditional way.

But when Jesse had tried to catch her eye that day, Bashful had looked away. He'd followed her gaze to the white man walking around the wagons, shouting, "Move along." Jesse felt as if an icy hand had gripped his heart, and he knew that he must act now, even though the log house he was building for her was not yet finished. He had only the faintest memory of unloading the wagon. What he remembered was stomping into the store, the chits damp with the sweat of his hand. He'd selected the finest pieces of calico from the piles on the counter. Then tins of tobacco, coffee, sugar, and slabs of bacon, as much as he could hold in his arms, aware of Bashful at the window, eyes hunting the white man outside.

Jesse handed his chits to Carrier Shotgun, the Arapaho who helped Burnet inside the store. He'd hurried across the porch and stored the purchases in the wagon. Then he drove out of the yard, willing the horses to fly over the prairie.

He'd found Stands-Alone waiting in the opened door of the big log cabin where he lived with his wife and children, close to the small cabin that Bashful occupied with Auntie Sara. The man had waved Jesse inside, as if he'd been expecting him. Jesse had followed him, his gaze fixed on the line of gray sweat that ran down the other man's white shirt, over the knobs of his spine. Jesse set the gifts on the table and waited until Stands-Alone straddled the wood bench and motioned him to sit down on the other side. It was then that he'd noticed Thomas, Stands-Alone's oldest son, on the chair in the far corner. He had tilted the chair back against the wall, his boots tucked behind the front legs.

"Why do you come?" Stands-Alone had not wasted time on the polite preliminaries, and Jesse understood that Bashful's brother already knew why he'd come.

He began slowly, reaching for the words in Arapaho. Stands-Alone was the son of a chief, and he, Jesse, was nobody, the son of nobody. He had no memory of the time when his mother had taken him from his father and fled Oklahoma with another man. Bravehorn, he was called. Bravehorn had never treated him like a son. In the warm months, Jesse had slept in the corral, and in the cold times, on a blanket in the kitchen. One day the priest had come to the house and said, "This boy should go to school. He's smart."

Bravehorn had laughed, but he didn't interfere when his mother took him to the boarding school at St. Francis Mission. He'd joined the other new children, all sniveling and crying. Jesse didn't cry. It was the day he started to become a man.

Bashful was one of the children, but she hadn't cried either. She'd been kind to him, telling him not to worry. They would learn to read and write and follow the white road, the way her father and Auntie Sara had said, and Jesse hadn't the heart to tell her that he wasn't worried.

84

He was free. He had started to love her then.

By the end of his school years, Jesse had read many books. He could figure numbers, build houses and barns and fences, and plant and harvest crops, and he had his height and strength. He could make his own way. He had his own allotment, one hundred and sixty acres on the reservation parceled out by the government in Washington to educated Indians. He'd focused his energy on proving himself worthy for a chief's daughter.

"For many years, I have loved your sister," he'd told Stands-Alone. From the corner came a low snicker. Jesse remembered trying to blot the sound from his mind. It made no difference what Thomas thought. "I ask your permission to take her as a wife." Jesse's tongue had felt dry, the words like chips of wood inside his mouth. He'd stumbled on, explaining that he'd had a fine crop this season, surplus oats and alfalfa to sell at the Mercantile, not mentioning that he'd used the profit to purchase the gifts. He had enough logs to finish the house he was building for her.

Stands-Alone was quiet a long time. Finally he struck the edge of the table with the palm of his hand. "You are a fool, Jesse White Owl. Do you think she cares about your crops and livestock and log house? She has her own allotment next to the land our father gave to her, with a fine house the relatives have built for her. She will go to the house when she marries."

"I wanted to give her a gift." Jesse had blurted out the words.

"You wanted to show her what a great man you are."

85

Stands-Alone got to his feet and leaned over the table, angry white light flicking in his dark eyes. "You speak too late. Another man will marry her."

The icy hand squeezed his heart. Jesse had to fight for the next breath. "The white man," he managed.

"He has been courting her, meeting her outside the Mercantile when they didn't think anyone was watching. While you were in Omaha selling your cattle, he came with a wagon-load of gifts, thinking he could purchase my sister." Stands-Alone threw back his head and guffawed. Another snicker erupted from the corner. "I told him to leave," Stands-Alone said. "Who is he? A stranger from a farm in Nebraska comes here to Indian country and gets himself a job at the Mercantile—that's all he is. He has nothing to give her."

"You told him to leave?" Jesse asked, his face warm with the flush of hope.

"Aunt Sara came to me and said, the girl is crying. Refuses to eat or leave the cabin. She said to me that Bashful will die if I don't allow her to marry the man she loves. What could I do?"

Jesse remembered leaving the cabin, legs wobbling beneath him. He'd managed to hoist himself onto the wagon bench and pull away, not looking at the cabin where she lived. He did not go to the wedding. He'd tried to stop up his ears when people gossiped about how Bashful had worn her mother's dress, deerskin as soft as silk with beads across the top and fringe along the hem of the skirt. Her black hair was pinned up with beaded combs and an eagle feather. She and the white man had gone to St. Francis church where the priest said they were now man and wife; but afterward, they'd gone to the two-story house that her family had prepared for her. She had stood in the doorway and invited the white man inside, the way her mother had invited her father inside the tipi her family had given her. The moment the white man had stepped across the threshold, they became man and wife in the Arapaho Way. All the relatives had crowded into the house, and Stands-Alone had spoken to Bashful and her husband in Arapaho. They should love one another, he'd said. They should live in peace; they should follow the white road and the good red road. They should love their children.

Now Jesse rocked back on his heels, his gaze fastened on the flowers, drooping and fading over the mound. He could feel the wetness on his face, taste the warm, salty moisture on his lips. It was his fault that she was dead. He saw the sequence of pictures, one after the other, like shadows flitting over the mound. He hadn't asked for her soon enough, and she had married the white man, who brought her and the child to Curtis's village. And there she was, cradling her child, when the fool . . .

The fool, Thunder, playing at being a warrior, riding down slope with the other fool warriors, shooting rifles into the air. Into the air! Except for Thunder, galloping through the village, forgetting it was a game, rushing toward her tipi and firing, firing. When was it? At what point had Thunder drawn a real cartridge from his pocket, slipped it into the loading port of the Winchester 73 and worked the lever? Just before he'd turned his pony toward Bashful's tipi?

Oh, there were witnesses who saw what happened

next. The white man himself told the agent what he saw—the fool firing the rifle at his wife. Firing close-up to make certain he wouldn't miss.

Jesse knew then what he had to do. The certainty rose up inside him and choked off the air until blackness started to circle him. The blackness didn't leave until he made his vow: "I will kill the man who killed you, Bashful."

9

VICKY SPOTTED T.J. waiting outside the glass doors of her apartment building as she drove around the corner. He had the look of a man who had stepped outside a bank after being turned down for a loan—slim and medium height, black hair combed back, hunching over the cigarette held close to his lips, taking quick puffs and staring into the vacant street. He had on blue jeans and the plaid jacket unzipped over a blue shirt. As she pulled up to the curb, he flicked the cigarette onto the sidewalk, got in beside her, and slammed the door hard into the silence.

He didn't say anything. The Jeep filled with the odors of aftershave and tobacco smoke.

Vicky made a U-turn and headed toward Main Street. "I hope you got some rest," she said.

"Listen, Vicky . . ." T.J. paused and made a sucking noise, as if he were taking another draw on the cigarette. "Forget what happened at your place, okay? I don't know what came over me. It's like the world is breaking off into little pieces. Denise shooting herself! Jesus . . ."

Vicky glanced over. He was shaking his head, running his eyes over the windshield in search of an explanation.

"I mean, Jesus, she was my wife, and she went and blew a hole in her head. I shouldn't have made a pass at you."

"It's forgotten, T.J." Vicky heard the sound of her own voice, tight and controlled. She'd been trying to forget all afternoon, but the image of T.J. pulling her into his chest rubbed in her mind like glass in an open wound. She'd trusted T.J. since they were kids. There had been times when she'd felt he was the only person on her side, the only one who faced the truth about Ben, about her crumbling marriage. T.J. who had said, "Leave him, Vicky. I'll help you."

She maneuvered the Jeep into a parking space in front of a row of flat-faced brick buildings with shops displaying an array of books, clothing, and gifts behind plate-glass windows. T.J. kept up a running explanation directed at the windshield: The truth was . . . Did she want the truth? The truth was he'd always found her very attractive. That was a fact. No way would he have gotten out of line if it hadn't been for the shock . . .

"I said, forget it." Vicky felt a prick of surprise at the sharpness in her voice. She turned off the engine and got out, grateful for the cold air washing over her, providing an invisible barrier between her and the man crawling out of the passenger seat.

"How long's this gonna take?" he asked as they started across the sidewalk, dodging a red leash that connected a black spaniel to a large, thick-waisted woman with a knit hat pulled down over her ears.

"Not long." Vicky opened the door wedged between two plate-glass windows and started up the narrow steps covered in black vinyl. There was a sense of the past in the building—the dim lights hanging from the high ceiling, the sheen on the brass hand rail, and the slight grooves worn into the center of the steps by decades of boots. T.J.'s boots scraped behind her.

"Gianelli's probably trying to figure out why Denise would want to end her life so he can tie this up." Vicky tossed the words over her shoulder as she reached the second floor. Several pebble-glass doors circled the wide hallway.

"She shot herself," T.J. spit out the words. "She had no cause."

"Take it easy." Vicky placed a hand on the man's arm. She could feel the tightness in the muscles beneath his jacket sleeve. He was still in shock. What took place earlier in her apartment was caused by shock. T.J. was an old friend, and she was beginning to regret bringing him for an interview this afternoon. She should have asked Gianelli to put the interview off until T.J. had the chance to recover his equilibrium. And yet, the family wanted to hold the funeral within three days.

Vicky guided the man to the door on the right and pressed the intercom on the wall. "Vicky Holden," she said, leaning into the speaker. "With T.J. Painted Horse."

Several seconds passed. T.J. was taking in gulps of air, like a runner getting ready for a sprint. Finally the door swung inward and Ted Gianelli—two hundred and fifty pounds, dressed in dark trousers and a light blue shirt opened at the collar—stood in the opening. He surveyed the hall a moment before nodding them inside.

"This way," he said, leading them down a hallway toward a pair of windows that overlooked the street. In front of the windows was a large wooden desk covered with folders arranged in orderly stacks. A computer stood on a table next to the desk, a scene of blue-and-white mountains fixed like a photograph on the monitor.

The fed walked over and picked up a file folder. "Have a seat," he said, pointing the folder toward two chairs on the other side of the desk.

Vicky took one of the chairs. T.J. didn't move, and for a moment she was afraid that he might whirl about and head back down the hall. The fed must have had the same thought because he waited until T.J. dropped into the other chair before he sat down behind the desk.

Gianelli opened the file folder and thumbed through the thin stack of papers inside, giving them his full attention. He seemed older all of a sudden, Vicky thought—brow more furrowed, squint lines cut more deeply, black hair streaked with gray. He was about her age, forty-five. He'd been assigned to the area for five years now, and in that time, there had been more homicides, burglaries, and rapes than she wanted to think about. They'd been on opposing sides most of the time: She, trying to protect a client's rights, and Gianelli, not letting go until he had the answers.

He swiveled toward her and pulled a yellow notepad from a drawer in the middle of the desk. "I'm going to be interviewing you about the death of your wife, T.J.," he said.

Vicky glanced between the agent and T.J. She could

sense the charge of electricity in the air. This was not a routine follow-up interview after a suicide.

"What are you looking for, Ted?"

Gianelli ignored the question, fastening his gaze on T.J. "What we have is a possible homicide. Let's go over again what you did last evening."

"Homicide!" Vicky heard the shock in her voice. She hurried on. "My client was at the office yesterday evening." Stalling, trying to get a grip on what was happening. God, suppose the coroner had determined somehow that Denise couldn't have shot herself—maybe by the entrance and trajectory of the bullet. Or the coroner didn't find her fingerprints on the gun, or any gunpowder residue on her hands. If Denise didn't kill herself, the first person Gianelli would suspect was T.J. This was the start of a murder investigation. "T.J. told you everything last night," she said. "There's no reason to go over it again."

T.J. sank against the back of his chair and spread his hands over his thighs. His fingers were twitching. "I knew it was gonna happen sooner or later."

"You knew your wife was going to be murdered?" Gianelli leaned over the desk.

"Hold on." Vicky shot a glance at T.J. "You don't have to say anything." Turning back to the agent, she said, "I want to see the coroner's report."

Gianelli shook his head. "Sorry, Vicky. I respect your request, but we're going to have to play by my rules. This is a criminal investigation."

T.J. threw out both hands, as he were fending off a blow.

"You think I don't want the fed . . ." he nodded toward the man on the other side of the desk, "to find the bastards who killed my wife? I got a whole hell of a lot I want to say." He scooted forward until he was perched on the edge of the seat. "They were coming after me. I wasn't home, so they shot Denise as a warning. I'm gonna be next."

"What are you talking about?"

"Phone calls in the middle of the night. Some hang ups; some just saying I'd better get off the rez. Letters with no names, saying they're gonna sic the dogs on me and burn down my house if I don't stop holding up the drilling out at the coal beds. One of those bastards finally came looking for me last night and found Denise."

T.J. dropped his face into his hands. A low noise, like a growl, erupted from his throat. His shoulders were shaking. "I'm the one supposed to be dead." The words were muffled against his fingers. "Denise was supposed to be in Casper for a couple of days. She wasn't supposed to be home. She must've changed the mind and decided not to go." He let a moment pass before he ran his jacket sleeve over his eyes, shifted back in the seat, and leaned his head against the wall.

"Let's go over this again," Gianelli said. "You said last night that you stayed at the office until about eight-thirty, then drove home. Is that right?"

Vicky got to her feet. "Nothing's changed, Ted. I think we're done here. T.J. needs to get some rest."

"You think I shot my wife, don't you?" T.J. was still reclining in the chair, and his voice came from some place deep in his chest.

"Nobody's ruled out yet," Gianelli said.

"Let's go, T.J." Vicky tried to wave the man out of the chair. She hadn't had the chance to talk to him, not as a lawyer to a client. They walked in here thinking Denise had taken her own life. Now they were dealing with homicide and T.J. was a suspect. And he was innocent. She couldn't imagine T.J. Painted Horse shooting anyone. She had to caution him, warn him against saying anything that might incriminate him or cause Gianelli to limit the investigation to him.

"I'm not afraid." T.J. was looking past her toward the agent. "You want me to take a lie detector test? Name the time. Ask me anything you want. Go ahead and ask me."

"Did you murder your wife?" Gianelli asked.

T.J. didn't move for a moment, then he bolted to his feet. His breath came in quick, loud jabs.

"Don't say anything," Vicky said.

"I loved Denise," T.J. said.

Vicky stepped in front of the man. "As your lawyer, I'm telling you this meeting is over. We're leaving now." Vicky took hold of the man's arm and steered him into the hallway.

"Your client wants to cooperate," Gianelli said from behind them. "Why won't you let him?"

"If you have evidence that my client had anything to do with his wife's death, then get a warrant," Vicky said, throwing a glance back at the large, dark figure standing behind the desk, backlit by the light shining through the window.

10

FATHER JOHN CROSSED the mission grounds and took the concrete steps in front of the church two at a time, his breath hanging like tiny gray clouds in the frigid morning air. A pink light was working into the eastern sky, and vehicles were still turning onto Circle Drive, headlights flashing through the cottonwoods. He and Father Damien took turns saying the six o'clock Mass each morning. This morning was Father John's turn. He felt the familiar sense of peace as he walked down the aisle. The warmth of the church washed over him. It was like coming home. Elders and grandmothers in the front rows, rosaries slipping through curled fingers, Leonard Bizzel behind the altar, large, brown hands smoothing the cloth, the faint odor of burning wax from the candles that glowed at either side of the sanctuary, and the stilled atmosphere of prayer.

He'd tossed and turned all night, trying to push back the images that ran through his mind like the continuous loop of a motion picture. Christine Nelson walking out of the museum and disappearing into the night. Denise Painted Horse's inert body on the bedroom floor. Homicide. The moccasin telegraph had been busy into the late evening, probably a dozen calls to the mission, the voices on the other end numb with shock. "Fed says somebody shot her, Father. You don't think it could've been T.J., do you, Father? T.J. don't seem like a murderer. Maybe he got mad at her or something . . ."

"T.J. was working late at the office," he'd said over

and over. Let that go out over the telegraph.

He genuflected in front of the tabernacle—the miniature tipi that the grandmothers had made from tanned deerskin—and went into the sacristy. So much to pray for, he thought, taking the chasuble from the hanger in the closet. He would offer the Mass for Denise's soul, and for T.J. and all of the relatives, and for Christine. He would pray that she was safe. *You can't pray too much, Father,* he remembered the elders telling him when he'd first come to St. Francis.

He pulled the chasuble over his plaid shirt and blue jeans, and it came to him again that this was not a job. Not something he did, being a priest. It was who he was, a man called out from other men for reasons he had given up trying to understand. Or was it that he'd been pushed out when he hadn't wanted to go? "Not me, Lord. Call somebody else." He'd had plans. He was heading toward a doctorate in American history, a teaching position in a small New England college, a wife and a couple of kids. He'd barely heard of the Arapahos. Out West someplace. One of the Plains Indian tribes? And yet, there were times now when it seemed as if all of his plans had been leading him here, that this was the place where he'd always been heading.

"People are sure upset about Denise getting shot." The sound of Leonard's voice surprised him, breaking into his thoughts. The Indian walked over to the cabinet and began taking out the Mass books. "Everybody liked Denise. She was a good woman. No call for somebody to kill her. We've been worrying about

96

Christine, too, the wife and me. Maybe somebody's gone and shot her."

"I hope not," Father John said. Another image now: Christine's house, the upended furniture and broken glass, the violence. It hung like a shadow at the edges of his mind.

"Wife'd like to get on with her own work, Father. What with making sure a lot of Arapahos show up for Senator Evans's visit, she's got a lot to do. Father Damien wants a big crowd cheering real loud, 'cause the senator wants to bring jobs to the rez, unlike some people on the business council." Leonard backed toward the door, holding the Mass books out like an offering.

Father John took the chalice from the cabinet and followed Leonard out to the altar. *I will go into the altar of God. To God, the joy of my youth.* He glanced out at the brown faces turned up at him, worry locked in the dark eyes. Another homicide on the rez, a white woman missing, and the FBI and police fanning out, asking questions, reminding everyone that a murderer was somewhere among them. The sense of unease was as palpable as the electric charge preceding a storm.

"Let us pray together," he said.

THE RESIDENCE WAS quiet, apart from the clank of a metal pan and the rush of water out of a faucet. Father John tossed his jacket onto the bench in the hall and walked back to the kitchen. Shafts of daylight worked their way past the white curtains at the window above the sink. The air was thick with the aromas of fresh coffee, hot oatmeal, and half-burnt toast. Walks-On pushed himself off the blanket in the corner and set a wet muzzle in the palm of his hand. Father John scratched the dog's ears, then stepped over to the counter and poured some coffee into a mug. Elena was at the stove ladling oatmeal into a bowl. Seventy-some years old, part Arapaho, part Cheyenne, the woman had been the housekeeper at St. Francis longer than she professed to remember. She ran the house like a drill sergeant, he sometimes thought, with the pastor and the assistant priest expected to march along in time. It wasn't a bad thing. It sometimes kept him on time.

He sat down across from his assistant, who was scraping the traces of oatmeal out of a bowl, the *Gazette* opened on the other side of his mug.

"My God! The paper says that the police think Christine was abducted." Father Damien thumped his fist against the paper, his eyes running down an article on the first page. The man's mind was like a shotgun—one barrel for the latest news, the other for conversation. "Paper says you were the last one to see her before she disappeared."

"Last one before whoever took her." Elena set a bowl of oatmeal in front of Father John. The steam curled over the rim and smelled of melted brown sugar.

"You don't think her disappearance is related to her job here at the mission, do you?" A note of incredulity worked into the other priest's voice.

"Of course it has to do with the mission." Elena patted at the white apron tied over her blue dress. "A lot of people come to see the Curtis photographs, and that white woman was like a chicken. Couldn't stop pecking. 'Who was your ancestors? When did they come to the rez?' "

"So somebody abducted her?" The incredulity in Damien's voice had slid into scorn.

"Look, we don't know what happened to Christine. Let's not jump to conclusions." Father John poured some milk into the bowl and took a spoonful of the oatmeal. "Thank you, Elena." He glanced up at the woman hovering at the edge of the table, her round face frozen with expectancy. "This is gourmet oatmeal, without a doubt."

"Now how would you know that?"

"Trust me, I'm a connoisseur of oatmeal."

"I don't see how Christine disappearing could have anything to do with the mission," Father Damien said, answering his own question and folding the *Gazette*. He got to his feet, as if the matter were settled. "I'll call Senator Evans's campaign manager right away and assure him that the senator will be perfectly safe at St. Francis. No doubt the poor woman had some personal problems . . ."

"We don't know that," Father John said.

"Process of elimination, John. If her disappearance isn't connected to the mission, where, need I remind you, she has been employed for one month, it must be connected to some problem she brought with her. I think I can make a strong case that will reassure the senator's people. By the way"—he tapped his knuckles against the table—"I've asked Leonard to repaint the front of the museum, so that when the TV cameras pan across, it will look spruced up. He'll have to cut back some cottonwoods so they don't throw shadows over the place."

"Excuse me, Father," Elena said. "There's no way Leonard's gonna paint the museum, cut down branches, and take care of everything else around here before the almighty senator shows his face. I got a leaking washing machine that Leonard's gotta fix." She swung to the counter, lifted the coffee pot and topped off Father John's mug.

He took a long swallow. "Ah, gourmet coffee," he said. It was hot and nutty-flavored, like the coffee she brewed every morning. He wondered if it really was delicious, or only familiar.

"Leonard has enough to do," he said, glancing up at the other priest. "Don't worry, the mission will look just fine on TV."

"When's the last time you took a good look around, John? How long you been here now?"

Father John saluted the man with his mug. "Took a look around this morning," he said. "Nine years next spring."

"Nine years? The provincial's left you here nine years?"

"He forgot about me." He hoped that was true, but every day, when he reached for the ringing phone, there was always the thought flitting at the back of his mind, like a pesky fly. This could be the call, this could be the order for another assignment.

"Good thing, too," Elena said, staring at the other priest. "You can't just come here and get a feel for our ways overnight."

"Do you think it's possible, John, that you've been here so long, you no longer see what must be done? That what you see is the image of the mission when you first arrived?"

Well, that was possible, Father John thought. He had to allow for the possibility. There was an image of St. Francis Mission that he would always carry in his mind. He set down the mug and went back to the oatmeal, aware of the other priest moving behind him toward the door.

Elena turned around, poured another mug of coffee, then took the chair that Damien had vacated. She laced her fingers around the mug as Damien's footsteps receded down the hallway and the front door opened and shut, sending a gust of cold air across the kitchen.

"Maybe Father Damien's got part of it right." Elena lifted her mug and stared at him over the rim. "Maybe that white woman showed up here with a load of personal problems. She used to work at fancy museums, right? Maybe she helped herself to some expensive art and somebody got real mad."

Father John locked eyes with the woman. Good Lord. It would explain the ransacked house. It made sense, except . . .

"Christine's a highly trained professional," he said.

"You know your problem, Father?"

"Which one?"

"You think everybody's honest as the day they come squawking into the world. Some folks are crooked as a dried, old tree, even highly trained professionals."

"Is that a fact?" Father John got to his feet and smiled

down at the woman rooted to her chair, hands wound around the mug. He'd probably heard more in the confessional than she could ever imagine. There had been times when he'd almost despaired that the light of God's grace could shine into the darkness.

"You hear what the fed's gonna do to T.J?" the woman said.

Father John sat back down. "Maybe you'd better tell me."

"Moccasin telegraph says the fed's gonna pin Denise's murder on him." She stared into the coffee mug, considering. "Poor Denise," she said. "I knew she wouldn't ever shoot herself. She loved her life. Always real proud of being Arapaho. Always wanted to make the kids proud." Letting out a long sigh, she brought her eyes back to his. "Fed's gonna take the easy way out and blame T.J."

"T.J. has an alibi," Father John said.

"Trouble with T.J.," the woman pushed on, as if she hadn't heard, "is that he's always wanting, wanting. He wants all the time, that man. Wasn't satisfied getting himself elected to the state legislature. He wants to come back to the rez and get on the business council so he can run things around here, show that he's a real big man. Folks are saying that now he wants to be a senator and go off to Washington." Elena shrugged. "I guess if Senator Evans gets to be the next president, T.J. can get himself elected senator." She didn't sound convinced. "T.J. might not be perfect, Father, but nobody on the rez thinks he could shoot anybody, especially not his wife."

Father John got to his feet again. He felt as if he'd

102

stepped off a riverbank and gotten caught in a current of rumors. "Gianelli's a good investigator." A one-man crusade, was more like it. Determined to rid the world, or at least the rez, of bad guys. "He'll find Denise's murderer."

IN THE OFFICE, Father John flipped through the papers waiting for his attention—yesterday's mail, bills to pay, phone messages to return, Sunday's homily to write—and tried to make sense of what Elena had said. The muffled sound of Father Damien's voice floated down the hall from the back office—reasoning, pleading. "No, no, no. Whatever happened to the curator has nothing to do with the mission." There was a pause, then Damien said, "Well, yes, it looks like T.J. Painted Horse's wife could have been murdered, but that wouldn't have any connection to Senator Evans's visit. She probably surprised an intruder." Another pause. "Yes, T.J. is a popular councilman. No. No. He couldn't have had anything to do with his wife's murder."

But the man could have had enemies, Father John was thinking. Nobody could speak out against the proposed drilling for methane gas, calling the environmental analysis "misleading and inadequate" and insisting on another study that could take months to complete, without making enemies. People were waiting on the jobs and the royalties. But T.J. had made some good points, Father John thought, talking about the millions of gallons of salty wastewater that drilling would pour onto grazing lands and hay fields, and the roads that would be cut through pastures for the heavy trucks and drilling equipment. The man wasn't afraid to stand up for what he believed in, even with a powerful man like Senator Evans on the other side. Father John admired T.J. for that.

"Thank God, things have been quiet lately on the rez," Gianelli had said. That was last Sunday, over spaghetti dinner at the agent's house. He'd helped Gianelli with a lot of cases over the last eight years. They were friends. Two transplants from the east. He, from Boston. Gianelli from somewhere in the Bronx. A baseball player who had once dreamed of the big leagues, and a one-time linebacker for the Patriots. Both opera fans, but Gianelli knew more about opera than he did by a long shot, a fact Father John didn't like to admit, certainly not to Gianelli. The man's wife made the best spaghetti in Wyoming, and dinner had been accompanied by the jabbering of four teenaged daughters and the music of "Madame Butterfly" in the background.

Three days ago. Everything had seemed normal and ordinary.

Father John pulled over the Rolodex and flipped through the cards until he had Vera's number. He picked up the phone and tapped the buttons. A half ring, then: "Hello? Hello?" Vera's voice, clipped with anxiety. "That you, T.J.?"

"Father John," he said, before launching into the purpose of the call. Now was not the time for polite pleasantries. "How's T.J. doing?"

"Grieving real hard for that wife of his, Father. Blames himself. Says some fool came looking for him and found Denise instead. Says he should've been there to protect her. Not bad enough Denise got herself killed. Now the fed thinks T.J. was the one that shot her in the head. Plain harassment, that's what I call it." There was a long intake of breath on the other end. "Easier to pin murder on an innocent Indian than go out and find the real killer."

"Where can I find T.J.?" Father John could feel a wariness settling inside him, like sand dropping into the pit of his stomach. The man was going to need somebody to talk to, somebody to reassure him. It would be easy in such a hard time as this—oh, he knew the truth of it—to look for reassurance in a whiskey bottle.

"T.J. took off early this morning. Didn't sleep all night. Crying and pacing the house like a caged lion. He chopped off his hair like a crazy man. He should've waited for the funeral when he could've sat in front of the casket, and the ceremonial woman with the special scissors would have cut off his hair. That's the Arapaho Way. I don't know what's come over him. He drove off with nothing but a sleeping bag. Oh, I know where he went. Up into the mountains to do his grieving." A short pause, another gasp of breath. "Like the ancestors in the Old Time."

Father John was quiet a moment, trying to pull from his memory what the elders had told him. How a man, grieving for someone he loved, went alone into the mountains. He smeared the dust of the earth onto his face and wailed into the wind, begging the eagle spirit to help him find the strength to soar above the grief, to be steadfast and sure. He stayed in the mountains until the spirit answered his prayer and he felt himself ready to return to his village and a new life. •

"Give me a call, Vera, when he returns," Father John said, ending the call. He hoped that T.J. didn't take a bottle of whiskey with him.

Gripping the receiver between his chin and shoulder, he dug through the notebooks and papers in the desk drawer and pulled out the local phone book. Then he thumbed through the pages until he had the listing for the Riverton Police and tapped out the number. Three rings, and a woman's voice came on the line. He gave his name and asked to speak to the investigator handling Christine Nelson's disappearance.

Four, five seconds passed. Father John drummed his fingers on top of the desk. Finally a man's voice: "This is Detective Porter. Any news on Christine Nelson?" he asked.

"I was hoping you'd have some news," Father John said. He could sense a feeling of dread coming over him like a dull ache.

"We're treating the woman's disappearance as an abduction, Father. Every law enforcement agency in the area is working the case, including the FBI. Tribal police are gonna have officers at the mission this morning to check out the museum. I've got my men canvasing the neighborhood and talking to neighbors. Somebody might've seen something and didn't realize what they were seeing. The state patrol's looking for the woman's Range Rover on every highway in Wyoming, and we're checking Teton County records for a line on the license plate. We could get lucky, Father. I'll let you know if there's any new developments."

Father John thanked the man and started to hang up.

"Hey, Father!"

He pressed the receiver against his ear and waited.

"You wouldn't happen to know if the lady kept a day timer or calendar, would you? Might be she wrote down the name of the person she was going to meet Monday night."

"If she kept a day timer, she probably took it with her," Father John said. He could still see her picking up her briefcase—the quick, impatient fluttering of her slim hands.

"Might be a big help, Father, if you come across any names the lady might've jotted down. Could be she told somebody at the museum where she was going."

"Could be," he said. He doubted it. He had the feeling that Christine Nelson told people only what she wanted them to know.

He told the detective that he'd let him know if he heard anything, then dropped the receiver into the cradle and swiveled sideways toward the window. Beyond, the cottonwoods shimmered in the sunlight; even the air was tinted gold. Maybe Detective Porter had a point, he thought. Maybe Christine Nelson had scribbled a note about the appointment she'd been eager to keep on Monday night.

Father John jumped to his feet, grabbed his jacket off the coat tree, and headed outside. He tossed his jacket over one shoulder and plunged through the corridors of sunshine and shade toward the museum.

11

THE MUSEUM WAS warm and bright under the white fluorescent ceiling lights. The murmur of voices mixed with the sound of hot air whooshing out of the vents. From the entry, Father John could see a scattering of visitors in the gallery—moving along the walls, pausing in front of the photos, nodding, smiling. Catherine stood near the photograph of the village. She reached out and swept her hand across the glass, making a point to the three middle-aged white women beside her. He smiled at the image. The woman seemed to be enjoying herself after all.

The door to the office was open, and he went inside and sat down at the desk. Telephone on the right. *The Plains Indian Photographs of Edward S. Curtis* on the left, and in the expanse of polished wood, a yellow notebook with two columns of names and telephone numbers on the top page. There were check marks next to the names. Parishioners. Catherine had probably been calling people, asking them to come for Senator Evans's visit on Monday. Damien wanted a crowd.

He opened the center desk drawer. Pens, pencils, paper clips, all arranged in neat compartments. No loose notes with the kind of scribbled reminders that he had left to himself. He slid open the side drawer. A few file folders arranged in alphabetical order. Budgets, expenses, inventory. Ah, here was something. An agreement with West Wind Gallery, the Denver gallery that had loaned the Curtis exhibit. He pulled the phone over and punched in the number on the letterhead. It was a long shot, but maybe somebody at the gallery might know something about Christine Nelson. He tucked the receiver into his shoulder and listened to the buzz of a phone ringing somewhere in Denver, thumbing through the pages for a name. There it was, on the last page.

The buzzing stopped, and a man's voice came on the line. Father John asked to speak to Linda Novak.

"Linda's on vacation at the moment." The words were precise and clipped. "Perhaps I can be of help to you?"

Father John gave the man his name and said he was calling about Christine Nelson, who had arranged for the Curtis exhibit . . .

"Yes, yes, yes," the man interrupted. "Linda is in charge of our Curtis collection. I'm afraid you'll have to speak with her. Shall I connect you to her voice mail? She sometimes checks her messages."

Father John repeated what he'd said into the vacuum of a machine, then dropped the receiver into the cradle and got to his feet. Apart from the abrupt sound of laughter that burst from the gallery, the office was quiet, an unoccupied feeling about it. Books stacked in the bookcase across the room, a pair of chairs with worn brown cushions pushed against the side wall. There was nothing of Christine Nelson, nothing she might have left behind. The woman might never have walked into the office, picked up her briefcase, grabbed her coat from behind the door. It was as if she was being erased from the image he carried in his mind, disappearing, the way she'd disappeared Monday night.

Well, that was crazy, he told himself. Christine Nelson

had to be somewhere, and chances were, whoever she'd gone to meet on Monday night knew what had happened to her.

He started across the entry toward the front door, the hum of voices floating around him like a familiar melody. He turned back and stepped into the gallery. Next to the door, on a small metal stand, was the guest book and a stack of brochures. He nodded at Catherine, who had thrown him a sideways glance before turning her attention back to the visitors. Then he picked up the book and a brochure and went back into the office. Settling into the chair he'd just vacated, he began glancing through the book, trying to make out the names scribbled down the left side of the pages. As indecipherable as hieroglyphics. The names of towns on the right were easier to read. Towns in Nebraska, Montana, Idaho, Colorado.

He hunted now for the local towns, checking the names next to Riverton, Lander, Fort Washakie, Ethete, Arapaho. Next to Arapaho, on the second page, was scribbled Eunice Redshield.

He stared at the name, another image beginning to take shape in his mind. Monday night, and the college students studying the photographs, jotting notes in notebooks, arguing. And the dark-haired young woman saying that one of the warriors was Thunder, her ancestor. Saying that her grandmother, Eunice Redshield, had told the curator.

"Here's the pastor." Catherine stood in the door, a group of women crowding around her. "These folks came down from Montana," she said, tossing her head

110

from one side to the other. "I've been telling them how Curtis could've been taking the photographs yesterday. Black Mountain looks just the same. Nothing's changed. That old log cabin that Curtis stayed in is still there."

"Good to have you here," he said to the visitors, who smiled and nodded before flowing back into the entry with Catherine. He was thinking that, like the log cabin, descendants of the people in the photographs were also here.

He picked up the brochure and folded it into his shirt pocket. Then he grabbed his jacket from the back of the chair and headed for the front door, giving Catherine and the group of women a little wave as he walked past. Back outside, he pulled on his jacket as he hurried toward the pickup.

12

THE REDSHIELD PLACE was at the end of a two-lane road close to the Little Wind River. Sheltered under a cottonwood was a small, rectangular house with brown siding and patterns of sunshine running down the sloped roof. There was a barn in the back that looked like a larger version of the house, and beyond that, nothing but the blue sky dipping down to the ground tipped in gold and red and vermilion as far as he could see, as if the earth were on fire.

Father John pointed the pickup into the tire tracks that crossed the yard and parked next to the house in a patch of dirt where a vehicle had obviously been parked not long before. He got out and slammed the door hard—a brittle sound that reverberated through the silence—to let whoever was inside know there was a visitor. He'd called Eunice from his cell as he'd turned out of the mission grounds. She'd be here, she told him. Maybe out in the barn.

Father John waited a moment, then headed down the side of the house for the barn. Through the open door that had scraped a half-moon into the dirt in front, he could see the woman moving about, a bucket hanging from one hand.

"Hello," he called, giving the door a rap and stepping inside.

Eunice Redshield lifted up the bucket, eyes round with fear, chest rising inside the folds of a denim jacket. "Oh, my goodness! Scared the bejeebers out of me, Father. How come I didn't hear that old pickup of yours? You didn't get yourself a new car, did you?"

"Afraid that's not in the budget." He laughed at the idea of a budget. Hay was scattered over the dirt floor, and the walls were covered with shelves filled with ropes, tack, and blankets. Two geldings bent into a trough of oats. The air was warm and humid with the horse's breath and the odors of manure and hay.

"Just got the boys their breakfast," she said, throwing her head toward the horses. She dropped the bucket on top of a large bin. "I got coffee brewing in the house."

He followed her across the yard and into the kitchen. "Have a seat, Father." Eunice nodded toward one of the chairs at the table, then hung her jacket on a hook behind the door and worked at tucking the ends of her

T-shirt into her blue jeans. She was a short woman with a squared look and thick legs encased in the jeans. Probably in her fifties, he was thinking as he draped his own jacket over the chair she'd indicated and sat down. She had a weathered look, with curled gray hair and worry lines etched into her forehead. Old enough that the kids on the rez would call her grandmother.

"You been doing okay, Father?" she asked, stretching upward on her toes to reach a shelf and pull down two mugs.

The question took him by surprise. "What makes you ask?"

"I hear that new priest you got at the mission is pretty much taking over. Got involved with the business council to get Senator Evans over to the mission." Eunice poured coffee into the mugs and set them on the table. Then she dropped with a loud sigh onto the chair across from him. "Gossip says you might be getting ready to leave. That true?"

"I'm not planning to go anywhere." He forced a little laugh and took a gulp of coffee. He could feel it burning somewhere deep inside his chest. The gossip on the moccasin telegraph that reached him was always about somebody else, never about him. He didn't want to think about leaving St. Francis. Fitting himself again into a teaching job at a Jesuit prep school or university. Finding his way again, his place somewhere else.

"Father Damien's a pretty good priest," she said. Then she took a sip of coffee and reached over and patted his hand. "People hereabouts like that other priest fine, but we'd sure hate to lose you, Father." She seemed to contemplate the possibility for a moment, the lines in her forehead frozen in concentration.

Sitting back, she worked at the coffee, then she said, "Hear that white woman at the museum went off somewhere. Hope nothing bad happened to her. She was one of them nervous types, you know, face all pinched and white like the blood drained out of her. Looked like she was running fast with an evil spirit right behind her. Hear somebody tore her place up. Think the police'll find her?"

He said that he hoped so, trying for as much reassurance as he could muster. Then he pulled the brochure on the Curtis exhibit from his jacket pocket. Smoothing out the shiny paper, he pushed it across the table. "I understand one of the warriors is your ancestor," he said, tapping at the photograph of the village on the front.

The atmosphere seemed to change, as if the warm air blowing through the vent had turned frigid. Eunice stared at the photo for several seconds before she started tracing the figure of the warrior on the right with one finger. "My great-grandfather, Thunder," she said. "Don't mind telling you I was real surprised when I walked into the museum and seen his photo. I went into the curator's office and told her she had my great-grandfather on the wall." The woman looked away, gathering the memory. "I remember she went on about how Edward Curtis never got around to identifying a lot of people in his photos, and she was sorry but the Arapahos weren't ever gonna be identified. I said, you got that wrong, 'cause I know my own great-grandfather. I got another picture of him. She got real interested then and said she'd like to see my picture, so I said, 'Come on over any time you want.' Hold on a minute, Father."

Eunice pushed away from the table, got to her feet, and disappeared through the archway behind her. There was the sound of drawers opening and closing, then she was back. "The lady came last week, and I showed her this," she said, slapping a large, sepia-toned photograph with curled corners next to the brochure. "Plain as day," she said. "Thunder had a real distinctive nose and big chin, and he had dimples in his cheeks. Don't see many Indians with dimples."

Father John pulled the brochure and photo in front of him. The man in the photo looked tall and muscular, with a clump of hair standing up from his forehead and thick braids that hung down the front of his fringed shirt. He smiled into the camera a hundred years ago, and the smile showed the dimples that made him seem relaxed and content. But in the dark eyes was a mixture of wariness and surprise, as if he wondered how much of himself the camera might capture. There was no doubt about it: The smiling man in the snapshot was the warrior with the feathered headdress and broad stripes of paint that looked like lightning zigzagging across his face and naked chest. Same forelock pulled up from his forehead, same nose and squared jaw and dimples.

"What did the curator say?"

"Oh, she got real excited. Wanted to know where I got the photo. 'Portrait,' I told her. Stories that come down in the family say that Curtis took the portrait in his tent out there by Black Mountain. Thunder got killed, you know, after Curtis set up that attack on a so-called Arapaho village. Other warriors got killed with him. Them others didn't leave any descendants."

"How did they die?"

The woman was quiet for so long that Father John wondered if she'd heard. He sipped at his coffee and waited. Finally she went on: "Wasn't something Dad wanted to talk about, but one time he told me that people said Thunder and the others killed a woman in Curtis's village. Told me the family had it real hard afterward, and no sense dwelling on the past. "She reached over, picked up the snapshot, and stared at it. "Dad said that Curtis took lots of portraits of people in his tent. Had people come in and dress up in fringed shirts and beaded necklaces that Curtis brought along, some of it from the Sioux. Even made the village look like a village in the Old Time. That's it right there." She tapped the brochure.

Father John was quiet a moment. "Who was the woman Thunder was accused of killing?"

Eunice shook her head and blew out her breath. "He was innocent, Father. All three of them warriors was innocent." She looked away a moment, then, bringing her gaze back to his, she said, "Name was Bashful Woman, the daughter of Sharp Nose. That's how come Thunder and the others had to die, I guess, 'cause people wanted revenge for a chief's daughter getting shot."

"You told Christine about this?"

The woman started nodding. "She wanted to know if I had a magnifying glass. So I went and found an old one in the desk and gave it to her. She stared at the village, moving the glass around, studying this and that, not saying anything for a long time. Then she handed me the brochure and the magnifying glass. 'You see the women in the village?' she says. I told her, 'My eyes aren't gone yet.' And she wants to know, who was the woman that got shot. I said, 'How would I know that?' 'Somebody must've told you what she looked like,' she says. I tell you, Father, I got fed up with that pushy white woman. I said, 'Excuse me, ma'am, but I showed you what I got, and I told you what I know.' I quit talking then, and that encouraged her to leave. But you know what she says on the way out? Says she could get me a thousand dollars for my photograph, and would I like to sell? I told her I wasn't selling any image of my ancestor. Then she wants to know who else on the rez has Curtis photos, and I told her, 'Nobody,' but that didn't satisfy her."

Father John picked up the brochure and studied the image of the village. He could make out the figures of women in the shadows. Black hair in braids, light-colored dresses with fringe that dropped over their moccasins. One carried an infant on her back; another sat in front of a tipi, cradling a small child in her lap. He could almost feel the curator's excitement at the possibility of identifying more people, of making sense out of what had happened.

"Let me guess," he said. "Christine wanted the names of Chief Sharp Nose's descendants."

"Oh, she wanted names, all right." Eunice shrugged. "I told her, 'That was a big family with descendants scattered around the rez. You can find lots of people that come down from Chief Sharp Nose. He was the last chief, and people got a lotta respect for the old chiefs.' "

"Did you give Christine the names of any descendants?" Father John could think of two or three elders who were great-grandsons of the last Arapaho chief—Max Oldman was one—but an outsider like Christine wouldn't know who they were unless someone told her.

Eunice shook her head. "Sharp Nose family's had enough trouble down the years, you ask me. Max Oldman's nephew got himself shot some years back, and now Denise . . ." She let the thought trail off.

Father John didn't take his eyes from the woman. Denise Painted Horse was also a descendant of Sharp Nose, and chances were good that Christine Nelson had gone looking for descendants with Curtis photographs. He swallowed hard against the gaps in the logic. There were probably dozens of Sharp Nose descendants on the rez, and Eunice hadn't given Christine any names. What was the connection? Where was the proof that Denise and Christine had even met?

He drained the last of the coffee and got to his feet. "Thank you, Eunice," he said.

"See, that's the difference between you and white people like her." The woman stood up next to him. She barely came to his shoulder. "They never say thank you for what they get. You think that white woman went looking for one of Sharp Nose's people and got herself into some kind of trouble? You think that's why she's disappeared?"

"I don't know," Father John said. The lines in the woman's forehead deepened, and he realized that it was now his turn to give the gift of information. He said, "I think she could have been on her way to meet someone on the reservation when she disappeared."

"If she asked any Arapaho that come into the museum about the Sharp Nose people, she would've heard about Max Oldman." Eunice stepped back and pushed her chair against the table. It made a sharp noise, like the ring of a hammer. "Oldman's head of the family now."

Father John pulled on his jacket, only half following what the woman was saying: something about how she hoped the white woman would turn up okay. He was thinking that he'd drive over to Max's place and have a talk with the elder. But before he did, he wanted to find out what had happened at Curtis's village.

He was outside and around the corner, following his boot prints along the side of the house, when he heard Eunice call out: "Come back any time, Father. I always got the coffee on."

He slid behind the steering wheel and, leaning across the seat, fumbled through the papers in the glove compartment for his cell. The cab was warm in the sun. He rolled down the window and pushed in the number for the mission.

"Father Damien." The voice on the other end was clear and confidant and . . . Dear Lord. Damien was at the mission and in control.

"Everything okay?"

"You had a few calls, but I took care of them."

"I'll be back in a couple of hours."

"No need to hurry," the other priest said.

Father John hit the end key and tossed the cell onto

the passenger seat. Then he started the engine and shot out onto the road. He had to laugh at the irony. Finally an assistant who took a real interest in the mission. It looked as if his prayers had been answered. The problem was, he now had an assistant who could replace him.

13

SOMETHING ABOUT THE sound of the front door opening, the scuff of footsteps on the wood floor, made Vicky glance away from the computer monitor. Beyond the beveled glass of the French doors was the tall figure of Adam Lone Eagle. The black hair smoothed back, blurring into the collar of his dark coat. She felt a jab of annoyance. Here he was, when she'd decided he'd probably never call again. Just walk away after a half-dozen dinners, the way you'd walk away from an acquaintance you ran into every time you went to the grocery story. The muffled sound of Adam's voice floated through the doors. Then Annie's, giggling and nervous.

Adam had a way of making women nervous, Vicky thought, just like he had a way of appearing at inopportune moments. She was about to leave for the reservation. She'd gotten to the office early and spent the morning finishing up some work—a lease for a client renting out an office in Lander, a threatening letter to an insurance company that refused to pay another client's claim—after spending most of the night pacing her apartment, her thoughts running in a continuous loop over the meeting in Gianelli's office. Always circling back to the beginning: T.J. was innocent. Somewhere in the night, with the green iridescent numbers on the clock blinking 3:10, she'd decided to check out T.J.'s alibi herself. One witness who had seen T.J. at the office Monday night, and Gianelli would have to look elsewhere for the killer.

Vicky got up and yanked open the French doors just as Adam was reaching for the knobs. "Got a minute?" he asked, his eyes traveling over her before coming back to rest on hers. He was smiling, as if he were pleased with the image he'd taken in.

"That's all I have," Vicky said, moving back toward the desk, annoyed at the way he made her stomach flutter with the way he looked at her, the most ordinary question he asked. The man always took her by surprise, as if there were things about him she'd forgotten since the last time she'd seen him. The determination in the way he carried himself: head high, shoulders square inside the black leather jacket. There was determination, too, in the set of his jaw, the sharp cheekbones and finely shaped nose with the hump at the top, the eyes like black stones that absorbed everything and revealed nothing. He might have been a warrior who'd stepped out of one of the old photographs.

He was still smiling at her. "It's been too long since I've seen you."

She gripped the edge of the desk. Dinner ten days ago, then nothing. "We're both busy," she said.

"Come on." He leaned close. The smell of aftershave on his skin mixed with the faint odor of leather. "You

121

didn't miss me a little?"

"Adam, I'm very busy."

He held up one hand, palm outward in the sign of peace. "How about tonight? We can have dinner over at Hudson. There's something I want to talk over with you. Seven o'clock."

"You don't give a woman a chance to say anything, Adam."

"Say yes. I'll pick you up at your place."

Vicky drew in a long breath. "I'll meet you at the restaurant," she said finally.

Adam reached out and ran a finger along the curve of her chin, a light touch that sent a jolt of electricity through her. "See you tonight." Then he was gone, striding through the outer office, letting himself through the front door.

Vicky gathered up the papers scattered over her desk and slipped them inside a folder. She was about to file the folder in one of the desk drawers when she realized that Annie was standing between the French doors, holding onto the knobs. She *was* young. Twenty-three years old, half of Vicky's age, the age of her own kids, Lucas and Susan, with an "I've seen it all" look on her face.

"That Lakota sure knows how to get what he wants," Annie said.

Vicky set the folder in place and slammed the drawer. She had no intention of discussing Adam with her secretary. She told her that a client would be stopping by to pick up the rental lease this afternoon, and the letter to the insurance company had to make today's mail.

"People been talking about . . ."

Vicky cut in. "I don't want to hear the gossip, Annie."

The woman's head snapped back as if she'd been struck. "I thought you'd want to know."

Vicky took her coat from the coat tree and shrugged into the soft gray wool. Oh, she could guess the gossip on the moccasin telegraph. Adam Lone Eagle, lawyer from Casper. Lakota. Handsome. They'd been seen together in restaurants, holding hands, and walking down Main Street. But there were days and weeks with no phone calls, when she wondered if she'd ever hear from him again, and she'd told herself it didn't matter. She wasn't sure whether she was attracted to him, or whether she'd talked herself into the idea because . . . because, at times, the man seemed so attracted to her and because he was available.

"I'll check in later," Vicky said, fixing the strap of her black bag over one shoulder and brushing past the secretary. She hurried across the office and let herself outdoors, pulling the door shut against the secretary's gaze.

She drove north on Highway 287, stomping on the accelerator to pass the old pickups lumbering down the middle of the asphalt. Clumps of brush floated past the window like bales of sunshine. She passed Plunkett Road and turned onto Blue Sky Highway. After several miles, another right into the graveled parking lot that wrapped around the squat, redbrick tribal headquarters building. She left the Jeep in a vacant space at the end of a row of vehicles and walked back to the entrance through the warmth of the sunshine washing over the sidewalk.

Across the tiled floor of the lobby, a wave toward the receptionist behind the desk, then down the hallway on the right past a procession of closed doors with panels of pebbly glass. Savi Crowthorpe's door was open. The councilman was curled over the papers spread across his desk. He was a slim man with muscular shoulders, a hawklike nose, and straight, black hair that hugged the curve of his neck. The capable, long fingers of the basketball player he'd been at Wyoming Indian High flipped through the papers. Glancing up, he waved Vicky inside with his eyes.

"Gotta make this short," he said, skipping the polite preliminaries. "I have a meeting in ten minutes. Take a seat."

Vicky sat down on the metal-framed chair halfway between the door and the desk. The office was stuffy, hot air angling like a blowtorch out of the overhead vent. She unbuttoned her coat. "I'm here about T.J.," she said.

"You and the fed." The councilman squared the edges of the stacked papers. "Gianelli was waiting in the lobby when I got to work yesterday. Wanted to know what time T.J. left the office on Monday. I'm gonna tell you the same thing I told him. After the council meeting, T.J. and I worked late on Senator Evans's visit next week. How we're gonna handle the crowds at Fort Washakie; how much food we gotta serve, 'cause people aren't coming out if they don't get fed; and how we're gonna end the program so the senator can get over to St. Francis Mission. Finished up about six-thirty, and I went home. It was the wife's birthday, so she wasn't real keen on me working late. Kept calling wanting to know when I was coming home."

"What about T.J.?"

"Still in the office when I left. Said he was gonna work on the comments he was gonna make at Fort Washakie about the importance of getting another environmental study before we start polluting the reservation. His exact words, as I remember. Like I told the fed, if T.J. says he worked late, that's what he did. Works all the time, that man. He's the one who discovered how the BIA was trying to push a weak environmental analysis on us that was done by a consulting firm hired by the oil companies, so the companies could start their drilling."

"Anybody else here?"

"At six-thirty?" The councilman gave her a crooked smile. "The place was a tomb."

Vicky shifted her gaze to the window. She could feel her heart pounding. T.J. had no alibi.

The phone had started to ring, and the councilman stretched out his long fingers and lifted the receiver. "Don't start without me," he said, jumping to his feet. He dropped the receiver back into place. "Sorry, Vicky. Gotta go."

"Thanks for your time, Savi." Vicky stood up and turned toward the door.

"He didn't kill his wife, you know," the councilman said. "Woman gets shot, the husband's the first one they're gonna suspect. Maybe T.J. isn't perfect, but he doesn't have killing in him. You gotta help him, Vicky."

"Look, Savi," she began. "If you think of anybody

who might have seen T.J. here on Monday night . . ."

"Patrol car," he cut in.

"What?"

"Police patrol comes around during the night, checks to make sure the building's locked up, everything's okay."

"Thanks." Vicky gave the man a wave and started down the hall, pulling her cell phone out of her bag. She stopped at the front door and tapped out a number, then stepped outdoors and retraced her steps to the Jeep, moving between the crisp cold of the shadows and the warmth of the sunshine, the phone pressed against her ear.

"Wind River Police." A woman's voice came on the other end.

"Let me talk to Chief Banner." Vicky got in behind the wheel and pulled the door shut. "It's Vicky Holden."

"Hold on. I'll see if the chief's available."

"It's important."

"I'm sure."

A couple of minutes passed. The Jeep came alive— engine running, cool air pouring from the vents. Finally the chief's voice: "Vicky? What's going on?"

"I'd like to talk to the patrolman on duty Monday night, the one checking the tribal headquarters."

"This about T.J.?" There was a clicking noise at the other end, as if the man was tapping a pencil against the phone.

"T.J. was working late. He needs a witness."

The tapping stopped. "Looks like my boy was on duty in Ethete that night. Patrick's real conscientious about checking on the tribal buildings."

"Can you connect me to him?"

"Doesn't come on duty until . . ." Tap. Tap. Tap. "He clocks in at five. Where you gonna be?"

She told him that she was on her way to Vera Wilson's place. Then back to Lander.

"Patrick'll find you. Take it easy, Vicky."

"Wait, Banner," she said. "There's something else."

"Shoot."

Vicky took in a gulp of cold air. "Were there any disturbance calls to T.J.'s house? Any records of domestic abuse?" Gianelli would ask, and she had to know what Gianelli knew.

A loud guffaw burst down the line. "A tribal councilman? If that'd happened, it would've been all over the rez. Next time he ran for election, people would've thrown his ass off the council. Look, I'll check the records for you, but I'm telling you, there's not gonna be anything there."

Vicky felt her muscles begin to relax. She thanked the chief, hit the end button, and slipped the phone back into her bag. Then she backed into the lot and lurched forward out onto the highway. She had to talk to T.J.

14

VERA STOOD IN the doorway, blinking with disappointment. Then she stepped sideways, her eyes running across the yard where Vicky had left the Jeep between two pickups. A cold gust of wind blew a cloud of dust across the stoop, and Vera lifted one hand and absentmindedly brushed at the front of her red blouse.

"Is T.J. around?" Vicky asked.

"I was hoping you was T.J.," Vera said, stepping back into the house. "Come on in."

Vicky followed the woman into the living room, warm and thick with the smells of fresh coffee and fry bread. There was nobody in the room, but Vicky could see three women seated at the kitchen table in back, a scattering of coffee mugs and plates in front of them. There was a sense of interruption, as if conversation had stopped in mid-sentence. The women were staring into the living room.

"I have to talk to T.J.," Vicky said. "Where is he?"

Vera threw a glance toward the kitchen, then took hold of Vicky's arm and steered her into the hall on the right. The woman's fingers dug through her coat sleeve and into her skin a moment before she let go and hurried ahead.

Vicky followed her into a small bedroom and shut the door as Vera perched on the edge of a narrow bed, next to a table covered with snapshots in plastic frames. Pictures of Vera with her husband, who'd died five or six years ago; Vera with two children, grown now and living someplace else. A snapshot of T.J., about eighteen, posing in black cap and gown, the wind sweeping the skirt of the gown back against his legs. A memory went off in her mind like a flashbulb. A June day, the sun beating down on the field where the graduation had taken place, her gown as hot and heavy as a blanket.

T.J. again, in an army uniform, taller, more confidant looking, a man standing in front of an old pickup. And

T.J. and Denise hugging on a door stoop. It was as if the moments had been stopped in time, the light and shadows and feel of the air, the angle of shoulders and arms, the hopeful expressions forever fixed in the image.

She realized that Vera was crying. "What is it?" she asked, sitting down on the bed beside her.

"I been so worried." Vera ran the palms of her hands over her cheeks. "T.J. went into the mountains this morning. Said he was gonna go crazy if he didn't get off by himself so he could mourn for Denise in the old way. He already chopped off his hair and he's gonna be crying and praying, all alone out there, blaming himself."

"Whoever shot Denise would have shot T.J. if he'd been there," Vicky said. It was just as T.J. had told Gianelli yesterday. Councilmen got threats all the time. T.J. had just never expected anybody to carry them out, but Monday night, that's what had happened.

Vera drew in a long breath that whistled in her teeth. "There's something else," she said. "The fed's gonna put Denise's murder on T.J., and the thing is . . ." She hesitated.

"What? What are you trying to tell me?" Vicky tried to keep the impatience out of her own voice.

The other woman shifted around until she was facing her. She closed her eyes a moment and took in another gulp of air. "Denise was gonna divorce him, Vicky."

Vicky didn't say anything. So that was what Denise had on her mind when she'd stopped her in the grocery store.

"T.J. told me Denise wanted to call it quits, but that's not what he wanted," Vera went on. "Said he'd made a mistake, but he wanted to work things out." The woman shrugged and looked away.

"Mistake? What kind of a mistake? Another woman?"

"It was over, Vicky. Didn't mean anything."

Vicky got up and went to the window. It was edging toward dusk, and the moon shone white against the silver sky. In the shadows, clumps of wild grasses turned blood red. T.J.'s alibi was as transparent as air. Unless somebody saw him at the tribal offices Monday evening, he had the opportunity to kill his wife. And now this—God, T.J. hadn't said anything about an affair. Opportunity and motive. Gianelli would have enough to get the grand jury to indict T.J. for murder.

"Who is she?" Vicky turned back to the woman hunched over on the bed, one hand clamped over her mouth.

"I never asked. I didn't want to know. She was nothing but trouble, you ask me."

"What about the gossip?" Vicky gestured with her head in the direction of the kitchen.

The other woman took a moment, clasping and unclasping her hands in her lap now. "Nobody says anything to me. I'm pretty sure she wasn't from the rez. T.J. was real careful, being on the business council. He had his reputation to think about. She called today."

"The woman called here?"

"Wanting to talk to T.J. Sounded real upset. I said he wasn't here, and she hung up. I knew it was her."

"Listen, Vera," Vicky began, trying for a confidence

she didn't feel. A sense of unease was working through her, as if T.J. had become someone else, not the image of the man she remembered. She stepped over and set her hand on the other woman's shoulder. "If she calls again, ask her to call me. Tell her I'm trying to help T.J. And as soon as T.J. gets back, tell him I have to talk to him."

It was a moment before they started back down the hallway. Shadows bunched against the walls. Ahead, a thin stream of light flowed out of the kitchen and across the living room. The house was quiet, and Vicky wondered if the other women had left. But they were still there, as still as mannequins at the table. Vera hurried ahead and yanked the front door open.

"Any news about T.J.?" a woman in a pink sweatshirt called out.

"Not yet," Vera shouted, beckoning Vicky through the door with her eyes.

"Try not to worry," Vicky said, stepping past the woman onto the stoop. The words hung between them a moment, limp and inadequate.

Vera mouthed a silent thank you, then shut the door.

The temperature must have dropped ten degrees, the moonlight swallowing the hint of warmth that had come with the sunshine. Hugging her coat around her, Vicky hurried for the Jeep. She was about to shut her door when the woman in the pink sweatshirt emerged from the house and ran over.

"You don't remember me," she said, opening the passenger door and leaning inside. Her long black braids dangled over the seat.

Vicky studied the woman's face in the glow of the dashboard lights. High forehead, prominent nose, and tight, determined mouth. "Nancy?" she said.

"Nancy Thomas. Used to be Whiteplume."

"I remember you." It was starting to come back now. They'd gone to high school together, and the woman was connected to T.J. Probably a cousin.

"I told Vera I needed cigarettes out of my pickup," the woman was saying. "I wanted to talk to you. You're defending T.J., right?"

Defending wasn't exactly right, Vicky wanted to say. T.J. hadn't been charged with anything. "He's my client," she said.

"Whatever. He's in a big load of shit, you ask me, and Vera's in total denial. She can't believe her important brother could be a bastard. He's been cheating on Denise for a year."

"Vera said it was over," Vicky said. She wondered if the woman knew how long the affair had been going on.

"Maybe you oughtta ask his girlfriend if it's over."

"Who is she?"

"I hear the gossip. Tall blond, a lot younger than T.J. That surprise you?" She gave a little laugh and pulled at the pink sleeves. "I hear she works for Great Plains Insurance over in Riverton. I figure T.J. didn't tell you about her 'cause he thinks it's some big secret."

"Thanks," Vicky said.

"Look, I love Vera. We been through a lot of shit together, and I'm gonna be here for her no matter what happens. I think T.J.'s gonna get his ass charged with murder, and that's gonna be real hard on Vera. Maybe

132

he did it, I don't know, but for Vera's sake, I hope you make sure he gets a fair trial or whatever." The woman backed away, closing the door as she went.

Vicky turned the key in the ignition and listened for a moment to the engine coming to life in the quiet. By the time she'd turned the Jeep around in the yard, the pink sweatshirt had disappeared into the house.

VICKY WAS HEADING south on 287, close to the boundary of the reservation, the yellow cone of headlights sweeping into the dusk, when she realized that blue and red lights were flashing in the rearview mirror. She eased on the brakes and guided the Jeep to the side, watching the lights pull in behind her. She waited until the policeman in a dark uniform had crawled out of the patrol car and walked up to her door, then she rolled down the window and looked up into the sculpted face of Patrick Banner.

"Dad said you want to talk to me," he said. "Mind coming back to the patrol car?"

Vicky turned off the engine and followed Chief Banner's son. He opened his door and waited until she'd slid into the passenger seat before he settled himself behind the steering wheel. "I take it this is about T.J.," he said, turning toward her. His dark blue jacket folded over the rim of the wheel. "What's going on?"

"He's out there"—Vicky waved toward the dark expanse of foothills rising outside her window— "grieving for his wife. He's not himself. He hasn't been thinking straight."

Patrick tapped the rim with a gloved finger. It made a

rhythmic, muffled noise. In the glow of the dashboard lights, he looked like a younger version of his father: the same long face and hooked nose, the hooded eyes settling on her. "Some guys like to go up to Moccasin Lake," he said. "I'll radio the sheriff up in Arapaho County. If T.J.'s in the vicinity, they'll check on him. That all you wanted?"

Vicky shook her head. "The chief said you were on patrol in Ethete Monday night," she began. "Did you see anybody at the tribal headquarters after six-thirty?"

Patrick stared out the windshield a moment, as if he were calling to mind the building and the parking lot. "Nope," he said finally. "Nobody around. Excuse me." He reached across her, opened the glove compartment, and drew out a black notebook. "Monday night," he said, thumbing through the pages. "Here it is." He shoved the notebook into the dashboard light. "Checked on the building at seven, nine, eleven, one A.M. Doors locked, lights off, and nobody around."

"What about the parking lot?"

"Like I said, nobody was around. So what's this all about? T.J. say he was at the office when his wife got shot?" He blew out a long breath. "They put me on the witness stand, I'm gonna have to swear that nobody was in the building that evening. Sure hope T.J. can come up with a better alibi. Maybe he'd better rethink where he might have been."

Vicky opened the door and started to get out. "Thanks, Patrick," she said.

Before she could close the door, he leaned across the seat. "Be careful, Vicky," he said. "A guy like T.J. has made enemies. If one of them killed his wife, the killer could still be looking for T.J. And if he doesn't find him, he could come looking for his lawyer."

Vicky shut the door and made her way back to the Jeep through the mixture of moonlight and headlights frozen in the cold air. She had pulled back into the lane and gone several hundred feet when she saw the headlights in the rearview mirror carve through a U-turn across the highway, leaving only the flickering red taillights that grew fainter and fainter until they disappeared into the reservation.

15

THE RIVERTON LIBRARY, a single-story expanse of red brick and peaked roofs, sprawled on the corner of a neighborhood of bungalows set back from tree-lined streets. Blue shadows crept across the lawn in front of the library. Father John parked at the curb and walked up the wide sidewalk to the entrance. It was quiet inside, except for the low voice of a woman reading to a small boy on a bench near the door. He crossed to the desk in the center of the large room. Book stacks fanned around the desk like the spokes in a wheel. The librarian, an attractive woman with dark hair and lively eyes—the same librarian who usually helped him when he came in—was already on her feet, watching him approach.

"Another research project, Father?" she asked.

"I'm afraid so," he said.

"What? You know you love researching the past. Once a history professor, always a history . . .

"High school teacher," he said, finishing her sentence.

"All the same. I have to confess . . ." She paused and laughed, shaking her head. "Not that I really intend to confess any sins . . ."

"I'm sure you don't have any."

"Exactly. Not having any sins, I can only confess to sharing your love for history. Finding a new research project is like setting sail on an unknown sea. Where are you sailing today, Father?"

"Back to 1907," he said.

"Ah, a very popular year."

"How so?"

"The curator from your museum—what was her name? Christine something came in to look through the newspapers for 1907. I saw in the *Gazette* that she's missing. My goodness." The woman lifted one hand, as if to ward off an invisible evil, and glanced about the library. There was comfort in the rows of books, the certitude and quiet. "I hope she's all right."

"Did Christine say what she was looking for?" The same thing he was looking for, he suspected. An explanation of what had happened in the Curtis village.

The woman shook her head. "I'm afraid I didn't ask, Father. She seemed very . . ." She hesitated. "I remember that she raced out of here after she finished her research."

"When was that?"

"Let me think." She studied the space above his head a moment. "Early last week, I guess. Sorry, I can't be more help."

He smiled at the woman. It was possible that Christine

136

had found the names she was looking for. A connection to the dead woman and the dead warriors, someone else to talk to, someone she might have been on her way to meet Monday night.

He said, "I think I'll take a look at the newspapers."

"You know where they are, Father." He was already heading across the room for the door to the basement. "Light switch is on the left," she called.

He flipped the switch and plunged down a flight of stairs into a maze of shelves stacked with thick, leather-bound books. He could smell the dust and the old leather—familiar odors coming to him—as he worked his way past the shelves. In the far corner was a reading table with books stacked along the side and, next to the table, a copying machine. He stopped in front of a shelf of tall, thin books, a patchwork of shadows falling over the early editions of the *Gazette*. His gaze ran over the gold-embossed dates on the spines. 1890s, then 1900s. 1905. 1906. The next space was empty.

He walked over to the reading table. Next to a sign that read LEAVE MATERIALS HERE was a stack of books, and on the top, a black leather book with golden numbers on the spine: 1907. He found a chair around the corner, sat down at the table, and opened the book in the middle. He smoothed the brittle, yellowed pages, feeling the old book begin to relax in his hands. He was thinking that Curtis had photographed the village in good weather. Cloudless sky. No snow on the ground. Which meant about a six-month window, from mid-May to mid-October. He eased the pages forward until the date at the top read May 16, 1907. His eyes hunted down the narrow columns, looking for a headline about the murder of a chief's daughter or the deaths of three Arapaho men.

Nothing. He kept turning the pages, working faster now, settling into a familiar rhythm from the hours he'd spent in archives, searching out obscure facts that made sense out of a small part of the past. The type was crabbed and hard-to-read. There were no photographs, only an occasional illustration to break up the small print. He had reached mid-September when he spotted a small announcement. *Seattle photographer Edward S. Curtis expected on the Wind River Reservation some time in the next weeks. He has informed the agency that he will require an assistant while in the area. Indians who can read and write may wish to apply for the position.*

He slowed the tempo, scanning each page until he'd reached the middle of October. There, on the front page in the lower right corner, a small headline: RESERVATION MURDER. He scanned the inch-long article that said an Indian woman had been shot to death while the photographer, Edward S. Curtis, was taking pictures of an Indian village. "There will likely be moaning and gnashing of teeth on the reservation, since it appears the woman was the daughter of the famous Chief Sharp Nose. Mike Fleming, the agent on the reservation, is conducting the investigation into the death and talking to many witnesses."

Father John flipped through several more issues to a front-page headline that ran across three columns: INDIANS GUILTY OF MURDER IN DEATH OF CHIEF'S

DAUGHTER. Below the headline were illustrations of three Indian men. Thunder was on the right, dimples etched into his cheeks. Father John read through the article. *Three Indians were found guilty of murdering an Arapaho woman and sentenced to be hanged at the Fort Washakie agency. The murder occurred while the photographer, Edward S. Curtis, was taking pictures of a mock attack on a village that resembled an actual Arapaho village. Many witnesses testified that Thunder, posing as a warrior, rode close to the woman with his rifle just before she was found shot in the chest. The other so-called warriors, Ben Franklin and Alvin Pretty Lodge, were also in the vicinity.*

Father John followed the article to the next page where there was a large illustration of a log cabin next to a small tent at the foot of what looked like a mountain slope scattered with pine trees. The caption read: LODGING PLACE OF EDWARD S. CURTIS. THE VILLAGE STOOD NEARBY.

Below the caption, the article continued: *After hearing the witnesses' testimony, the magistrate had no choice but to find Thunder guilty of first-degree murder and the other two Indians guilty of being accessories to the heinous crime. The executioner has been sent for and should arrive by train on Tuesday next.*

Father John glanced over the paragraph again. Something was missing. The magistrate had pronounced the men guilty and sentenced them to death, but . . . there was no mention of any defense lawyers.

He let out a long, slow breath and read on: *The murdered woman was Bashful Woman, the daughter of*

Chief Sharp Nose, much revered among the Indians. She married a white man from Nebraska, Carston Evans, who runs one of the area's biggest cattle operations on his ranch southwest of Thermopolis. Mr. Evans said that his wife was a good wife and mother to their two-year-old daughter. He said that his wife lived the Arapaho Way.

Evans. Father John leaned back against the chair and stared into the shadows of the stacks. Senator Jaime Evans operated a large cattle ranch that the man who was probably his grandfather had started. And his grandfather had been married to an Arapaho. They'd had a child. He wondered if the senator was also descended from Sharp Nose, then discarded the idea. If the man had any Indian blood, he would have made the most of the fact. Especially Senator Evans. He always portrayed himself as a man of the people, a Westerner, an ordinary rancher. Never mind that his ranch rode on top of an ocean of oil.

Father John closed the book and pushed it to the edge of the table, trying to work out what Christine Nelson might have made of the articles. She'd found the names of the other two warriors, Alvin Pretty Lodge and Ben Franklin, but Eunice Redshield had said that neither man had any descendants on the rez. Still, Christine had found illustrations to prove their identities in the Curtis photograph. But there were no illustrations of Bashful Woman, nothing to prove which woman in the village had been murdered.

And Christine had found something more: Senator Evans's grandfather had been married to an Arapaho woman, the daughter of Chief Sharp Nose. Random pieces of history that might add up to nothing, he realized, except that Denise Painted Horse was part of the Sharp Nose family, and it was possible that Denise had owned a Curtis photograph, perhaps a portrait of Bashful Woman.

He made his way back along the stacks and up the stairs. When he flipped off the lights, a well of darkness opened below. For a brief moment, he felt as if he were standing over an abyss, like the past itself. He walked out into the library and waited while the librarian checked out a couple of books for a gray-haired woman.

Finally, the librarian came along the counter toward him. "Any luck in the dusty archives, Father?"

"What do you have on the Evans family?" he asked, dodging the question.

"Senator Evans? You mean the next president of the United States? He's coming home to announce his candidacy in Cheyenne next Monday. Imagine having a Wyoming rancher in the White House. Are you a supporter?"

"He's scheduled a visit to the mission," he said, still dodging.

"Oh!" She nodded, as if that explained why he'd asked about the Evans family. "I think we have what you're looking for." She stepped around the corner and made her way down a row of shelves, her gaze traveling over the spines of books. Finally she pulled one free and walked back. "This should tell you everything you'd like to know," she said, handing him the large book with a photograph of cattle grazing on the plains. "I had the pleasure of meeting the senator last year. He's certainly a nice man. I can tell you, he has the support of everybody around here. After all, he's one of us."

Father John gave the woman a little smile and took the book over to an upholstered chair. He sat down and turned to the index. The Evans Ranch was listed on page forty-four. He thumbed the pages backward until he came to a full-page color photograph of a two-story frame ranch house with the peaked roof and wide front porch of another era. It looked as if other rooms had been built on through the years, attached to one side, then the other, stamping their own era onto the house: 1930s, 1950s.

On the next page, inside a box marked with thick, black lines, was the Evans family tree with the names Carston Evans and Matilda Hunter at the top. Other lines dropped to the names of three children: James, Mary, Barbara. It looked as if neither daughter had married, but James had fathered one child: Senator Jaime Evans.

Father John skimmed through the chapter on the family history. Carston Evans, raised on a farm in Nebraska, had come to Wyoming in 1904 looking for opportunity. Starting with a few head of cattle, he had built the Evans Ranch into one of Wyoming's largest cattle ranches. Ten years after he began ranching, the elder Evans had discovered oil seeping into the pasture. Today the ranch is one of the state's major oil producers. The Evans family has been active in local politics. Carston Evans's son, James, served twenty years as county commissioner, and his son, Jaime Evans, continuing the family's commitment to public service, was elected to represent Wyoming, first in Congress, then in the United States Senate.

There were photographs taken through the years. A head shot of Carston Evans: medium height and slight build, with a long face and prominent nose under a wide-brimmed cowboy hat. Casual photographs of his son and grandson posing on the front porch. And a full-page photograph of Senator Jaime Evans surrounded by a crowd of people on a stage, arms raised in victory, banner stretched overhead with large black letters that read EVANS FOR U.S. SENATE.

Father John closed the book. There was no mention of Bashful Woman. It was as though any image of the murdered Arapaho woman had been erased, as if she had never existed.

He considered this for a moment. If Christine wanted to identify the murdered woman in the Curtis photograph, she'd had to look elsewhere for a likeness.

Father John carried the book over to the desk and waited until the librarian uncurled herself from the computer and swiveled toward him. "Find what you were looking for?" she asked.

"Any chance that Christine Nelson looked at this book?" He tapped the cover.

The woman held his gaze a moment. Finally, she said, "I remember pulling the book for her. She sat over there"—a nod toward the chair he had just vacated. "She seemed disappointed."

"Disappointed?"

"I don't think she found what she was looking for."
She leaned toward him. "You didn't, either, did you?"

"Not yet," he said.

16

FATHER JOHN FOUND the CD he was looking for and inserted the disc into the player on the book shelf. He adjusted the volume until it was just right. Not too loud, or Damien would come down the hall to complain. He faced the bookshelf, allowing the music to float over him and lift, for a moment, the worry weighing on him all day. There was comfort in Verdi. You could count on the man to deliver the kind of music that was like a prayer, the way it seemed to put things into perspective and bring about a sense of peace.

He went back to the work at his desk that he hoped to finish before he headed over to the residence for dinner. A few more payroll checks to write, watching the balance drop closer to zero with each entry. It was like watching a thermometer drop outside. He was writing out the check payable to Christine Nelson when a gust of icy air swooped through the office and the front door thudded shut. He looked up as Ted Gianelli appeared in the doorway, clutching a thick, blue-covered book.

"Looks like we've got a lead on your curator," he said, strolling across the office and dropping the book on Father John's desk.

Father John pulled the book toward him. The cover was iridescent blue, with the name Eric Loftus in large, white letters across the top and *The Secret War* in gold letters on the bottom. The book must have been two inches thick.

"Help yourself to coffee." Father John nodded toward the small table with Styrofoam cups and cartons of sugar and powdered cream stacked in front of the coffee pot. The coffee was starting to smell like burned sugar.

Gianelli walked over to the table and took his time pouring the coffee, stirring in cream and sugar, his head bent in the direction of the CD player. *Deserto sulla terra*, he said.

"You're pretty good." Was there any opera music the man didn't recognize?

"Damn straight." The agent settled into one of the chairs Father John kept for visitors and dropped his nose close to the Styrofoam cup. He sniffed a couple of times. "Brewed last week?"

"It'll put hair on your chest, Ted." Father John thumped the top of the book. "You bring me some bed-time reading, or does this have something to do with Christine?"

"Ever heard of Eric Loftus?"

"Must be a famous author." Father John gave the book another thump.

"Famous rogue CIA officer, stationed all over the world. Moscow, Paris, Mexico City. The kind that knows better than his superiors and the whole damn United States Congress. Liked to take matters into his own hands. Retired from the agency five years ago and been living in Jackson, running a gallery of Plains Indian art and artifacts and writing his memoirs. God knows how they got by the CIA's publications review board."

"Why am I interested in Eric Loftus?"

"Your interest would be in the man's wife." Gianelli was enjoying this. "Attractive woman, brown hair, green eyes, good figure, and brains. Her name is Christine Loftus, otherwise known as Christine Nelson." He paused, allowing the news to mingle with the melody of the aria. "We managed to connect the first three numbers on the license plate to a light tan Range Rover in Teton County, registered to Eric Loftus. Happens to own the gallery in Jackson. The agent up there paid the gallery a visit a couple of hours ago and had a chat with the man. Loftus claims his wife is the art expert, he runs the business side. Seems the woman has a history of bipolar illness. Goes like a house afire when she's up, becomes suicidal when she crashes. Seems she also has a history of driving away when she's in the manic stage, which comes on as soon as she decides she's cured and stops taking her meds. Six weeks ago, she got in the Range Rover and drove off. Loftus never reported her missing. Said she's done it before and always comes home."

Father John took his eyes away and stared out the window a moment. The streetlamps around Circle Drive had come on, sending dim flares of yellow light into the curtain of dusk. The mission looked strange in the light, like the surreal vision in a dream. In years of counseling and hearing confessions, he'd convinced himself that he could gauge people, that he had his own inner lie detector. He'd been wrong about a woman who called herself Christine Nelson. He'd thought she was high-spirited, energetic, a workaholic. He'd missed that she was ill.

"Look, John," Gianelli's voice cut into his thoughts. "Is there anything else you can tell me about the woman?"

Father John locked eyes again with the man sprawled in the side chair, a notepad balanced on one thick thigh. He knew nothing about Christine Nelson, Father John was thinking. No, that wasn't exactly true. "She's good at her job," he said. "She's a professional with enough contacts in the art world to bring the Curtis exhibit here from the West Wind Gallery in Denver."

Gianelli started scribbling on the pad as Father John explained that Christine had been trying to identify Arapahos in the photographs. She'd visited Eunice Redshield, and she was probably trying to find someone in the Sharp Nose clan who could identity one of the women in the photograph, the daughter of Chief Sharp Nose. And something else. Christine had tried to buy a photo from Eunice for a thousand dollars.

Gianelli stopped scribbling and leaned back in his chair. "Thousand dollars for a photograph?"

"An unknown photo taken by Edward Curtis."

"So she could have met somebody in the Sharp Nose clan Monday night. How many people we talking about?"

"I'm not sure. There are probably numerous descendents. Denise Painted Horse was one of them."

Gianelli let out a little whistle and went back to the scribbling. Scribbling and nodding. "Woman murdered, another woman missing on the same night. First thought I had was, maybe there's a connection." He looked up. "I checked the guest book from the museum after Banner's men picked it up. Denise Painted Horse's name isn't there. Was there any connection, as far as you know?"

Father John shook his head. That was the problem. He couldn't get the possibility out of his mind. Denise could have visited the museum, but if she didn't sign the guest book, where was the evidence? Where was the evidence that Denise and Christine had ever met?

He said, "T.J. might know."

"I wouldn't say that T.J.'s being cooperative, thanks to Vicky." The agent slipped the notepad inside his jacket and got to his feet. The features of his face seemed to lock together, as if he'd pulled a tight mask over his head.

"People here don't think T.J.'s capable of killing anybody," Father John said. "They know the man, and they twist him."

Caro nome was playing now, filling up the silence a moment. Finally Gianelli nodded toward the CD player. "Well, Gaultier Malde wasn't who he appeared to be, was he? Gilda was taken in by a handsome face. She trusted him."

The fed started for the door, then turned back. "Problem is, T.J. lied about his alibi. If he can't account for his whereabouts when his wife was shot . . ." He let the thought merge into the aria. "You can tell people that I have no intention of railroading T.J., but I'm not going to let a murderer walk away. If you learn anything . . ."

"I'll get in touch," Father John said, but the agent had

already disappeared into the corridor. There was another *whoosh* of air, and the *thwack* of the door shutting reverberated through the floorboards.

Father John scooped the book off the desk. The metallic gold letters blinked on the blue cover. In the center was the shadowy figure of a man in a black coat, looking away from the camera toward what might have been a half-destroyed building in some Third World country.

Father John thumbed through the pages, scanning the first chapters. The path of a spy, from Cornell—political science, government studies, finance—to Harvard graduate school, zeroing in on foreign affairs. Graduation with honors and on to the CIA. They didn't recruit him. Eric Loftus recruited the CIA, burning to defeat the enemies of his country.

Father John skipped over the next chapters—early years of training, first postings—and stopped at the chapter titled, VANISHING THE OPPOSITION:

Upon occasion, it became necessary to deal with a foreign agent in such a way that the security of our operations would be protected. Such an agent was a Mexican official that I shall call Señor Gomez. Señor Gomez had been one of our trusted assets for many years. The time arrived, however, when we discovered he had sold himself to a major drug cartel. In return for his assurance that a truckload of cocaine would not be stopped at the border, the drug cartel had arranged to place large sums of money in a Swiss bank account for Señor Gomez.

Since Señor Gomez had been useful to us, I naturally tried to convince the man that his best interests lay with the Americans. I had obtained photographs of him in his casita with a beautiful woman, whom I shall call Maria. In the privacy of Señor Gomez's office, I laid the photographs on the desk. To my surprise, he started laughing. He laughed so hard that he began to choke. For a brief moment, I thought that our problems might solve themselves.

When Señor Gomez recovered his equilibrium, he told me to take the photographs to his wife, because she also enjoyed a hearty laugh. It seemed that the señor and his wife had a mutual understanding. She would look the other way when he visited his casita, if he looked the other way when she visited a two-bit bullfighter with a gored right arm. The señor flung the photographs at me and threatened to expose our operatives.

After serious consultations at the highest levels, it was decided that the matter of Señor Gomez had to be resolved. No matter the cost, we had to protect our operatives. Through a deep-cover asset, I passed the word to the leaders of the drug cartel that Señor Gomez had double-crossed them and the next drug shipment would be seized at the border by the U.S. Drug Enforcement Administration.

On a Monday morning, Señor Gomez's car arrived at his home to take him to his office. There was a new driver who explained that he had been sent by the government carpool. This did not alarm the señor, since his regular driver could be unreli-

able after the weekend. Señor Gomez got into the back seat of the Lincoln Town Car, which curved around the driveway and turned onto the major thoroughfare.

It was the last time that Señor Gomez was seen.

Father John closed the book and pushed it across the desk, a new picture taking shape in his mind. A small, dark-haired woman climbing into a Range Rover and driving away from Jackson. Away from a man who knew how to handle people who displeased him, away from a trained killer, a man who didn't blink at having someone killed. Suppose she'd gotten as far as she could go with whatever money she'd managed to take with her? Over the mountain to a job at an Indian mission where Eric Loftus might never think to look. Suppose she was hiding, waiting for the opportunity to go even farther, looking for a way . . .

Then she'd stumbled on an unknown Curtis photograph and the possibility of more photographs on the reservation. Perhaps a lot of photographs. A woman with Christine's background would know the value, and she'd know art dealers willing to purchase the photos. She could arrange the deals, take the commissions, and perhaps make enough money to get far away from Eric Loftus. She could lose herself and become someone else, someone Eric Loftus couldn't find.

Except that Eunice Redshield wouldn't sell.

But Christine had met someone who would sell—he was sure of it now. Someone willing to sell photographs of the ancestors.

17

October 1907

JESSE WHITE OWL squinted into the cold and, hunched inside his canvas great coat, guided the mare through Fort Washakie. Past the Wind River boarding school, the agent's cabin, the stone dormitory where the soldiers lived. The brittle air deadened the sound of the mare's hooves. He reined in at the hitching post in front of the yellowish stone building that was the Wind River Agency. In the yard off to the side, clumps of wooden beams held upright with iron plates stood silhouetted against the gray sky. Hanging from the beam, moving in the wind, were three ropes frozen into nooses.

Jesse looked away from the scaffolding. Yesterday after he came down from the mountains, he'd stopped at the Mercantile store. He'd wanted the news, and Indians were always hanging around the Mercantile ready to pass on the gossip. The magistrate had come from Lander the day before yesterday, he'd learned. People had jammed the agency building and crowded onto the porch and spilled out onto the grounds, demanding justice for Bashful.

It had given Jesse a sense of relief—the anger that had swept over the reservation. He'd felt the force of the anger in the men leaning against the counter, telling what had happened. Witnesses had stood up, one after the other. They had been in the photographer's village, they said. Even Carston Evans had stood up. They had all seen what happened, and they spoke the truth of how the warriors had galloped into the village, pointing their Winchester 73s into the sky, firing blanks—cartridges of black powder and wads of cardboard—and how everyone had started screaming and running, death at their backs.

It was Thunder who had galloped up to Bashful's tipi. When he rode off, Bashful was dead. The magistrate said Thunder was guilty of murder. The other warriors were accomplices, were they not? They rode with Thunder, didn't they? They must have known what Thunder intended to do. Everyone at the agency had shouted, "Yes! Yes!" The magistrate had handed down the sentence: The three warriors would be hanged the day after tomorrow.

Now Jesse made his way across the porch of the agency building and let himself through the heavy wooden door. The hinges squealed like a trapped animal. The killers would not be needing the contraption outside. He could feel the weight of the Colt .32 automatic pistol—no bigger than his hand—jammed inside his boot against his ankle.

Inside, boots had carved a groove down the middle of the wood floor all the way to the office on the far side of the entry. Jesse could see the agent, Mike Fleming, a slight-framed white man with strips of gray hair combed over the top of his scalp. He was seated at the desk, pouring over an opened ledger book.

"What is it?" The white man did not look up. "Can't you see I'm busy?"

"It's important, Mr. Fleming," Jesse said.

The white man lifted his head, a slow movement that looked as if it took place with some pain. "Jesus, Jesse. You know you Indians need an appointment." He peered over the top of round, rimless spectacles and drew his mouth into a thin line of disapproval. "You can't barge in anytime the mood strikes you. I got work to do. We got three executions scheduled for day after tomorrow. Where were you during the trial? You seen it all, I dare say, working with Curtis like you was. Could've been some help if you'd been here to tell your story. You get scared of talking to the federal magistrate?"

Jesse held his cowboy hat in both hands in front of his stomach, the perfect picture of contrition, he thought, the image of a humble, hapless Indian the agent wanted to see. "I feel real bad about it. I hear Bashful's killers are gonna get what's coming to them."

"You bet they are. Magistrate wants to make an example of them. We can't have Indians getting themselves up in regalia and acting like savages. Attacking village . . ." He broke off, shaking his head. "If I'd had any idea what Curtis was up to, I would've put a stop to the project, that's for certain. What d'ya want, Jesse, now that you're here?"

"I was thinking to have a few words with Thunder and the others," Jesse said, bending forward a little, not as straight and tall as usual.

"Can't happen, Jesse. You know the rules. No visitors except family before an execution." The agent looked down at the ledger book and gave him a little wave, as if he were flicking away a pesky fly. "Go on, get outta here."

"I got a message for Thunder," Jesse pushed on. "It's from Bashful."

"You got a message from Bashful?" The white man's head jerked back up. "Before she was killed?"

"Day before yesterday," he said.

"You got a message from a dead woman?"

"I been in the mountains and I had a vision. Bashful come to me and give me a message for Thunder. Man's gonna die in two days . . ." He could sense the agent's interest. It was a wedge that he pushed into. "Man's gonna die, could give him some comfort, Mr. Fleming. Let the poor man die with a little comfort."

"I never know when you Indians are bullshitting me, Jesse. You on the level?"

Jesse waited a couple of beats. "I want all of 'em to pay for Bashful's death," he said. "Still, won't do no harm to let 'em go into the sky world feeling a little better."

"I suppose she forgives them?"

"She was a kind woman."

"You loved her, didn't you? Always thought you and Bashful should've gotten married, but her being a chief's daughter made her pretty high up." He laughed, his head bobbing in rhythm to the guttural noises coming from his throat. "Even Indians got their upper classes. So what happened? Her brother, Stands-Alone, refuse to give you permission and married her off to a white man instead?"

The agent pushed back from the desk and lifted himself to his feet. His chest looked caved in below the chickenlike neck. Arms as thin as twigs inside the sleeves of his white shirt hung at his sides. He could crush the man, Jesse was thinking, with his hands.

"What do you say, Mr. Fleming? Can I have a few minutes with Thunder?"

"Yeah, what the hell. Messages from the dead." Shaking his head, the agent came around the desk. His face was so close that Jesse could smell the sourness of the man's breath. "Five minutes, Jesse. You sure you ain't up to something?"

"Just delivering a message."

"Well, I gotta pat you down. Spread eagle . . ." The agent nodded toward the wall. "Gotta make sure you ain't packing any weapons."

Jesse turned around and, spreading his arms and legs, set his hands hard against the wall. The agent's bony fingers ran down his arms, punched through his jacket into his stomach and ribs, and started working along his pant legs. Jesse held his breath. The fingers were on his calves now, above his boots.

They stopped moving.

"Okay, you're clean." The agent's voice sounded hollow behind him. "Watch yourself. Jesse. You're going in with three killers."

"I know them," Jesse said. He followed the man down a hall to the back of the building. In the corner was a door made of iron bars. The agent yanked at the gold chain on his belt until he was fingering a long, gold key at the end. He jammed the key into the door and kicked it open.

"This is your lucky day," he shouted. "Jesse White Owl's here with a message from the beyond, where you bastards are going real soon."

Jesse stepped past the man into a room about the size of the agent's office. He could feel the pistol scrape against his ankle. Thunder stood at the small window, staring past the bars at the scaffolding outside. The other warriors were on the bunks against the stone wall on the right. Ben Franklin sat on the lower bunk, his face in his hands. On the top bunk, Alvin Pretty Lodge was curled toward the wall. The strip of brown skin between the tail of his shirt and the band of his blue jeans made Jesse wince. He didn't know these men at all. They weren't brave warriors, with paint on their bodies and rifles waving overhead. This was who they really were: cowards who attacked villages and killed women.

Cowards who killed Bashful.

He would have to make the shots count. One shot in the forehead for each of the cowards; one for himself.

Thunder was coming across the cell toward him, arms outstretched. "I do not come as a friend," Jesse said.

The Indian stopped in place, surprise flowing through the despair in his expression. Everything about him looked hopeless: the angle of his shoulders, the slight bend in his back, the way his face fell forward, black eyes studying the ground. "I'm sorry for your loss, Jesse," he said. "She was beautiful, and I know you loved her."

"Why?" Jesse heard the hopelessness in his own

157

voice. "I want to go to the sky world with her. I want to tell her why she died. What happened? Did you punish her for marrying a white man?" Jesse went on, all the explanations that he'd gone over in his mind. He was barely aware of Franklin getting to his feet, Pretty Lodge pulling himself upright against the headboard. He moved in closer. "You loved her, too, didn't you, Thunder? Is that why you shot her? Because her eyes never looked on scum like you?"

Thunder moved backward. "You're a crazy Indian, Jesse. You'd better go on and get outta here."

"I have to know!" Jesse was shouting now, the words spitting like gravel from his throat. Pretty Lodge jumped off the top bunk and lined up next to Franklin, cowards all of them.

"Everything okay back there, Jesse?" The agent sounded far away, his voice muffled and thin.

"Yeah, everything's fine," Jesse yelled. "Just having a last talk."

"Two more minutes and you gotta wind it up."

Jesse glanced from Thunder to the other Indians and, reaching down, pulled the pistol out of his boot. He straightened up slowly, keeping the gun on Thunder. "Tell me," he said, his teeth clenched. "In the name of the Creator and all of the spirits, before we all die, tell me why you killed Bashful."

Thunder didn't take his eyes from the pistol. "You gonna shoot us, Jesse? Go ahead. Pull the trigger." He threw his head toward the window with the bars across the glass and the scaffold beyond. "You think we want to die out there, get our necks broke like sheep? Go ahead and kill us now, Jesse. You'll be doing us a favor."

Jesse let his gaze take in the cowards on his right, perspiration rolling on their foreheads. Then he locked eyes again with Thunder. "Why did you kill her?"

The Indian drew the palm of his hand down over his nose and chin. "Our families were in them tipis, Jesse, our little children. Don't matter how authentic the photographer wanted the photos, we was shooting blanks into the air."

"You can't fool me, Thunder." The trigger felt like ice against Jesse's finger. "There were witnesses that saw you riding up close to Bashful."

"I got my wife and little boy in the tipi next to Bashful's. You think I was shooting when I rode close?"

The smallest pressure, Jesse was thinking, a tightening of his forefinger and the bullet would smash into the man's head.

But he didn't know . . . he didn't know the man.

"I swear to you by the ancestors," Thunder said. "I swear I didn't kill Bashful."

"How did it happen?" Jesse heard the crack in his voice. They were coming to him again, the images he'd tried to block from his mind. The warriors racing into the village, people scattering. The rifle blasts, one on top of another, the sounds of screaming, the puffs of gray smoke and the odors of rotten eggs. He'd been concentrating on the glass plates. Removing the holders with the exposed plates from the camera, shoving other holders into Curtis's hands as fast as he could, so that the photographer could make his images. Shooting off his own rifle when the photographer yelled, "Stop." He hadn't *seen* . . .

"Shoot us, Jesse." Thunder said. "Be done with it."

Jesse dropped his arm. The Colt brushed against his pant leg. "I swore to kill the man that killed Bashful," he said. "We're gonna leave here now. I'm gonna tell the agent I'm all done. Soon's he opens the door, I show him the gun and we'll go."

"Where we gonna go, Jesse?" Thunder asked. "There'll be a posse out before we get half mile down the road. If the posse don't get us, Bashful's clan'll come after us. Stands-Alone'll hunt us down. Where we gonna hide? We're dead men, Jesse, and you'll be dead with us. Stay alive, Jesse. Find Bashful's killer so folks'll know who did that terrible thing."

Jesse turned toward the bunks. "You wanna come?"

The other men were shaking their heads in unison. "We ride with Thunder," Franklin said.

Jesse jammed the pistol into his jacket pocket, then stepped back and shouted out into the hallway. He grabbed hold of the bars and leaned his forehead against the cold iron.

It seemed a long time before boots clacked on the plank floor, coming closer. Finally, the clink of the key in the lock, the door squeaking open. Jesse made his way back down the hall and out the door into the cool afternoon.

18

VICKY SPOTTED ADAM through the dim light and the blue smoke hanging over the tables in the restaurant. He was in the last booth along the left wall: Indian man in mid-forties, black-haired, square-jawed, wearing a dark sweater with the light collar of his shirt visible, emphasizing the copper tone of his skin. He looked self-possessed and strong. She couldn't imagine Adam Lone Eagle ever doubting himself.

"I'm meeting a friend." Vicky smiled at the heavy-set blond hostess with bright red lipstick who had lifted a menu off the podium at the entrance.

The woman threw a glance over one shoulder toward the dining room. "The gentleman in back?" she asked, the faintest note of disappointment ringing in her tone.

Vicky shrugged out of her coat and hung it on a rack with the other coats, then she started into the dining room, working her way past the tables covered with plates of steak and baked potatoes and baskets of bread. Candles flickered in tiny, round vases. Most of the diners were white—a mixture of couples and families—but a few Indian families were scattered about. Dishes and silverware clanked over the din of conversation. The whole room was wrapped in the odors of seared meat, melted butter, and smoke.

Adam was on his feet when she reached the booth. "Sorry I'm late," she said, aware of the heads swiveling around, the eyes trained on them as Adam leaned toward her and brushed his lips against her cheek.

He ushered her into the booth, then slid across from her. "I was starting to worry that you wouldn't come," he said, before launching into the small talk—the polite preliminaries to whatever he'd wanted to talk to her about. Recommending items on the menu. Commenting that winter was on the way. Vicky tried to follow along. Nodding. Nodding. It was no good. The image of T.J. insisting that he had an alibi was burned into the inside of her eyelids.

"What is it?" Adam asked, after the waitress had taken their orders: two small filets, medium. There were pinpricks of candlelight in his brown eyes.

Vicky sat back. "Am I so transparent?"

"Like the glass around this candle," he said, running a finger around the rim of the vase.

"What happens," she began, "if you find out a client has been lying to you and . . ." She hesitated, then plunged on. "He could be guilty."

"We're talking about T.J. Painted Horse?"

Vicky glanced away. She shouldn't have started this. "A hypothetical question, Adam. Forget it. It's not important."

"Not important? I can see it all over your face." Adam sat back, not taking his eyes from her. "It's filled up your thoughts. So let's talk about this hypothetical client of yours. He's lied to you, which means he hasn't admitted to committing the crime. So you give him the best damn defense you can. Make the prosecutor prove the case point by point." Adam shifted forward, a defense lawyer warming up to the summation. "Even guilty clients have the right to a fair trial and a damn good lawyer."

The waitress emerged out of the blur of diners beyond the booth. Hosting a tray with one hand, she opened the stand with the other, slid the tray on top, and began delivering plates of filet and potatoes, sides of salads, a basket with bread poking out of the napkin.

"It's not that simple, Adam." Vicky sliced into the potato and watched the melted butter and sour cream dribble into the slice. *T.J. killed his wife!* "I don't want to help a murderer go free."

"Well, we don't always know who's guilty, do we?" Adam shrugged and gave her a smile that, she realized, was meant to encourage her. "I have a proposal for you," he said. "I think that we'd make an unbeatable team."

Vicky took a bite of her own steak. She had to force it down. "Team?" she said after a moment.

"We complement each other." He leaned over the table, so close that the candle light danced over the tiny scar that ran along his cheek. "I always liked that word. Complement. Complete. You're a sensitive lawyer. You don't like the idea of murderers running around. I'm the pragmatic type. Sometimes murderers go free. That's the way it is." Moving even closer, lowering his voice until it was almost a whisper, he said, "I'm making you a business proposal, Vicky. I've been thinking about leaving my firm in Casper and concentrating on Indian law. How about forming a firm together in Lander?"

"A business proposal." Vicky repeated the words, trying to wrap her mind around the idea. She shifted her gaze to the top of the booth beyond the man's shoulder.

What had she been thinking? That Adam was interested in her? Attracted to her? Dinners together, telephone calls. The friendly kiss when she'd arrived, and all the time he'd been scouting out a new law partner, a business associate.

"Strictly business. We can make ourselves experts in Indian law. Water. Oil. Gas. The Arapaho tribe will no longer have to go to Cheyenne to find experts. We'll be stronger together than alone. You're Arapaho, but you're a woman. I'm an outsider, but I'm still native. We cancel out each other's weaknesses." He paused for a moment, then hurried on. "And we'll be able to talk to each other about our cases. No more hypothetical clients. Think about it, Vicky. It's not easy practicing alone."

"All finished here?" The waitress appeared and began clearing the table. Another moment and she was setting down cups and saucers and pouring coffee.

Vicky stared at the steam curling out of her cup and waited until the waitress had walked away. "You surprise me, Adam," she said.

Adam clasped his hands and leaned toward her. "Don't get me wrong, Vicky. I'm attracted like hell to you. This would give us the chance to spend time together, get to know each other. Come on, aren't you attracted to me? Just a little?"

Vicky laughed and nodded toward the dining room. "Every woman in this restaurant is attracted to you, Adam."

"I don't care about them. What do you say?"

Vicky sipped at her coffee a moment. "I've worked

alone now for most of the last five years." *Hi sei ci nihi,* Woman Alone, the grandmothers called her. "I'm used to being alone."

"No you're not." Adam reached out and placed his hand over hers. "Think about it, Vicky, that's all I'm asking."

She heard herself promising to give the matter some thought, then she sipped at the last of her coffee and waited while Adam paid the bill. "A business expense," he said, winking at her and waving away her efforts to retrieve her wallet from her bag. They walked back through the restaurant, found their coats, and, pulling them on, stepped outside. The evening was silent in the cold. There was the faintest smell of moisture in the air, like the promise of snow banking over the mountains, preparing to sweep down over the reservation. The moon had broken through the clouds, casting a pearl-gray light over the parking lot and throwing long shadows around the vehicles.

"I'll follow you home." Adam said.

"No need to. I'll be fine."

"You'll call me soon?"

"I'll call you," Vicky said, sliding behind the steering wheel of the Jeep.

THE AA MEETING had let out at nine, but it was ten minutes later before Father John had helped Leonard finish locking up Eagle Hall and started for the residence. He looked forward to the meetings every week—the sense of purpose and resolve that permeated the atmosphere. He felt stronger afterward, the thirst weaker, receding into the past where it belonged.

Three pickups were still parked in Circle Drive, and Leonard and several others who had been at the meeting huddled together close to the vehicles, their voices cutting through the moonlight that flooded the grounds. Father John gave them a wave as he walked past, then thrust his hands into his jacket pockets and dipped his chin into the folds of the collar. His boots scraped against the ice-hard ground.

He was halfway across the field enclosed by Circle Drive, the frozen stalks of grass snapping under his boots, when he noticed the light glowing in the corner window of the museum. Catherine must have forgotten to turn off all the lights. And yet, he hadn't noticed the light on his way over to the meeting earlier.

He veered left toward the museum, ran up the porch steps, and tried the door. Locked. He fished the key ring out of his jeans pocket, moving sideways down the porch toward the glowing window as he did so. Everything looked normal in the entry, except for the light spilling from beneath the closed door to Christine Nelson's office. His breath made a little smudge on the glass pane. Christine Loftus, he reminded himself.

He walked back to the door, jiggled the key in the lock, and stepped inside. A rush of warm air came at him like wind out of a tunnel. In the gallery ahead, a residue of light played over the photographs of long-dead Arapahos. He started toward the office and stopped. A sound, almost imperceptible, like the sound of snow. He stood very still. The next sound, when it came, was the hard, definite thud of a drawer pushed shut.

He moved closer, took hold of the knob, and threw the door open. Seated behind the desk was a large man who looked to be in his early fifties, with a squared-jaw; dark, bushy eyebrows; and reddish, short-cropped hair. He was thumbing through papers in one of the folders scattered over the desk.

"What are you doing here?" Father John said.

"Father O'Malley, the pastor, I presume." The man flipped over a page, not looking up. "I've been expecting you." He lifted his massive chin and stared across the desk with eyes as opaque and steady as stone. "Where's my wife, pastor?"

"Eric Loftus. How'd you get in here?"

Loftus threw back his head and gave a loud guffaw. "Took about half a second to get through the lock on the front door. Could've cleaned out your precious artifacts and all those Curtis photos before anybody knew I was here. I want my wife, pastor, and you were the last man to see her."

"The FBI and police are looking for her."

A bushy eyebrow shot up. "A fed assigned to an Indian reservation, a detective in a two-bit town, a bunch of Indian policemen. Give me a break, pastor. They're chasing their asses around. Some bastard took her and trashed her place. I figure you got a good idea who it was."

"You figure wrong, Loftus. If I had any idea of what happened to your wife, I'd take it to the fed."

"Think about it pastor. You know the people on the rez. A lot of them came to see the photographs, judging by what people here been telling me." The man

167

drummed his knuckles on the desk. "Maybe somebody started hanging around, getting interested in the curator. You understand what I'm saying? Some Arapaho having fantasies about my wife. Maybe he followed her out of here Monday evening. Anybody like that come to mind, pastor?"

Father John didn't take his eyes away, a new picture emerging in his head. The man who made people disappear had a face. "Maybe you followed her out of here," he said. "Maybe you wanted her to come back to you and she refused."

Loftus broke into what passed for a smile. Only the right side of his face changed, as if the left half were paralyzed. Knuckles popped white out of the hand bunched into a fist on the desk. "You're a brave man, pastor. You don't know how brave. If I wanted my wife to disappear, she would have gone on a long trip. At least that's how it would've looked. No apartment trashed. The work of an amateur!" He threw his head back and emitted a grunting noise. "I assure you I am not an amateur."

Loftus leaned back, set one elbow on the armrest, and began rubbing at his chin. The room was stuffy. From outside came the murmur of voices, brittle in the cold. "I'm going to let your remark pass," he said. "What I want is my wife. I had her figured for Europe, traipsing around the museums. Maybe Mexico City. Sooner or later she'd come to her senses, or run out of whatever money she stole from me, whichever came first. Call me up and beg to come back, like she always does." The half-smile returned. "Never figured she'd hole up in an

Indian museum across the mountain, but Christine is full of surprises. Explains why I could never get her out of my system. So what do you say, pastor? Maybe somebody else couldn't get her out of his system."

"It's your theory," Father John said. He was thinking that the man could be right. Christine could have attracted a stalker. She was a striking woman. But Loftus was a one-man vigilante committee, and he had no intention of encouraging the man.

"Let's consider other possibilities." Another thump on the desk. "Maybe she went to meet somebody. Notice anybody hanging around that evening?"

"Take your theories to the fed, Loftus. I want you out of here."

"So you're not going to help me." Loftus pushed himself to his feet. He was close to Father John's height, about six foot four, and outweighed him by thirty pounds. A big man with pawlike hands and a neck like a tree stump. "I heard about you, the Indian priest. You're gonna protect those Indians no matter what. But if one of them is responsible for hurting my wife . . ." He drew his mouth into a tight line a moment before going on. "I'm gonna hold you responsible." He picked up the folder. "This here stuff about the exhibit is mine."

"Leave the folder and get out of here."

"You think you're man enough to take it away from me?"

"Don't try me, Loftus," Father John said, locking eyes with the man. God, it was like facing a stone wall. But this was a game of bluff, like the games on the streets of Boston when he was a kid and some bully blocked his way home from baseball practice in the half-light of dusk, traffic screaming by. Whoever blinked lost the game, and he'd learned not to blink. He had the sense that Loftus had learned the same lesson.

There was the *swoosh* of the front door opening, the click of footsteps crossing the entry. Father John kept his eyes on the man a few feet away. He could sense the weight of bodies displacing the air behind him and hear the quick intakes of breath.

"Everything all right, Father?" Leonard's voice.

"This man's just leaving," Father John said.

Loftus shrugged and set the folder on the desk, his gaze on the four Arapahos in the doorway. "Next time I'll remember that you have body guards," he said. Then he swung around and, shouldering his way past, walked into the entry. The front door slammed shut, rattling the window.

"You okay, Father?" Leonard patted Father John's shoulder as if he were checking for some injury.

"I'm fine," he assured the Indian.

"We seen you going to the museum and decided we'd better check, make sure everything was all right. Museum's supposed to be closed this time of night. Who was he?"

"Eric Loftus. He's married to the curator."

The man's eyes softened. "Poor sonnabitch. He's gotta be worried sick."

"He's looking for her." Father John flipped off the light switch and walked the Indians across the entry and out onto the porch. They waited while he locked the door. "Thanks for coming in," he said as they started

170

across the grounds in a perfect V, Leonard and the others heading down Circle Drive for the pickups, Father John cutting through the field toward the residence. Through the cottonwoods across the grounds, he could see the lights of an SUV turning onto Seventeen-Mile Road.

LIGHT FLICKERED FROM the living room into the dimness of the entry. The television was on, a low growl of voices talking over one another. Father John pitched his coat onto the bench and went into the room. Damien was slouched on the sofa, gripping the remote in one hand. On the television screen, Senator Jaime Evans flashed a smile from across the country, dodging down a corridor past a cordon of reporters who thrust out microphones and shouted questions: "Is it true you intend to announce your candidacy for the presidency, senator?" "Senator, senator, will you be making the announcement next week in Wyoming?" "What chance do you have of winning your party's nomination?"

"Gentlemen!" The senator stopped walking and slowly turned toward the crowd of reporters. He lifted one hand, palm outstretched, patience and exasperation mingling in the handsome face. His light-colored hair looked wind tossed, as if he'd just gotten in from riding across the pasture. But he looked comfortable in a dark suit and white shirt with a red tie knotted smartly at his throat. He waited until the medley of voices subsided. "I see we have ladies here." He flashed another smile. "Gentlemen and ladies, all in good time, all in good time. I will announce my decision next Monday in my home state of Wyoming. As for my chances of winning my party's nomination, let me say that should I seek the nomination, I would fully intend to win. Thank you!" He gave the crowd a wave and slipped inside a massive door that closed behind him.

"And there you have it." The scene switched to a reporter standing on the grounds of the capitol. "Senator Evans has refused to confirm the rumors that he already has a campaign staff in place and will formally launch his bid for the nomination next week. Back to you . . ."

Damien clicked the mute button. "There goes the next president," he said.

19

FATHER JOHN PARKED in front of the small house that might have erupted out of the plains, with siding the caramel color of the bare dirt yard. He left the engine running, the tape player on the seat beside him still playing the selection of Verdi arias he'd been listening to on the drive from the mission. The duet, *Deh! la parola amara,* was about to end when the front door opened. The bent figure of an old man stepped out of the shadows into the sunlight splashing over the stoop and motioned for him to come in. Father John turned off the engine and the tape player on the last haunting note.

"Hungry, Father?" Max Oldman wanted to know as Father John walked past him into the living room.

Father John laughed. Arapahos were always trying to feed him. "Elena made her usual delicious oatmeal this morning."

"You're a lucky man, Father. Even when Josephine was alive, I didn't get delicious oatmeal every morning." The elder headed across the small room, dodging a coffee table covered with newspapers and Styrofoam cups. There was a jump in his walk, as if he were dragging his left hip. He was close to eighty, Father John guessed, frail and calloused looking, with deep wrinkles in the back of his neck between the frayed collar of his blue shirt and the uneven line of his gray hair.

"Take a load off your feet." Max flicked a bony hand at the sofa under the window before dropping into a recliner that still bore the imprint of his back and thighs.

Father John sat down. He pulled off his jacket and cowboy hat and piled them on the cushion beside him. "How are you holding up, grandfather?" he asked, using the term of respect for an Arapaho elder, moving slowly into the reason for the visit.

"Okay, I reckon." The elder nodded, then he went on about the way fall was hanging on real pretty this year, the whole earth turning red and orange, with ripples of frost cutting across the open prairie. Then he was onto the wind storm a couple of weeks ago and the broken cottonwood branches. Had to get out the ladder and cut the branches off before they crashed down onto the roof.

Father John winced at the image of the old man up on a ladder. "Call me next time," he said. "I'll come over and help you." He waited a moment until the time seemed right, then he said, "I'm sorry about Denise."

A moist film glistened in the elder's eyes. They were

light colored for an Arapaho, hazel shading into green and lit with intelligence. They gave him a startling appearance, unexpected in the wrinkled brown face. "Sure tough to lose one of the younger generation. She was the granddaughter of my brother, you know."

Father John nodded. That also made her Max's granddaughter, in the Arapaho Way.

"Looks to me like you got your own problems, Father." Max laid his arms over the armrest and tapped his fingers on the front edges. Long blue veins bulged on the top of his brown hands. "I hear that curator lady that was working for you went missing."

"She's the reason I wanted to talk to you," Father John said.

"You think she got enough of Indian ways and took off?"

Father John said that he didn't think so. He started to explain that Christine's apartment had been ransacked, then realized by the impatient way Max was bobbing his head that he'd already heard the gossip.

"Don't wish that white woman no harm," Max said, head still bobbing. "But don't surprise me that she ran herself into trouble. She was a pushy lady."

"She came to see you?"

"That what you want to know about?"

Father John smiled at the old man. It wasn't polite to push and prod. He was asking for a gift.

The elder shifted his frail body in the recliner, reached down along the side and pulled a handle. The footrest jumped up, and he crossed his legs and settled back. "The lady calls me last week and asks if she can come over and see me. Says she has respect for Chief Sharp Nose and being I come down from the chief, she's got respect for me, too. Says she's doing research and needs help. So I told her to come on out anytime she saw fit. Two hours later, she was sitting on that sofa, same place you're sitting. Says she's looking for old photographs. Called them vintage photographs. Says the photographs could be portraits of people in the photos at the Curtis exhibit."

Father John leaned forward and clasped his hands between his knees. "Did she say she was trying to identify Sharp Nose's daughter in one of the photographs?"

An absorbed look came into the old man's eyes, as if he were watching a movie inside his head. "Her name was Bashful Woman," he said, a note of reverence sounding in his voice. "The curator lady said she wanted to give Bashful Woman proper recognition. She was gonna identify her so her story could be told, one way or another. Went on and on like that. I didn't say nothing. Just sat here in my recliner and let her go on and nodded the way she'd think an old Indian like me oughtta nod."

Father John laughed and waited while Max recrossed his legs and cleared his throat. Finally, the old man said, "Lady wants to know if I got any of them vintage photographs. Maybe one of Bashful Woman? Said she'll get me maybe a thousand dollars for one. A thousand dollars for an old photo? That's right, she said, and I oughtta be ready to sell right now. She knew galleries that was lining up to pay. Maybe I could use the money, she said, and she gives my place the old eyeball, like maybe things wasn't up to her fancy standards. All I had to do was get my old photos. Well, I got real tired of her pushing. I said, 'That's all very well and good, lady, but I don't got any of them vintage photos, and if I did have images of my ancestors, I guess I wouldn't be selling them to no galleries.' She didn't like that none."

Max cleared his throat again, and for a moment Father John thought that the story had ended. Then Max said, "That lady kept right on pushing. Wanted to know who else come down from Sharp Nose that might have old photos. I said, 'Nobody, lady. Nobody's gonna sell photos of the ancestors.' I didn't like getting impolite, but I figured she was gonna sit on my sofa all day. So I said, 'That's the end of the story, lady. That's all I got to say.'"

"Thank you, grandfather," Father John said. Quiet settled around them a moment, except for the faint ticking of a clock somewhere in the house. "I'm worried about her," he went on. "The police and the FBI are looking for her, but she seems to have vanished into thin air. I keep thinking that maybe Christine's disappearance and Denise's murder are connected somehow." He shrugged. It was a hunch, that was all, the old urge to find a pattern in random events. "Is it possible that Christine went to Denise looking for old photos?"

Max was shaking his head before Father John had finished the question. "Denise wasn't gonna sell that lady nothing, so she would've been wasting her time. I sure wasn't gonna send her to Denise. More than likely, somebody got real mad at T.J. for holding up jobs out at the gas fields. People need jobs around here, you know.

I figure somebody was out to teach T.J. a lesson. Man's pretty broken up. Blames himself 'cause Denise was the one who got killed when it was supposed to be him."

He cleared his throat and peered into the space between them, as if a new thought had pushed into his mind. Then he said, "You probably heard, Father, things weren't so hot between her and T.J. Now he's gone off to the mountains to grieve. Vera's been calling all over the rez, asking if people seen him anywhere, wanting him to come home. She don't understand how it is with warriors. T.J.'s blaming himself 'cause it was his job to protect his wife. So he's grieving hard. He's asking the spirits for a vision so he can know what he's gotta do next. He's gone where nobody's gonna find him, and he'll come back when he's good and ready."

What the elder said made sense, Father John thought. It was logical. And yet, he had a sense of things left unsaid in the way that Max kept his eyes on the vacant space, as if there was more—something he didn't want to put into words. Father John felt as if he'd run into an alley, certain of a way out only to find a brick wall that he couldn't get around.

After a long moment, he gathered up his jacket and hat, got to his feet, and thanked the elder for the information he'd chosen to give. "Please don't get up, grandfather," he said as the old man fiddled with the handle to the footrest. "Stay where you are."

"Come back anytime, Father," Max said.

They might have spent the time discussing the weather, Father John thought, waving his hat toward the old man. He let himself through the door and hurried through a corridor of sunlight to the pickup, shrugging into his jacket as he went. A sense of futility weighed on him, a heavy load. He'd had a hunch, and the hunch was wrong: Max Oldman hadn't sent Christine to Denise. Christine could have been on her way to meet any one of dozens of Sharp Nose descendents when she disappeared.

20

VICKY SPOTTED THE large, black letters painted across the plate glass window at the end of the strip mall: GREAT PLAINS INSURANCE. She drove down the row of vehicles in the parking lot, past a dress shop with naked mannequins in the window, past a beauty salon with heads bobbing under the dryers inside, past a deli where a man in a leather jacket was holding the door open for a little kid with yellow, curly hair. She pulled into the vacant space with a sign on the sidewalk: RESERVED FOR GREAT PLAINS.

The evergreens in the planters on the sidewalk seemed greener in the October sun, the leaves on the spindly trees around the periphery of the lot were a deeper shade of red. Even the air seemed lighter, tinged with gold. Vicky made her way to the glass door and stepped into an entry with plastic chairs pushed against the window and a counter blocking the way to a corridor. On the wall behind the counter were five or six black-and-white photographs of smiling faces with a row of names below. Over the photographs, a banner read, TRUST YOUR FRIENDLY GREAT PLAINS AGENTS.

A short, pudgy-faced woman who looked as if she'd been a teenager not long ago emerged from the corridor. "How can we help you?" she asked, setting both hands on the counter and pulling herself upward, as if eagerness had propelled her to her tiptoes.

"I'd like to see one of your agents," Vicky said. She had no idea of the agent's name. White woman, blond, works at the insurance agency in the strip mall over in Riverton, was all that Vera's friend had said.

"Mr. Ringer isn't busy at the moment. I'll take you to his office." The receptionist rolled back on her heels, shrinking at least an inch as she moved to the end of the counter and reached for the wood gate.

Vicky glanced at the photos. Four men, three women. Two of the women were brunettes. One was blond. Below the photo was a name.

She said, "I'd like to speak with Marnie Rankin."

"Marnie? She's on conference call." The receptionist walked back and peered down at a phone on the ledge below the countertop. "Looks like she might be done. I'll check to see . . ."

"Oh, Val!" Another woman came down the corridor, waving a sheaf of papers. She was tall—about T.J.'s height, Vicky guessed—with long blond hair cut in layers about her face and the kind of makeup that made her face look flat and colorless, except for the black mascara on her eyelashes. "I'd like you to contact . . ." She looked up. "Sorry, I didn't realize you were busy."

"This woman"—a nod toward Vicky—"wants to see you, Marnie. You got the time?"

Vicky could almost see the image of herself in the

179

woman's eyes: Indian, dark skin, black hair, nicely enough dressed in a dark wool coat, possibly able to afford insurance.

"Follow me, please." The woman thrust the stack of papers at the receptionist, then opened the gate and led the way down the corridor. The sound of men's voices—a loud bark of laughter—floated through the walls. "Call me Marnie." She threw a glance over one shoulder. "Our agency does a lot of business on the rez. I'm sure we can help you."

Vicky followed the woman into an office with a pair of small chairs in front of a desk wedged between two filing cabinets. Sunlight flared across the papers on the desk and dropped onto the floor, carving out a white triangle in the blue carpet. Behind the desk, the window framed a view of the green Dumpster in the parking lot.

"Have a seat," Marnie Rankin said. She perched on the chair behind the desk, pushed an assortment of papers aside, and clasped her hands over the blotter. "I'm afraid you have me at a disadvantage. You know my name, but I don't know yours."

"Vicky Holden," Vicky said, dropping onto one of the visitor's chairs and fishing a business card out of her bag. She handed the card across the desk. The office was suffused with an aroma of flowery perfume. She unbuttoned her coat and watched the other woman's expression cloud with wariness as she studied the card.

"So you're a lawyer?" Marnie Rankin tapped the card against her palm. The wariness gave way to a blank, unreadable expression, as if she'd taken out a towel and wiped all reactions from her face. "What can I do for you?"

"I'm here about T.J. Painted Horse," Vicky said. No sign of recognition, not the faintest twitch of a muscle.

Vicky pressed on: "I believe you know T.J." A leading question, she knew, but all she had was gossip, a rumor passed on by a friend of T.J.'s sister. Rumors could be wrong.

The business card stopped tapping. "I know a lot of people on the rez. I told you, we have a lot of Indian customers. Mostly we sell them auto insurance."

"I believe you know T.J. personally."

"I may have sold him an insurance policy. Look . . ." A new energy surged through the agent's voice, propelling her forward against the desk. "I read the newspaper about T.J.'s wife getting murdered last Monday night. So what if I knew T.J.? What's this all about?"

Vicky allowed the silence to settle between them a moment before she said, "You and T.J. were having an affair, isn't that right?" A desperate gamble, she knew. She was playing hunches, probing for anything that might prove T.J. couldn't have murdered Denise and stop the concern gnawing like a tiny animal inside her.

Marnie Rankin got up and marched around the desk. For a half second, Vicky expected the woman to ask her to leave. Instead, she closed the door and went back to her chair. "What did T.J. tell you?" she asked, something new—fear? nervousness?—leaking into her tone. But her face remained unreadable, a chalk-white mask.

"T.J.'s been protecting you," Vicky said, still probing for the truth, waiting for the slightest crack in the mask.

"Protecting me!" The crack started to appear now, a slow shattering until the mask dropped from the woman's face. She tossed her head and gave a howl of laughter. "Oh, that's rich," she said, wiping at the moisture in her eyes, creating little dark smudges around the rims. "If T.J.'s protecting me, how the hell did you know to come here?"

"T.J. didn't involve you," Vicky said. "I've heard the gossip on the rez."

For a moment, Vicky thought that Marnie Rankin might burst into tears. The woman slumped against the back of her chair and closed her eyes for several seconds. "I don't know what I was thinking to get involved with a man like that. Married. Indian. Where was it going to go? We'd have to keep it secret forever." She fixed her gaze at some point behind Vicky. "Oh, I can see my mother's face if I ever brought T.J. to her house."

"T.J.'s family would have felt the same way."

"What?" The woman locked eyes with Vicky a moment, then shrugged and looked away. "It doesn't matter. T.J. and I are old history, he says."

"Why don't you tell me about your relationship," Vicky said.

"What happened between us is nobody's business."

"It could be your business."

"What are you talking about?"

"Sooner or later the FBI agent is going to hear the same gossip that I heard and he's going to be at your front door."

The woman winced, and Vicky pushed on. "A mistress might equal a motive for T.J. to kill his wife. The fed might even start thinking that the mistress was an accomplice."

Marnie opened her mouth as if she were about to laugh. A tight, strangled noise erupted from her throat. "How dare you accuse me . . ."

Vicky cut in: "I'm telling you what the fed might conclude. I want to help T.J., Marnie, and I might be able to help you. When did you and T.J. get involved?"

Vicky could see the argument playing out behind the woman's eyes. There was a moment when she thought again that Marnie Rankin would tell her to leave. Instead, the woman looked away and said, "T.J. came to the agency about six months ago looking for insurance."

"What kind?"

"A life insurance policy." The agent hesitated, then went on: "On Denise, for one hundred thousand dollars."

Vicky felt her heart lurch. God, T.J., she thought. What have you done?

The woman was still talking, and Vicky tried to follow. Something about T.J. saying they were going to buy policies on each other. In case anything happened, they wanted to be sure their families were taken care of. "They always helped their families," she said. "I liked that about him. We started talking, and we ended up going over to the deli for coffee. We hit it off. He's smart and ambitious. Handsome," she said, smiling at whatever memories were washing over her. "He was very interesting."

"So he started calling you?"

"I called him." Marnie gave her a frank look. "I'm not ashamed of it. If a woman finds a man attractive, there's no reason she can't call him."

"He was married."

"He wasn't committed to her." The woman spit out the words. "The marriage was over, except for the divorce."

"Divorce?"

"T.J. didn't tell you about that? Denise was going to divorce him. She'd had enough of his . . ." She paused. "Cattin' around, she called it."

Vicky fingered one of the buttons on the front of her coat. Another motive. Motives piling up like bricks. Denise had wanted to talk to her about filing for a divorce. What if T.J. hadn't wanted a divorce? What if he'd thought that if Denise divorced him, it would hurt his chances of being reelected to the council?

T.J. had come over, the woman was saying. Tapping the business card into her palm again, punctuating her words. They'd gone to dinner, and one thing had led to another.

"You went to bed together."

"What are you, a nun? What do you think happens when two people find each other attractive?" She shoved the business card into the pocket of the blotter. "The problem was . . ." she broke off, moisture pooling again in her eyes. "I fell in love with the bastard, which turned out to be just about the stupidest thing I ever did, but I couldn't help it. I still can't help loving him."

"What about Monday evening, Marnie? Did you see him then?"

184

The other woman raised her eyes to Vicky's. "What does he say?"

"I'd like to know what you say."

The woman swallowed once, twice. "He must have gotten to my place about six and he stayed late."

"He didn't leave the office until after six-thirty," Vicky said.

"So he got to my place later. Maybe around seven." The woman shrugged. "I don't remember exactly." She slumped back against her chair again. The tears were starting now, like water spurting out of a faucet. "He told me it was over between us. What we had was . . ." She ran one hand over her face—eyes, nose, mouth. "It was nothing. He said what we had was nothing."

"Why, Marnie? What happened?"

The woman gave a strangled laugh. "If you think he wanted to fix things with his wife, you're dead wrong. He found somebody else. I knew that's what it was all about. I always know," she said, glancing away. "Somebody else comes along that's sexier, better looking. I told him that whatever happened, whatever he decided, I would always be here for him. He can always count on me."

"Can he count on you to lie for him?"

"What do you mean?"

"Can he count on you to give him an alibi?"

The mask returned, frozen and white, except for the black smudges below her eyes. "T.J. was at my place Monday evening. How could he murder his wife when he was with me?"

The question hung between them a moment, like sunshine drifting over the desk. Vicky stood up, pulled on her coat, and started for the door. She turned back. "I suspect the fed will be around to talk to you. My advice would be . . ."

"I didn't ask for your advice." The other woman was on her feet, like a martinet, stiff-necked and unflinching behind the desk.

". . . to tell the truth." Vicky finished the thought. "For your own sake, Marnie. Making a false statement to the fed in an investigation is a felony offense." She wheeled around, opened the door, and started for the front. A door slammed shut behind her, and a gust of cold air whipped down the corridor.

In a couple of minutes, Vicky was turning into the thin line of traffic on Federal. Her heart was beating in her ears. She wanted to believe in T.J.—God, she wanted to believe in the man. He was an old friend. He'd stood by her in that dark time. He'd always been a man she could trust. She *needed* him to be innocent. Not a cheater and a liar. Not a man who'd bought a hundred thousand dollar insurance policy on a woman who was later shot to death.

God. God. God.

She pulled her cell phone out of her bag on the passenger seat and, stopping for a red light, tapped out Vera's number. The minute that Vera picked up, Vicky knew by the tone of the woman's voice that T.J. was still in the mountains. She went through the motions: asking about T.J., reminding Vera to have him call when he got back. Then she hung up and headed south out of town.

Turning into the reservation now. On automatic, it seemed, as if the vehicle had received an electrical impulse that sent it into a right turn, then, after a mile, a left into St. Francis Mission without any direction from her. She was holding her breath. She had to talk to John O'Malley.

"Be here, John," she said out loud over the noise of the tires churning over the asphalt on the straightway through the cottonwoods to Circle Drive, sun and shadow rippling over the mission grounds ahead. She could almost sense his presence—the calmness and strength of him—as if he were sitting in the Jeep beside her.

21

FATHER JOHN TOOK the curve on Seventeen-Mile Road and eased on the brake, *Giorni poveri vivea* playing on high volume. Looming over the road ahead was the sign for St. Francis Mission. As the Jeep in the oncoming lane, red signal blinking, swung across the road, he saw Vicky at the wheel: the shape of her head, the set of her shoulders. He would know her anywhere.

He drove after her through the tunnel of cottonwoods, golden in the sun, and out onto Circle Drive. Vicky was getting out of the Jeep in front of the administration building as he parked next to her and hit the off button on the player, the notes of the aria lingering in the cab for a half-second, like a memory. It took him by surprise, as it always did, at how beautiful she was.

"I've got to talk to you, John," she said when he

walked around the front of the pickup. "As a priest. In private."

He threw a glance at the SUV and three pickups parked on the other side of the Jeep. Father Damien had called a meeting of the volunteers who had agreed to help with the senator's visit. There could be people in the corridor, craning their necks to see who was in the pastor's office and speculating on the reason. Then he remembered that Catherine had an appointment at Indian Health Services this afternoon, and he'd told her it was okay to close the museum for as long as she needed.

"I know a quiet place," he said. He took Vicky's arm and guided her into Circle Drive. She seemed small and light beside him. He made himself turn away from the sun dancing in her black hair and from the familiar aroma of sage about her. He'd told himself that he'd forgotten all of that.

The museum was cool, with shafts of sunlight falling into the shadows and the dusty odor of the old building. Father John shut the door behind them and ushered Vicky into the office on the right. The instant he flipped the light switch, the fluorescent fixture overhead suffused the room in a white glow.

"Have a seat," he said, but she was already pacing. Desk. Door. Window. She always paced when she was upset, or trying to work something out. How well he knew her, he thought. So many little things about her memorized.

He perched on the edge of the desk, not taking his eyes from her. "Talk to me," he said.

"T.J.'s disappeared." She stopped pacing for half a second, as if to make sure he'd heard. Her eyes were clouded with worry, and little worry lines dug into her forehead. Then, moving again: "I talked to Vera a little while ago. She's beside herself with worry. T.J.'s been gone for almost two days. I think he's cleared out of the area."

"Why would he do that?" Father John asked, but he was beginning to understand. There was only one reason for T.J. to flee, and that was why Vicky was here.

"Suppose he's guilty, John." Pacing again, combing her fingers through her hair.

"Wait a minute," he said, arranging the facts in his mind. Logic was in the facts. "T.J. was at his office when Denise was killed. I talked to him after he'd found her. He was devastated. He blamed himself . . ."

Father John broke off. Vicky was staring at him with such intensity in her eyes that he had to force himself not to look away. It couldn't be true, he thought. He'd known T.J. and Denise for eight years. He couldn't imagine that it was true.

"He wasn't at the office Monday evening," Vicky said. Her voice was low, almost apologetic. "His alibi isn't worth dirt, and he knows it. It's taken me less than a couple of days to prove he was lying. It probably took Gianelli less time than that. T.J. took off because he knows he'll be indicted."

Vicky walked over and stood in front of him. He could feel the charge in the air between them, his own worry mixing with her anger and disappointment. "What T.J. doesn't know is that he has another alibi. All

189

he has to do is come back and explain that he'd been protecting his girlfriend in Riverton. Marnie Rankin. An insurance agent. Blond, beautiful, and stupid about men. She'll swear to anything that T.J. says. All I'd have to do is put her on the stand and listen to her lie. Someone on the jury will believe her and persuade the rest of the jury of reasonable doubt. T.J. will walk out of the courtroom a free man."

"You spoke to the woman?"

Vicky nodded and went back to pacing. "I could feel her desperation. She'd do anything to keep T.J."

"Okay, Vicky," Father John said, trying to arrange what she was saying into a logical order that made sense. "Let's say the woman is lying and T.J. wasn't with her Monday evening. That means T.J. hasn't told the truth about where he was. It doesn't mean he killed Denise."

Vicky walked over and stared out the window. "Eight months ago, T.J. bought one hundred thousand dollars worth of life insurance on Denise. That isn't all. Denise found out about Marnie Rankin and intended to divorce him. T.J. wouldn't have wanted a divorce. He was proud to be married to the great-granddaughter of Sharp Nose. It gave him status. So, he has motive and he had the opportunity."

She turned back to him, and for a moment he thought she might start to cry. "I had this crazy idea that I could become a lawyer and make a difference. I could help people who didn't have anywhere else to turn—Indians who didn't know they had any rights. I wanted to make sure the system recognized their rights." She looked away again and ran the palm of one hand across her cheeks. "I didn't become a lawyer to help wife murderers walk free."

He understood now. "Listen, Vicky," he said, his voice low and calm. "This isn't about you and Ben. T.J. isn't Ben, and you aren't Denise."

"Oh, God." Vicky dropped her face into her hands a moment. "I'm supposed to be professional. When I think of T.J. now, I see Ben's face. He would have killed me if I hadn't left."

"You're human, Vicky, that's all. A human lawyer." He let the quiet settle around them a moment. "You could tell T.J. to find another lawyer."

She started pacing again. Shaking her head. Pacing. "Believe me, I've thought about it. But everyone on the rez would think that I knew that T.J. was guilty. Even if he was acquitted, no one would ever believe him or trust him again. He'd have to leave the rez."

"Well, that's the point, isn't it? You don't know that T.J. is guilty." He paused. "You don't have to be the judge, Vicky. You just have to make sure that the man's rights are protected."

Vicky threw her head back and laughed. It sounded like a strangled cry. "You sound like Adam," she said.

Oh, yes, Adam. There was Adam Lone Eagle now, hovering like an invisible presence beside her. Father John looked away. He wanted her to be happy. He prayed for her to be happy and at peace. He wanted her to go on with her life and have a future. He just hadn't counted on Adam Lone Eagle as part of the future.

Father John stood up and walked over to the window.

Walks-On was stretched into a patch of sunshine on the sidewalk in front of the residence. Gold flashed in the cottonwoods, and in the distance, the mountains looked purple, rimmed in orange. Of course there would be another man for her, he thought. There would be Adam.

"Guilty or innocent," Vicky was saying behind him. "Adam says it doesn't matter. Just give the man the best defense possible."

And then she was next to him. He felt a jolt of surprise at the sadness in her eyes when he turned toward her. "Is anybody what he seems, John? Is everyone just a collection of images that they project to hide who they really are? I've known T.J. most of my life, but I didn't know him at all. He could be a murderer."

She turned and went back to the desk. "I thought I was getting to know Adam. We've gone to dinner, talked a lot. Two lawyers, both lonely, looking for true love and all the other clichés. That was us, I thought." She waved one hand, as if to dismiss the whole of it. "The only thing Adam's interested in is a law partner. He thinks we should start a firm together." She gave a little laugh. "What is it you baseball players say? I'm striking out here. Marnie Rankin and I, both holding onto some image in our head that has nothing to do with reality. She's convinced herself that T.J. loves her, even after he's broken up with her." She stopped. "What, John? What is it?"

The questions took him by surprise. It was if she had seen the questions forming at the edge of his own mind, no more than shadows. "Did the woman say why T.J. had wanted to end the relationship?"

"Another woman. What else?"

Father John went back to the desk and sat down in the chair, trying to remember what Damien had told him: how he'd gone to the tribal headquarters to see T.J. and Savi Crowthorpe in an attempt to include St. Francis Mission in Senator Evans's visit to the reservation. Suppose Christine had gone along to talk about the Curtis exhibit and the way it combined Arapaho culture and history. Suppose she'd mentioned that she wanted to identify people in the Curtis photos and was looking for members of the Sharp Nose family. Suppose T.J. had introduced her to his wife.

"What are you thinking?" Vicky asked, the same intensity lighting her eyes.

"The curator at the museum disappeared Monday night," he began.

"Oh, John." She interrupted. "I'm so sorry. I read about it in the *Gazette*. You must be very worried, and here I am, going on about . . ."

"Vicky, it's okay." He held up the palm of his hand. "It's just that she disappeared the same night that Denise was murdered. I've been trying to find a connection between them."

Vicky kept her eyes on his. "T.J.," she said.

"I'm starting to think so." He hesitated. "Turns out that Christine is married to a former CIA agent by the name of Eric Loftus, who isn't happy that his wife drove off and left him. She was here, trying to get on her feet. She'd tried to purchase vintage Curtis photographs from Eunice Redshield and Max Oldman, probably hoping to sell them."

193

Vicky seemed to take this in for a moment. Then she said, "If she found photographs, there could be more."

"Exactly. I think she figured that someone in the Sharp Nose family might own photographs since . . ." He broke off. "Come on, I'll show you," he said, getting out of the chair and ushering her ahead into the entry. The clack of their footsteps reverberated off the wood floor into the silence of the old building. He flipped the light switch in the gallery and kept going—past the hundred-year-old images of Plains Indians posing for the camera, solemn-faced and dignified, as if that were the image they wanted the future generations to know them by.

He stopped in front of the photographs of the Arapahos and lifted one hand toward the village. "Christine wanted to identify the woman in this photograph who was killed while Curtis was shooting the scene."

"Another woman murdered?"

"Bashful Woman," he said, tapping the glass. "The daughter of Chief Sharp Nose. She was in the village."

Vicky didn't say anything for a long moment. "I remember hearing about her. The chief's favorite child. She died young. I remember the elders didn't like to talk about it. They said it was not good to dwell on the bad things in the past, that dwelling on old evil might invite it back."

He told her that the woman had married Carston Evans, Senator Evans's grandfather, and that they'd had a child.

Vicky lifted her chin and stared at the ceiling. "I never heard that the senator is descended . . ."

"He's not," Father John cut in. "I don't know what became of the child, but the senator is descended from the second wife, a woman from Nebraska. The man was in the village when Bashful Woman was shot." Father John let his own gaze run over the figures in the village, so small and distant, yet so real and alive looking. Most of the faces of the men were shadowed by cowboy hats. It was impossible to distinguish a white man from an Arapaho.

Father John moved his hand over the warriors riding down the slope. "Christine was able to identify the three men," he went on. "Thunder is on the right. He's Eunice Redshield's ancestor. The others are Alvin Pretty Lodge and Ben Franklin. Eunice says they don't have any descendants on the rez. All three men were hanged for Bashful's murder, but Eunice says they were innocent."

Vicky frowned. "There must have been a trial, John. If Bashful Woman was shot in the village, there would have been witnesses. Surely if there was any evidence the men were innocent, it would have been presented to the magistrate."

He waited a moment before he said, "They didn't have a lawyer, Vicky."

She turned away from him then and faced the portraits on the side wall. When she turned back, he saw the flash of light in her eyes, and the calm resolve moving through her expression.

"They might have been innocent," she said. "T.J. might be innocent."

"Yes," he said.

22

THE BUNGALOW HAD the vacant end-of-the-day look, with the light fading in the dusk and the moon already bright, sending dark shadows over the lawn and obscuring the words ATTORNEY AT LAW, on the sign. Vicky parked the Jeep and hurried up the sidewalk. Work had been piled on her desk—leases to review, a will to draft—when she'd gone to see Marnie Rankin in Riverton. She'd intended to be back in the office by late afternoon, but she'd gone to the mission instead, as if the Jeep had driven itself, propelled by the turmoil in her mind. It always came down to John O'Malley. She could trust John O'Malley, and who else could she trust? No one, no one.

She started to unlock the front door, then realized that the door was already unlocked. It wasn't like Annie to forget to lock up. Vicky pushed the door open and stepped inside. Seated in one of the visitor's chairs was a large man with reddish hair, cropped short, wearing blue jeans and a dark sport coat over a turtleneck sweater. Legs crossed, elbows set on the armrests, a cigarette in the thick fingers curved next to the side of his head. He moved the cigarette to his mouth and inhaled. The red tip glowed in the dim light.

"Who are you?" Vicky said. She held the door open, conscious of the cold air sweeping past her legs.

Puffs of gray smoke came from the man's nostrils. "I was beginning to think you'd knocked off for the day."

He had a gravelly voice and little eyes, black pebbles lodged beneath bushy eyebrows and the thick wedge of his forehead. "Another ten minutes and I would have had to seek you out at your apartment."

"You haven't told me who you are." Vicky held her place and gripped the door knob.

The man took another drag from the cigarette. "Let's say, a husband searching for his missing wife."

"Eric Loftus." The words came in an exhalation of air. "You should try the FBI."

"Nobody around here knows shit." The man's mouth widened in a parody of a smile. "They don't know where your client, the tribal official, has gone off to either, but I think you know."

"How did you get in here?"

Loftus gestured toward the door with his cigarette. "You must have left the door unlocked."

"The door was locked."

"Well, it is a mystery, isn't it?"

"It's breaking and entering."

He laughed at that. "I prefer a mystery, like the disappearance of my wife and T.J. Painted Horse." He shook his head and laughed. "First thing he'll have to do is take a new name, like Christine did. Oh, I taught that woman well."

"Please leave." Vicky pushed the door back toward the wall. A dog was barking somewhere, a sharp sound wave breaking through the atmosphere.

Eric Loftus considered the cigarette burning into a small stump in his fingers. "Do you believe in coincidences?" he asked.

"Get out."

"I've read the local paper and talked to a number of people around here." The man's eyes were still riveted on the cigarette butt. "I've discovered a remarkable coincidence. Take last Monday night, for example. My wife left a museum on the reservation and drove off. On that same night, another woman on the reservation was shot in the head. The two instances occurred a few miles apart. Remarkable, don't you agree?"

Vicky tightened her fist around the door knob. *Someone else,* T.J.'s mistress had said. She realized that it had probably occurred to John O'Malley that the new woman in T.J.'s life might be Christine Loftus. But where was the proof? The woman could be anybody in Fremont County.

"What makes you think your wife knew T.J. Painted Horse?"

"It's been my experience that coincidences don't exist." Eric Loftus squeezed the burning tip of the butt between his finger and thumb, his eyes not leaving hers. A trail of gray smoke curled over his hand. "Coincidences are a façade, a mask, if you like, that only appears to be the truth. The truth is something else altogether. I asked myself, What is the truth behind this façade? What is the relationship between two events on the same evening, which appear to be unrelated?"

"There's nothing I can tell you, Loftus.

"We can stay here all night, if you like." He let the butt drop into the glass vase on the table next to the chair.

"Get out now." Vicky gestured with her head toward the outdoors.

"It strikes me that they could be together, your client and my wife. Christine was always attracted to the dark, swarthy types. One time in Mexico . . ." he shook his head and stared across the room. "A little incident, best forgotten. In any case, I removed the temptation from my wife's line of vision, shall we say." He brought his eyes back. "I figure your client and my wife are holed up together in a cheap motel. A replay of Mexico, I'm afraid, and I assure you that it will end the same way. My wife is a very sick woman, counselor. Oh, when she's up, she's higher than the moon. She can do anything, climb right into the sky. But when she crashes . . ." He shook his head. "All you have to do, counselor, is tell me what your client said about my wife. It could be the information I need to find them."

"You're crazy if you think I'm going to tell you anything," Vicky said.

Eric Loftus uncrossed his legs and got to his feet, a slow unfolding of muscles and strength a few feet away. "Don't say that to me." His voice was tight and controlled. "Don't ever say that."

A ringing phone burst through the quiet. Vicky glanced over at the desk, her hand still gripping the doorknob. A second ring. Third. She let go of the knob and began moving sideways, away from the door and into the office. Without taking her eyes off the man on her left, she reached for the phone and pressed the receiver to her ear. "Vicky Holden," she said. She could hear the tremor in her voice.

"Vicky?" It was Adam's voice. "What's wrong? Are you okay?"

"I'm not okay, Adam."

"I'm over on Main. I'll be there in two minutes."

"I'll see you in two minutes." Vicky stared at the man across from her.

"Very clever," Loftus said as she hung up. "Don't think that this is over. When you don't expect me, when you think you're all alone, I'll be there. I'll be watching you until you lead me to T.J. Painted Horse."

He stepped past her through the open door, and Vicky slammed the door behind him and threw the lock. She moved to the window and watched Loftus walk down the sidewalk, cross the street, and get into a dark-colored SUV, assuring herself that he was gone. The SUV pulled into the street as Adam's green Chevrolet truck came around the corner. For a half-instant, she thought the two vehicles would collide, but Adam swerved out of the way and slid to a stop at the curb. The SUV was gone.

Vicky opened the door as Adam was running up the sidewalk. "What the hell's going on?" He stepped inside and slammed the door behind him. "Who was that guy?"

"Eric Loftus." A blank look came into Adam's eyes, and she started to explain that the curator who'd disappeared from St. Francis Mission was the man's wife. He laid a finger over her lips.

"I don't care about the man's wife," he said. "What happened here?"

Vicky took hold of his wrist and pulled his hand away. She managed a smile. It seemed so silly, putting out an SOS, calling in a warrior. Loftus would have eventually left on his own. The man was swagger and bravado, the kind that liked to intimidate people. Maybe he liked that more than he wanted to find his wife. Or maybe . . .

"What is it, Vicky?" Adam leaned so close that she could make out the faint strands of gray hidden in his black hair and the worry moving in his dark eyes.

Vicky glanced away, letting her gaze rest on the chair where Loftus had sat, the back cushion still folded in on itself from his weight. The odor of smoke hung in the air. "Maybe Loftus knows where his wife is," she said, bringing her eyes back to Adam's. "Maybe he's responsible for her disappearance, and all of this"—a wave toward the chair—"is just the image of a concerned husband looking for his wife."

"You wouldn't be alone so much if . . ."

"I know," Vicky said. "I've been thinking about your offer." A business proposal, that was all, and the reminder bit into her like a wooden splinter. "I don't believe it's a good idea, Adam."

"You're wrong, Vicky. It's the best idea either of us has had in a long time. Look," he hurried on. "I have an appointment with a realtor to see some office space tomorrow, so I'm staying in town tonight, and I was hoping you were free. We can argue about it over dinner."

23

A PHONE WAS ringing across the distance. Vicky felt paralyzed, frozen to the door, fixed in place by the icy glare of the man looming over her. If she could get to the phone, Eric Loftus would leave the office. It was John O'Malley calling. No, that wasn't right. Adam was on the line. She had to pick up the phone and tell Adam . . .

Vicky sat up in bed. She was shivering, her nightgown clinging to her like an extra skin. It was a half-second before she realized that the ringing phone was on the nightstand. She threw herself across the bunched pile of blankets and grabbed the receiver. The green iridescent numbers on the clock looked shimmery, like numbers blinking under water: 2:39.

"Hello," she managed.

"Vicky? Is that you?"

The familiar voice made a clean cut through the fog in her head. "T.J.? Where are you?" A sense of relief washed over her, then gave way to discomfort and dread.

"I've got to see you right away," he said. "I know what happened."

"What are you talking about?" Vicky could hear the sleep still in her voice.

"I know who shot Denise."

Vicky swung her legs over the bed and pressed the receiver tight against her ear. She'd left a window open a little, and the cold draft blew across her bare legs. "Tell me what you know."

"In the mountains." His voice cracked. "I went up into the mountains and fasted and prayed for a way out of all this. I kept hoping that it was somebody who'd come after me and killed Denise 'cause I wasn't home. But all the time, I knew the truth. I just didn't want to see it. But up in the mountains, it was like I could *see* Denise getting shot right in front of me. That's what the spirits gave me, Vicky, the true thing, and I saw what I had to do. I have to tell the fed the truth, even if I don't have the evidence. I gotta say what is true. It can't be a secret any more. Oh, I know they don't think I'm ever gonna tell the truth. They think I'm scared shitless, and truth is, Vicky, I was scared, but the spirits gave me strength, and it's time everybody knows what happened."

"Listen to me, T.J.," Vicky began. She could picture the man in her head, gaunt, dehydrated, hungry, and probably drinking. He was drinking. "You're not making sense," she said. "Try to eat something and get some sleep. We can go over this in the morning."

"No, you listen to me, Vicky." The words came down the line like shots bursting out of a shotgun. "I know where the evidence is." He coughed into the line. It sounded as if he was choking. "This is big, Vicky. I'm telling you, this is big. I gotta see you right away."

Vicky was quiet a moment. "Where are you?"

"At the house."

"The house! It's a crime scene, T.J. It's still part of the investigation. The fed hasn't released the house yet. Go to Vera's, and I'll meet you there."

"No! Leave Vera out of it. It's enough that they killed

my wife. You want them to kill Vera, too?"

"Who are you talking about?"

"Just get over here, Vicky, before I lose my nerve."

"You're asking me to violate the crime scene, T.J."

"You're my lawyer. You've got to help me. The fed's trying to get me indicted for Denise's murder. That'll be just perfect. They kill Denise and I go to prison. You've got to come now, Vicky."

Vicky let a couple of seconds pass. She kept her eyes on the shimmering numbers. 2:45. "I'll meet you in front of the house," she said finally.

She was about to hang up when he shouted, "Hurry. You have to hurry. They're waiting for me somewhere. I know that's what they're doing, 'cause I know the truth."

Vicky cradled the receiver between her shoulder and ear. "I'll be there as soon as I can," she said.

The line went quiet, and for a moment she thought they'd been disconnected. Then T.J. said, "There was something else I saw in the mountains, Vicky. The moon was swirling through the sky, laughing and taunting me. Moon was daring me to tell the truth about Denise's murder. It's like Moon wants to kill me, too."

Vicky was on her feet, struggling to pull her robe around her shoulders. The man wasn't thinking straight. "Listen to me, T.J.," she said. "Just stay quiet and wait for me. I'll hurry."

SHE WAS OUT of the apartment in ten minutes, driving north on 287, the moon white and bloated looking in the silver sky. She could imagine T.J. in the mountains—

204

three days with a bottle of whiskey and no food or water, the moon hovering overhead, growing fatter each night. No wonder the man believed that the moon was taunting him.

She'd stared at the phone a moment after she'd hung up, debating whether to let someone know where she was going. Adam, maybe. She'd discarded the idea. If they were partners, she could call and leave a message, but they weren't partners. In the end, she'd headed out, she realized now, leaving nothing behind that might hint to her whereabouts.

God, she was as crazy as T.J. She stared at the asphalt unfurling into the headlights. Off to meet a client in the middle of the night, a man who might be a murderer. She should have told him she'd see him at the office in the morning and hung up. Why hadn't she? What was it in his voice—the desperation beyond the words—that had made her agree?

Vicky turned onto Blue Sky Highway, eating up the miles, flashing past the little houses set back from the road, silent cubes washed in the moonlight, nothing but open spaces spreading through the darkness. Outside Ethete now, she took a dirt road on the right, then drove into T.J.'s yard and stopped close to the house, the front fender bumping against the yellow police tape stretched between stakes in the ground. The windows were dark. No sign of anyone around, and T.J.'s pickup was nowhere in sight. It occurred to her that this was a joke, a sick excuse to lure her out here perpetrated by a desperate man.

Then, at the far edge of the yard—the pickup,

merging with the elongated shadow of a cottonwood. She bumped across the hard ground and drew up at a right angle to the pickup, her headlights splayed across the cab. She got out and opened the passenger door. There was no one inside.

She glanced around, jamming her hands into her coat pockets and shivering in the cold, half-expecting T.J. to appear, but nothing moved. Except for the high-pitched wail of a coyote in the distance, there was no sound. She got back into the Jeep and pulled a U-turn toward the police tape, then stopped, her fingers wrapped around the steering wheel, the engine humming into the void. T.J. must be inside.

Inside, sitting in the dark. Frightened. She'd heard the fear running through his voice. He'd parked the pickup in the shadows, hard to see from the road. He might have fallen asleep, she thought, exhausted from spending days in the mountains.

Vicky got out and stepped across the tape. The toe of her sneakers caught the edge, and she had to catch herself from falling. She walked up to the concrete stoop and knocked. A hollow sound, as if she were knocking on a false door with nothing but space behind it. She started pounding with the heel of her fist. "T.J.," she called. "Are you there?"

The coyote cried again, closer now, as if the animal was circling it's kill. Vicky tried the doorknob. It turned in her hand, a cold and inert ball of metal. Shoving the door open, she called out again: "T.J.?"

Still no answer. She stepped inside and reached around, patting the wall until her fingers found the light switch. A dim light cascaded from a globe in the ceiling down over the center of the small living room. She stood perfectly still, struggling to make sense out of the chaos before her: overturned sofa and chairs, foam leaking from the cushions, lamps twisted and smashed on the vinyl floor, picture frames strewn about, shards of glass twinkling in the light.

She started to back through the door when she saw something—the smallest movement—through the doorway to the kitchen in back. "T.J.," she called again. God, he could be in the kitchen. He could be hurt.

She flung the door back against the wall, willing the cold air to fill the room, and began picking her way through the chaos toward the kitchen. She stopped in the doorway and, leaning sideways, fumbled for another light switch. A fluorescent bulb on the ceiling flickered into life. Vicky stared at cabinet doors hanging open, drawers tossed upside down on the floor, utensils poking from beneath the sides, broken dishes and glasses scattered among the jumble of papers. Across the room, the back door stood open a few inches.

In the far corner—something moving. Vicky stood frozen in place, her breath a hot coal in her throat. A cat meowed, and she exhaled as the cat skittered past, its fur like a whisper against her jeans. The animal fled through the back door, pushing it open another couple of inches.

It was then that she noticed the glint of light outside. She stepped across the debris and peered past the door. Light from the kitchen flared out into the yard toward a small shed. The door was ajar, and inside she could see something small and metallic caught in the moonlight.

She hesitated. She should go back to the Jeep, she told herself. Lock herself in and call the police on her cell. But an hour ago, T.J. had called her from the house. He wanted to tell her the truth about Denise's murder. In that hour, something terrible had happened. T.J. was still here somewhere; she could sense his presence.

She gripped the doorjamb and pushed off across the yard. She stepped into the shed, taking in at a glance the cartons stacked in neat rows on the shelves and hanging from a hook, the silver harness glinting in the light.

She took another couple of steps and gasped. T.J. lay face down on the dirt floor, his body wedged against the lowest shelf on the right. Blood pooled around his head, matting his hair and soaking like spilled black paint into the dirt. He was naked from the waist up. Arms pulled behind him; shoulders out of the sockets, jutting like knobs against his skin. A brown belt wrapped around his wrists. She couldn't take her eyes from the bronze arms glistening in the dim light and the black gashes cut into his arms like graffiti.

She flinched backward, her body moving on its own, her eyes still locked on the body, as still as a log washed out of the abyss. She couldn't breathe. She felt as if all the oxygen had been sucked out of the shed. It was a half a moment before she managed to pull her gaze away from the body. She pivoted around and ran outside. Across the swatch of light, around the corner, and down the side of the house. She was almost to the front when she dropped onto her hands and knees and vomited until she felt empty inside and there was nothing but the sound of her own dry retching in the quiet.

She lifted herself upright and leaned against the rough siding a long moment before she felt sure enough to start for the Jeep. She crawled behind the steering wheel and, hands shaking, dug through her black bag until her fingers wrapped around the cold plastic of her cell. She tapped out 911 and pressed the phone hard against her ear while trying to steady her hand. "This is Vicky Holden," she managed when the operator came on the line. "I'm at T.J. Painted Horse's place. Send an officer right away. Someone's been killed."

T.J.'s been killed, she thought. She pressed the end key, dropped the phone into her lap, and wrapped her hands around the steering wheel, holding on as hard as she could. She couldn't stop shaking. This was crazy. She'd gotten everything wrong. She'd been so sure that T.J. had killed his wife, and now T.J. was dead. And whoever had killed Denise had been waiting, biding his time, like a mountain lion watching its prey. The moment T.J. had returned to the house, the lion had pounced.

It hit her that Eric Loftus could have found her client after all and tortured him. Tortured T.J. until he had told Eric everything he knew about his wife.

Vicky stared into the moonlight skittering over the house, trying to see past the images imprinted on the back of her eyes. The gashes on T.J.'s arms, the welts blossoming around the brown belt tightened on his wrists. She was going to be sick again. She held onto the steering wheel and made herself take in several breaths and exhale slowly. God, would the images ever go away?

She peeled her fingers off the wheel and picked up the cell. Her fingers pushed in a number—working on their own, as if they knew what was necessary. She listened to the buzzing sound of the phone ringing at St. Francis Mission, and after the third ring, the familiar voice: "Father O'Malley."

Sleepy and disoriented and matter-of-fact at the same time, as if he were used to answering the phone at four o'clock in the morning.

"T.J.'s been killed," she said, her own voice seemed to come from a vacuum.

"Where are you?"

"At T.J.'s place. I found him in the shed." There was the cry of a coyote, she thought, or a siren. She couldn't be sure, it sounded so far away. She said, "The police are coming."

"I'm on my way," he said.

24

THE HOUSE WAS ablaze in the darkness. Light spilled through the front windows and the opened door. Blue, red, and yellow lights flashing from the roof of a police cruiser spiraled across the front of the house, and dark uniforms moved past the windows inside. A photographer was also moving about, snapping pictures, the white light flashing intermittently into the living room. Vicky watched Ted Gianelli walk in from the kitchen, like a shadow moving through the light.

She stood outside between the Jeep and John O'Malley's pickup, gripping the fronts of her jacket, struggling against the sense that she'd wandered into a nightmare and couldn't find the way out.

The police had come—three cars, one after the other racing down the road and turning into the yard, yellow headlights jumping over the ground, officers spilling out of the opened doors. She'd gotten out of the Jeep and stumbled into the headlights. "He's in the shed," she'd heard herself shouting, and finally the officers had turned away and started around the corner of the house toward the back, leaving her alone again with the images in her head.

After a long while, one of the officers returned and began asking her questions. What had brought her here? When did she arrive? Was anyone else here? She was trying to find the answers, gripping her jacket to keep from floating away, when John O'Malley's pickup pulled in next to the cruisers. The door slammed shut, and he darted around the cars, plunging past the head-lights toward her.

She collapsed against him, grateful for the strength of his arms, the warmth of his breath in her hair.

"Are you okay?" he said.

"She's had a bad shock," said one officer.

"You're shivering. You should be inside."

"No." Vicky shook her head against his chest, then stepped back. Something was warm on her cheeks, and she realized she was crying. She wiped at the moisture. "It's horrible what they did to him."

"She found T.J.'s body, Father," the officer said.

"Around in back, in case you want to say some prayers. The fed's on his way, and the coroner'll be here any minute." He nodded toward the house, as if he were urging him on. "Up to you."

"Go ahead," Vicky said when she saw Father John hesitate.

She could sense his reluctance in the way he removed his hand from her shoulder. "Why don't you wait in the pickup? It's still warm. Start the motor." He pulled a key out of his jacket pocket and tried to press it into her hand.

Vicky waved it away. "It's okay." She stopped herself from saying, 'The cold air is real.'

A moment passed before she felt him take his eyes from her and start for the shed, the officer in step behind. And she was alone again. He had his responsibility, she told herself. There were the prayers, the rituals, all the trappings that he brought with him wherever he went. It was who he was—a priest. He could never leave them behind.

It was then that Gianelli's SUV came bumping across the yard. It stopped next to her Jeep, and he was out in a second, ducking around the hood. "Vicky? That you? What the hell happened?"

He stopped, like a bronco jerked backward. "Are you hurt?" he asked, his tone softer, suffused with concern.

She shook her head. "The officers are out back," she said.

"Can you tell me about it? You want to sit in the car where it's warm?" He tossed his head toward the SUV.

Vicky shook off the suggestion. They were the same,

she was thinking. Gianelli and John O'Malley. All she had to do was get warm and she'd be fine. She didn't want to get warm, to have the image settle in. "T.J. called me two hours ago. He asked me to come to the house, but when I got here, he was already . . ." She could feel the warm moisture on her face again.

"Let me take a look," Gianelli said. "We'll talk later."

She wasn't sure how many minutes had passed— twenty? thirty?—before Gianelli stepped through the front door, took her arm, and guided her into the living room. It was as cold as the outdoors. They sat on the sofa and he produced a notebook that he placed on the table in front of them. "Tell me what you know about this, Vicky," he said, his pen poised over the white page. "Start at the beginning. Why did you come here?"

She started going over it all again, the images flashing in her mind as she talked: the phone call in the night, the fear and urgency in T.J.'s voice, the house, the shed. All of it.

When she finished, the agent stopped writing and glanced around at the uniforms and the plain-clothes policemen still milling about the living room. Then he asked, "What exactly did T.J. say when he called?"

"That they had killed Denise."

"He said *they?*"

She nodded. That was right. T.J. had said *they*. "They tortured him, didn't they? He held out, didn't he? He didn't want to tell them whatever they wanted to know until . . ." She gulped back the sob erupting in her throat. "Until they made him."

"What else did T.J. say? What did they want from him, Vicky?"

"I think they were looking for old photographs." It was John O'Malley's voice coming through the blur of the living room.

The agent swiveled his head around. "Old photographs?" He shook his head. "So now you're telling me that somebody cut T.J. and put a bullet into his brain for old photographs?"

"It's probably what they were looking for at Christine Loftus's apartment." Father John sat down beside her, and Vicky felt his arm slip across her shoulders again. "Are you all right?" he asked. When she nodded, he said to Gianelli, "They didn't find what they wanted at Christine's, so they came here. They waited until T.J. showed up so he could show them where the photographs were."

"Jesus, John." The agent threw back his head and stared up at the ceiling. "What are you saying? Somebody killed both Denise and T.J. for old photographs that are worth what? A thousand dollars each?"

"Maybe a lot more."

Vicky glanced at Father John. She could almost read the tracks of thought crossing his face. He had put it together.

"Eric Loftus owns a gallery in Jackson," Father John was saying. "People there can afford to pay a lot of money for vintage photographs. The man's been trying to find his wife."

"Tell me about it. He's all over the place, intimidating people, making the investigation into her disappearance more difficult. After people meet up with Loftus, they're afraid to open their mouths about anything they might know. Suddenly the Arapahos who signed the guest book never heard of the Curtis exhibit."

"Maybe he found her, Ted," Vicky said. "Maybe she told him about the photographs."

The agent began rubbing his hands together, and Vicky sensed that he was shivering. Death was like that. It froze something inside.

"Okay," Gianelli said. So, you're telling me that the Painted Horses had some of those old photographs, and Loftus came here looking for them? You're saying that he killed Denise Monday night, then came back tonight and killed T.J.? Only one problem with this scenario, John. Last Monday night, Loftus had an opening at his gallery in Jackson. Probably a hundred people will swear that he was there."

"It's a short drive over the mountain," Vicky said.

Gianelli went on, as if he hadn't heard. "The agent in Jackson said that Loftus was distraught about his wife missing. Said she'd walked out on him six weeks ago, and he'd been discretely trying to find her since, calling around, asking art dealers if they'd heard from her. Said she had a history of going off for long periods. Now you're suggesting he found her on the rez and learned that she'd gotten onto old photos that might be valuable. Okay. Okay." The fed leaned over and scribbled a couple of more notes on the pad. "I'll lean on Eric Loftus and find out where he was this evening."

He paused, his attention turned toward the open door and the van pulling into the yard. "Coroner's here," he said. "No sense in you two hanging around, but . . ." He turned to Vicky. "I'll want to talk to you again tomorrow, see if there's anything else you remember after you get some rest. Try to get some rest," he said.

"Has anyone told Vera?" Father John said. The tone of a priest, Vicky thought.

"I was hoping that you'd . . ." The agent shrugged. "Poor woman. First her sister-in-law, now her brother. It'll be a blow."

Vicky could feel John O'Malley's gaze on her face. "I'll follow you home, first," he said.

Vicky pushed herself to her feet and went outside, heading for the Jeep, aware that Gianelli and John O'Malley were close behind. *First,* John O'Malley had said, but then he would have to do his duty. He would go to Vera and deliver the horrible news and comfort the poor woman with his prayers and platitudes and tell her how God was with her, no matter what. She knew the words by heart; there had been times when he had used them on her, and she wondered if God had been with T.J. when they were cutting his arms to the bones.

"You're a priest," she said, glancing over her shoulder. "You have your responsibility. Vera will need all the comforting she can get. I can get home just fine."

She had the sense that he was going to say something, that he was swallowing the words. Then he turned and walked over to the pickup. In a moment, the vehicle heaved itself out onto the road, taillights blinking like exploding firecrackers. "I can have an officer follow you home," Gianelli said.

"No need." She gave him a wave, then walked around

216

the Jeep and got behind the steering wheel. She was pressing the keys on the cell as she shot past the cruisers and turned onto the road; the image of Gianelli in the lights streaming around the house flashed in the rearview mirror. She pressed the phone hard against her ear, afraid she might lose courage and grope for the off key, and waited for the ringing to stop.

"Hello," Adam said, an edge of impatience in his voice.

"It's Vicky." It was hard to keep the wheel steady. She was shaking again.

"Vicky! It's not six o'clock yet. What's going on?"

"I'm sorry. I shouldn't have called." God, why had she called? Her index finger was dancing over the keys, searching for the feel of the off key.

"Don't hang up, Vicky!" Adam shouted through the phone. "What's happened? Are you all right?"

She held the phone close again and told him about T.J.

"Where are you?" he asked.

When she said that she was on her way back to Lander, Adam said that he'd be waiting at her apartment.

25

MADNESS! WHAT HAD she been thinking? Vicky lay very still, the sheet tangled about her, watching the daylight move past the curtains. It must be mid-morning. God, what had come over her? She'd seen dead bodies before. She'd seen people shot and beaten, but T.J. . . . . The sight of him had unhinged her, and she'd fallen into

Adam's arms, as if the warmth of his body could banish the images.

She made herself turn slowly, trying not to tug at the sheet. Adam was gone. His side of the bedcovers thrown back, the pillow still bunched up around the indentation of his head. The scent of him still in the air. A wave of relief came over her. She'd have time to make sense of what had happened before she had to face him again.

A cabinet door cracked shut deep in the apartment. Metal pans clanked together. "No," she said under her breath. Adam was still here. She crawled out of bed and rummaged through the dresser drawers for clothes, then carried her horde into the bathroom, like a thief escaping into the night, and turned on the shower.

Ten minutes later, in blue jeans and a sweatshirt, her hair still wet, she padded barefoot into the kitchen. She smoothed her hair back behind her ears as she slid onto the stool at the bar across from the stove where Adam Lone Eagle was scrambling eggs.

"Hungry, I'm sure," he said, glancing sideways at her.

"Adam," she began, stumbling for the words, combing her fingers through one side of her hair. "Last night was not a good idea. It shouldn't have happened."

Adam kept his eyes on the lumpy yellow eggs blossoming in the pan. Finally he laid the fork down, stepped over to the bar, and leaned down so that his face was level with hers.

"Wrong on two counts," he said. "It was this morning. And it was meant to happen."

His gaze was like a laser boring into her, and Vicky

struggled not to turn away. "The wrong time and the wrong reason, Adam," she said. "I shouldn't have called you. It wasn't fair to you."

"I'm glad you called."

"I wasn't thinking straight. I wasn't myself."

"I'd say you were very much yourself." Smiling, tilting his head, as if she'd just said something ridiculous.

"We can't work together and sleep together."

"Does that mean you're saying 'yes' to the partnership? I don't see any reason why we can't practice law and be lovers. We're good at both."

Now she looked away to keep from smiling at him.

Adam turned back and began dishing up plates of scrambled eggs, which he set on the bar. Then two mugs of coffee, a pile of toast, jam from the refrigerator, knives, and forks. God, the man thought of everything.

He pulled over another stool and perched across from her. "You should eat," he said, waving his fork. "You'll feel better."

Vicky worked at her coffee and pushed the eggs around her plate for two or three seconds, wondering at the newness of the moment, like trying on new clothes and wondering how they might fit. She made herself take a bite of eggs.

"Would you like to talk about what happened to T.J.?" Adam asked.

Talk about it? She had to stifle a laugh. There was no talking earlier. She'd been crying, and Adam had been kissing her.

She said, "What they did to him was terrible."

"I'm sorry you had to see it, Vicky."

"I was sure T.J. was guilty, and all the time he was innocent."

"You think you're the first lawyer to have that happen?"

"Is that supposed to make me feel better?"

She got to her feet, carried her plate over to the sink and turned on the water, watching the last trace of yellow egg wash into the garbage disposal.

A jolt of surprise. Adam's fingers digging into her shoulders. She hadn't heard him come up behind her. "Stop blaming yourself," he said. "Someone wanted T.J. and his wife dead. There's nothing you could have done to prevent what happened." He led her back around the bar. "Councilmen have to make decisions that get a lot of people mad."

Vicky crawled back onto her stool. "John . . ."

"John?"

"Father O'Malley thinks that T.J. and Denise might have had Curtis photographs that could be valuable," she said. Then she told him about Christine Loftus, missing for four days now. How the curator had been looking for Curtis photographs taken at the same time that Curtis had shot the photographs of Arapahos in the museum exhibit. How she'd identified three warriors in the staged photograph of a village under attack. How she wanted to identify the woman who had been killed in the attack. "Her name was Bashful Woman," Vicky said. "The daughter of Chief Sharp Nose."

Adam held his coffee mug in both hands, his eyes watching her over the rim. "A chief's daughter killed.

The people must have been outraged."

"All three warriors were hanged at the agency. Witnesses swore they'd seen one of them ride up to Bashful's tipi before she was shot. The others were found guilty of conspiracy." Vicky paused. "They claimed they were innocent, and none of them had a lawyer."

"Whew!" Adam shook his head and stood up. He refilled their mugs. "That's a lot of outrage," he said, straddling the stool again.

Vicky sipped at the hot coffee a moment. "Bashful Woman was the wife of a white man, Carston Evans. Senator Evans's grandfather, the man who started the Evans Ranch. It's not what you think," she hurried on, reading the conclusion in his eyes. "After Bashful was killed, Carston married a white woman from Nebraska. The senator doesn't have a drop of Arapaho blood in him. What I don't understand . . ." Vicky hesitated. "A chief's daughter could have had her pick of handsome warriors on the rez. Why would she marry a white man?"

Adam laughed. "I'd call that a no-brainer, Vicky. She wanted everything that went with being a white man's wife. He was a rancher. He knew how to raise cattle and grow crops. He knew how the markets worked, things that Indian men were just learning. A white man had rights and freedom. He could move about, do what he wanted, live anywhere. He didn't have to worry about signs that read, NO INDIANS ALLOWED. He didn't have to ask the agent for permission to leave the reservation to visit relatives somewhere else. Wherever the white man went, his wife could go."

"She was still Indian," Vicky said.

"And he was a squaw man. But if he knew how to make money, white people might've swallowed hard, but they would've accepted him no matter who his wife was." Adam focused on his coffee a couple of moments before he said, "The real question is, why did Carston Evans marry an Arapaho woman?"

"How about, she was beautiful?"

"No beautiful white women around?"

"She came from a respected family."

Adam got up and walked back across the kitchen. He set both hands on the counter and stared at the empty egg carton and the bowl with a yellow line of raw egg hardening on the side. A small blue vein pulsed in his temple. Finally he brought his eyes back to hers. "How did Evans get his ranch?"

"Probably purchased it from the government," Vicky said. She felt her own muscles tense. "A lot of local ranchers purchased reservation lands after the Dawes Act allotted lands to Indians and allowed the federal government to buy the excess lands and sell them to outsiders. We lost a million and a half acres from the reservation at that time."

"Forget the Dawes Act." Adam walked back and leaned toward her again. "The Burke Act of 1906 modified the Dawes Act. Indians deemed competent by the federal government were allowed to own their allotments in fee simple. If they'd gone to school and could read and write, the government considered them competent. They could buy and sell land like white people. They could inherit land and pass it on to their heirs."

Vicky stood up. She felt as if an invisible horror had invaded the space between them. "You're suggesting that Carston Evans married an Arapaho woman for her land?"

"A chief's daughter probably went to school. She was literate. Most likely she had her own allotment, and her father might have given her some land."

"My God, Adam, what are you saying? That Evans hired the three men to kill his wife?"

Adam shook his head. "You said they claimed they were innocent, and they didn't have a lawyer. Maybe they were innocent . . ."

"And Evans shot his own wife," Vicky heard herself saying.

"What do you think went on in the West after the Burke Act was passed? White men saw a way of getting ranch land without laying out any money. All they had to do was court an Indian woman who'd been to school and convince her she'd have a better life married to a white man. It probably didn't take much convincing. Do you think Bashful was the only woman to fall for a white man's promises? There was an epidemic of Indian women who died mysteriously after marrying white men. An epidemic, Vicky. And what did the white authorities do? They believed whatever the white husbands said: 'My wife fell off the porch. Fell off a horse. She was cleaning my gun when it went off.' And all those white husbands inherited the lands allotted their wives."

"Carston Evans testified that he saw Thunder shoot his wife. The magistrate believed him." Vicky felt cold and nauseated, the way she'd felt last night after seeing T.J.'s body. She crossed her arms and, hugging herself, turned into the living room and started pacing. Back and forth between the front door and the bar.

Look at the moon sideways. Grandmother's voice was in her head. *You can sometimes see the face of a white man with bushy eyebrows and down-turned mouth.* She stopped and found Adam's eyes again. "My people have a legend," she said. "In the time before the Old Time, a beautiful woman was sitting outside in the evening with her friends. She looked at the moon and said, 'I wonder what it would be like to marry Moon?' Moon heard her. He looked down and told her to climb into the sky, so she started climbing a lodgepole pine. The pine grew taller as she climbed, until she was in the sky. She married Moon. Soon she grew sad and longed for her people, but Moon refused to let her return to earth. So one day, she dug a hole through the clouds, found the tree, and started to climb down. Moon saw her. He threw a large boulder through the hole and killed her."

In the quiet that engulfed the apartment, Vicky could almost sense the past—their past, hers and Adam's— invading the space around them, as if it was always a part of the present but only revealed itself in brief moments. She closed her eyes a moment, the sense of Bashful Woman's presence so real that it seemed she could reach out and touch her.

After a moment, Vicky walked back and sat down again across from Adam. "They had a child," she said.

"What happened to the child?"

"God, maybe he killed the child, too." Vicky had to look away from this new image flitting across her mind. "What if Curtis happened to take a picture of Evans shooting his wife? What would a photograph like that do to Senator Evans's presidential ambitions?"

A couple of seconds passed before Adam said, "It happened a long time ago, Vicky. The senator isn't responsible for anything his grandfather might have done. It might embarrass the senator if it became public, but he would apologize and say how much he hated his grandfather's actions. The publicity might even help him."

"The senator has Arapaho land, Adam. He has oil and gas that should have stayed with the tribe."

"We're speculating here, Vicky. We don't know if Bashful's land became the Evans Ranch. You said yourself that Carston Evans could have purchased the ranch."

"Maybe," Vicky said. "But now I know where to look for the truth."

26

THE WIND RIVER agency building was a gray, cinder block affair off a side street in Fort Washakie. A jumble of pickups and cars straddled the parking lot next to the building, and other vehicles hugged the curbs in front. Vicky waited for a white SUV pulling away, then maneuvered the Jeep into the spot and walked up the sidewalk to the glass-front door. Broad, flat clouds floated close to the tops of the cottonwoods sheltering the building. The temperature was falling. It was colder on the reservation than in Lander, sixteen miles to the south. The warm valley the Arapahos had called Lander.

Vicky let herself into a lobby with offices behind the glass cubicles on either side. There was the dissonant clang of ringing phones, the murmur of voices. Aromas of stale coffee and half-eaten lunches drifted toward her. At the far end, rows of plastic chairs faced each other across the tiled floor. Beyond the chair, windows framed a view of the stone dormitory that had housed soldiers at Fort Washakie a century ago. Charged with protecting the Arapahos and Shoshones from the white ranchers in the surrounding area, Vicky thought. Charged with keeping the Indians on the rez.

She rapped on the opened door of the first cubicle on the left. LOUIS FOXWORTHY, ASSISTANT SUPERINTEN-DENT, was stamped in black letters on the pebbled glass. Inside, a slim, muscular Indian with short-cropped black hair leaned back in a chair, phone glued to one ear. He was nodding and waving her inside at the same time. "The FBI is handling the investigation," he said. "We believe this is an isolated incident. There's no cause for alarm." Nodding. Nodding. "Yes, of course. We'll keep you posted of any developments."

He slammed the phone into the cradle and leaned over the desk. "T.J.'s murder's got everybody's attention," he said. "Phone hasn't stopped ringing. Newspaper, radio, television reporters wanting to know if a councilman's murder has anything to do with the senator's upcoming visit." Foxworthy wiped his flattened hand across his forehead. "That was the BIA," he said, nodding toward the phone. "Even they're in on the act. Want to make sure we don't have anybody out here who might assassinate a senator like they assassinated the councilman. Wouldn't want anything to happen to Evans while he was on BIA turf."

"Assassinate?" Vicky dropped onto the edge of the plastic chair pushed into the corner and ignored the impatience that crossed the superintendent's face.

He said, "T.J. was shot in the head. What would you call it?"

"He was tortured."

"Yeah, I heard. So we got crazy people running around. It's Gianelli's job to find whoever did it, then we can all relax and get back to normal. BIA aren't the only ones worried. The senator's people are making noises like they don't want to send their man to the rez after all. What message will that send to the national media? Home of Arapahos and Shoshones unsafe? I hear you were the one who found T.J."

Vicky nodded.

"Pretty bad, was it?"

"T.J. didn't deserve what happened to him."

"That's the truth." He was quiet a moment, sucking in his lower lip. "Lots of people don't deserve what they get, right? What can I do for you?" The phone started ringing. "Hang on." He reached over and picked up the receiver. "This is Foxworthy."

A couple of seconds passed before he said, "No comment. There's nothing new. The investigation is in the hands of the FBI." He paused. A phone was ringing somewhere down the hall, and red lights were flashing on the phone on the desk. "That's right," the man said. "Ted Gianelli. Call him." He slammed down the phone. "Okay, so where were we?"

Vicky sat back in the chair. "I need your help, Louis."

"Hey, Vicky." The man planted his elbows on the desk and folded both hands back. "We're here to serve, you know that. I'm always happy to help you, but today is not the best of times, as you can see. T.J.'s murder has the whole office upset. We're not getting any work done around here today. How about you come back next week?"

"It's about the murder."

"You should talk to Gianelli," he said.

Vicky pulled a small notepad and a pen from her bag. "First I need some information."

Foxworthy let out a long sigh and leaned back. He swiveled to the right, then to the left. "Okay, provided it's quick and easy."

Vicky scribbled down the name Bashful Woman. Then she wrote: *daughter of Chief Sharp Nose.* She tore off the sheet of paper and handed it across the desk. "I need to know if Bashful Woman had an allotment, and if she did, where it was located."

The superintendent crumbled the paper into a tight ball and rolled it across the desk. "Of course she had an allotment. All of the chief's children received one-hun-dred-and-sixty-acre allotments soon's they turned twenty-one. They were considered good Indians, trust-worthy. They learned to speak English and read and write over at the mission school."

"Where was the allotment?"

"Not quick and easy, Vicky." Foxworthy threw a glance at the bank of file cabinets lining the wall behind his chair. "Current records are here," he said, "but we keep the old records in the probate files. Take a while to dig them out."

"It's important, Louis. T.J. and Denise were murdered. There could be more murders, unless the killer is stopped."

"Jesus, Vicky. You're really making my day here. All we need are some more murders and the senator and everybody else in Washington will write us off as hopeless. Not like appropriations haven't been cut enough. We don't need any more cuts."

"There has to be somebody here who can get me the records," Vicky pushed on.

The phone started ringing again. Once, twice. Foxworthy reached over and jabbed a button. The ringing stopped, and a little yellow light lit up. The answering machine, Vicky guessed.

It was a moment before Foxworthy said, "I'm not making any promises, but I'll see what I can do. You want to come back later?"

Vicky got to her feet and started for the door. "I'll be waiting in the hall," she said.

She walked toward the blue plastic chairs. The sound of the man's voice on the telephone behind her mingled with the ringing phones, the clack of keyboards, and the low undertow of conversations. Through the glass walls, she could see dark heads bobbing toward computer monitors. A woman raised her eyes and smiled.

Vicky stopped at the window. The wind was blowing, speckling the glass with dust. The dormitory looked still and frozen, almost ghostlike, in the wind. Across from the dormitory was a two-story white frame house where the government agents assigned to the reservation had once lived. Between the two buildings was an open space with brush and grasses pushing up from the earth, tipped with the faintest trace of frost. The scaffold had been there, she thought. She could imagine the scene: three men swinging from their necks, heads bent forward, the toes of their boots dropped toward the plank floor, and groups of people standing about, staring, waiting for the last twitch of a muscle, the final stillness of death.

God. She wondered if Carston Evans had been in the crowd. Was there no one else who knew the three men were innocent? No one else who knew the truth?

Vicky sank down on one of the chairs and dragged a news magazine off the nearby table. She began leafing through the pages, trying to focus on first one article, then another, wondering if the murder of a tribal councilman would attract the national media, as Foxworthy feared.

She stopped. Senator Evans was grinning at her from the glossy page. Grinning and waving his hat overhead, like a rodeo cowboy swinging a rope. "Tossing a Cowboy Hat into the Ring," the headline read. She glanced through the article below the photograph. "Will the cowboy senator from Wyoming announce that he intends to run for president? When asked about his intentions, the maverick senator said, 'Stay tuned.

You'll be the first to hear.' Insiders are betting that the announcement will come during the senator's trip home next week. Since the senator entered Congress as Wyoming's sole representative fourteen years ago, he has announced his political intentions from the steps of the Wyoming state capitol in Cheyenne. Twelve years ago, he went to the state capitol to toss his hat into the ring for the U.S. Senate.

"Despite the senator's record as a friend of oil and gas corporations, Senator Evans has maintained a strong following throughout the western states. Polls place his approval rating at seventy percent. Part of the senator's appeal, analysts say, is his outgoing personality and down-to-earth manner. 'When the senator talks to you,' one woman said, 'you think you're the only person he cares about.' Fifty-eight years old and trim, the senator is an early morning fixture jogging in Rock Creek Park before he puts in a twelve-hour day on capitol hill. 'He works for us,' the woman stated, although Robert Burnhart, a Washington bus driver, disagreed. 'You ask me, big corporations are the senator's best friends.'"

"Vicky?"

Vicky looked around. Foxworthy was leaning outside the door to his office. She tossed the magazine onto the table and walked back down the hall. "You're in luck," he said, leading the way back into the office. "One of my old Army buddies agreed to take the time to pull the records. I owe him, he says, so he'll be expecting me to return the favor one of these days." He thrust two sheets of paper at her.

At the top of one, in thick black letters, were the

words *Sharp Nose Family.* Below that was Bashful Woman, twenty-one years of age. The next lines gave the legal description of the allotment.

Vicky glanced at the second page. The name on top was Sharp Nose, and the text detailed the description of the chief's allotment.

"See there." The superintendent stood next to her and tapped at the sheet with Bashful Woman's allotment. "She had one hundred and sixty acres, not bad for a young woman. When the chief died, his lands were divided among his children and she received another forty acres adjacent to her own allotment."

Vicky was still reading through the legal description—even more obtuse than the descriptions she was accustomed to. "Where exactly were the allotments?" she asked.

"Vicky . . ." There was a pleading note in the man's tone. "I've had to turn off my phones. You know how many calls I have to return already?" He exhaled and, pushing the side chair out of the way, threw open a filing drawer. In a moment he'd flopped a large folder on top of the papers on his desk. "Maybe we can pin down the sites by this map," he said, pulling a map of the reservation free from other maps in the folder. "Read off the description," he said.

He was bent over the map, both index fingers on fixed points. As she read, his fingers began to move toward each other until they stopped at two points near the top of the map. Keeping one finger on the map, he rummaged under the folder and brought out a pencil. He made a small mark on both points.

"Read on," he said, and they went through the same motions: She, calling out the descriptions, he, bringing his index fingers together, except that now he was working from the top and bottom of the map. Again the fingers halted at two points about an inch apart, and holding the places with thumb and finger, Foxworthy placed the pencil marks on the map.

Vicky read off the descriptions on the second sheet, and four other pencil marks appeared next to the first marks. "Take a look," Foxworthy said, glancing up from the map. "The lady ran a decent ranch."

Vicky went around the desk and peered down at the map, trying to get her bearings. The ranch was southwest of Thermopolis in the Owl Creek mountains. The Evans Ranch was in the vicinity. "One more question," she said.

"Come on, Vicky." The man's voice was so tight that, for a moment, she feared he would announce he'd run out of time.

She hurried on: "Where exactly is the Evans Ranch?"

"You know the ranch is in the same area."

"I want to know if it's the same land. Bashful Woman was Carston Evans's wife."

Foxworthy flinched backward, as if she'd slapped him. "We don't need this, Vicky. We can't go around accusing the senator's ancestors of taking ownership of Arapaho land."

Vicky cut in: "Two people have been murdered, Louis. A white woman is missing. It could all be tied to the Evans Ranch. We have to know the truth."

"Boy, this just isn't my day." The man was shaking

his head. After a moment, he shouldered past her and went back to the filing cabinet. He pulled out another brown file and flopped it on top of the map. He was breathing hard, gasping, she thought, as he rifled through another stack of maps before he pulled one free. "Without the legal description of the Evans Ranch," he said, studying the map, "no way can we be definite. You'll have to get the description at the county clerk's office. All we can do is compare the locations based on the number of miles per inch on each map. Let's see . . ." He'd found a ruler somewhere and was measuring from the margins. "The northern line of the reservation is here." He pointed to a dot. "It looks like the Evans Ranch starts about here, thirty or forty miles west of Boysen Reservoir, then south another fifteen, twenty miles, probably make a five mile adjustment to the east."

Vicky was jotting down the miles as he worked. After a moment, he jerked the first map out from beneath the other file and went back to sliding the ruler around and calling out the miles. Vicky kept taking notes. The miles were almost exactly the same. It would take a legal description of the Evans Ranch to verify that Carston Evans had inherited his wife's lands. What she had was close enough, though. Close enough to know the truth.

"What's this prove?" Foxworthy asked. "There's any number of ways that Evans could have accumulated the land. He could have purchased land from the Sharp Nose family," he went on, his voice growing fainter, as if he realized the weakness of his own argument.

"He could have killed his wife," Vicky said. "Tell me,

Louis. How many other Arapaho women were killed for their land? You have the records."

"What difference would it make? Nobody's going to be getting any lands back after a century. Nobody cares, Vicky."

"I think Senator Evans cares."

The superintendent dipped his head into one hand and rubbed at his eyes. "Jesus, Vicky. You know what kind of dynamite you could be setting off here? Evans is a powerful man. There's no telling what he might do if he thought you were going to expose something like this."

"There's no telling what the man has done already," she said.

27

HE WAS RUNNING, chasing after the figure that ran ahead, disappearing as soon as he caught up. A specter dissolving away from him, like an image dissolving from a photograph.

Father John sat up in bed. Startled, only half awake. It must be mid-morning. Sunlight streamed past the curtains, and the bedroom felt warm and stuffy. He was a man obsessed, he thought. Obsessed by a woman in shock and grief—alone outside the house of a murdered man, a woman he couldn't comfort.

He'd driven over to Vera's and stayed with her until daylight had begun to glow in the windows and the sky beyond had turned pink and gold. Vera, sobbing on the sofa, and he, trying to find words of comfort, finally letting the stillness settle in, more comforting than words.

Gradually relatives and friends had arrived until the living room was crowded with people standing about, occupying every chair. He'd driven back to the mission, the moon still faintly visible in a sky that had changed into milky blue, and fallen into an exhausted half-sleep, the unwanted dreams crashing over him.

He got out of bed, showered, and shaved. In the kitchen, he made himself a couple of pieces of toast, aware of the washing machine rumbling in the basement and Elena scurrying about with a dust mop. She'd make him some oatmeal, she said, reminding him that breakfast was three hours earlier. He waved away the offer, and washed the toast down with strong, lukewarm coffee.

Ten minutes later, he was in the administration building, passing the door to his own office, on his way down the corridor to Father Damien's office. The other priest was at the desk, head bent sideways into a phone call. Father John swung a wood chair around and straddled it backward. He waited until the call ended and Damien hung up.

"You've heard about T.J.?" Father John nodded at the phone. The moccasin telegraph had probably been working for hours.

Damien raked his fingers across his thinning hair—a gesture of discouragement. "First his wife. Now the poor man himself. It's terrible, John. T.J. was a dedicated councilman. He struck me as someone with a far-reaching vision, and he had the courage to stand up against his own people, not to mention a powerful man like Senator Evans, over the methane controversy. The senator's campaign people are making noises about canceling the senator's visit." The other priest had the pained look of a man watching the barn he'd been constructing start to collapse.

"What do they say?" Father John gestured with his head toward the phone.

"A lot of mumbo jumbo about the senator's busy schedule and pressing demands. A fool can read between the lines. Quinn is convinced that the senator could be in danger. Did I think that the murders of a councilman and his wife were coincidence when the councilman had been helping to plan the senator's visit? I explained that the murders, as tragic as they are, don't have anything to do with the mission. I told him that even if he decides that the senator shouldn't go to Fort Washakie, there's no reason to cancel the visit here. Catherine's already lined up dozens of people. The TV cameras will be here. Finally Quinn agreed to stop by this afternoon and take another look. Okay, I admit . . ." Damien shrugged. "It took another phone call from Dad. Frankly, the murders aren't the only thing Quinn's worried about. He keeps asking me if we've had any word on Christine. What have you heard?"

Father John shook his head. Then he said, "Tell me, Damien. Did Christine go to any of the meetings with T.J. at the tribal offices?"

"You think there's a connection?" The other priest jerked backward, as if he'd gotten an electrical shock. "Look, John," he said, patting the side of his head now. "We had two meetings, both unsuccessful. T.J. and the other councilman, Savi Crowthorpe, kept insisting there wouldn't be enough time for the senator to visit schools and tribal offices and still get over to St. Francis. So I asked Christine to come along for another meeting. You know how excited she was . . . is." He corrected himself. ". . . about the Curtis exhibit. I figured she could convince the councilmen that the senator would enjoy the photographs."

"That was it? One meeting?"

"It went pretty well," Damien said, nodding and glancing about the office. "I was going over some details with Savi afterward, and Christine and T.J. walked out together. They were still talking in the parking lot when I came out. I'm sure that the councilmen suggested the mission to the senator's people, even though nothing happened. Not until Dad called the senator himself."

Father John stood up and turned the chair back into place, only half aware of the phone ringing and the other priest picking up. He had the connection now, Father John was thinking. He could imagine the scenario: Christine and T.J. talking in the parking lot. She saying that she was looking for Sharp Nose descendants, and T.J. telling her about Denise, a woman who loved history and who most likely had some old photographs. His theory was correct. He felt a heaviness coming over him, like a weight pressing down.

"For you." Damien pointed the receiver in his direction.

"I'll take it in my office," Father John said.

THE WOMAN'S VOICE coming down the line was high-pitched and stiff. "Linda Novak, returning your call," she said. It was a half-second before Father John recognized the name of the Curtis expert at the West Wind Gallery in Denver.

"How is the exhibit going?" she asked, after he'd thanked her for getting back to him.

He told her the exhibit had brought in a lot of visitors, and the woman went on—a softer tone now, obviously settling into a familiar rhythm—about how the prints had been pulled from original copper plates etched a hundred years ago at a studio in Boston. How they were almost indistinguishable from the first prints made, except, of course, with the latest technology, they were even more beautiful.

Father John waited for a break, then told her that the curator had been missing since last Monday and that the police and FBI were investigating her disappearance.

"Missing!" She shouted the word. "I hope Eric isn't involved. I'm sure you know, Father, that Christine is married to a brilliant man who is very controlling." She hesitated, as if she were considering whether to go on. A couple of beats passed before she said, "Christine told me that she'd left Eric again. Oh, I didn't take it seriously. She's left him before, but she's always gone back. Of course I promised not to tell Eric where she was if he called the gallery, which he did about a day later. I figured she needed some time to sort things out. Shall I send someone to dismount the exhibit after Senator Evans's visit?"

The question took Father John by surprise. "How did you know about the visit?" he asked.

"It's all Christine talked about the last time she called," the woman said. "It was an opportunity to show the Curtis photographs to the next president of the United States. There would be media attention, which will only increase the demand for Curtis's work. Naturally, I was very pleased at the prospect of new customers for the gallery."

"I was hoping you could tell me," Father John began, "how valuable an original Curtis photograph might be."

"Original? As I said, Father, the photos in the exhibit were printed from the original copper . . ."

"Vintage Curtis photographs," he said.

"Well, that would depend." A keyboard clacked on the other end. "Curtis shot forty thousand images, which have been copied and reproduced for years. That doesn't mean the earlier prints are necessarily the most valuable. The price is pegged to the subject. Show me a vintage print of Chief Joseph or Geronimo or the Canyon de Chelly, and I could get you twenty thousand dollars. But an unknown subject, well . . ." The clacking stopped. "Anywhere from several hundred dollars to several thousand. Naturally, buyers would want proof that the photographs dated from Curtis's own time."

"Did Christine mention finding any vintage photographs on the reservation?" Father John asked.

Another pause before the woman said, "I'm sure if she had made any such find, she would have told me. I suppose it's always possible that Curtis left prints with Indian people. They'd be of historic interest, even if they weren't particularly valuable. Of course, a real find would be the original glass plate negatives that Curtis exposed. Hardly likely that he left any of those behind. He always carried the exposed plates out of the field. Unfortunately, the plates were later destroyed. Smashed, I'm afraid."

"What are we talking about?" Father John said. "How valuable would a glass plate be?"

The clacking resumed again. After a moment, the woman said, "It would be a rare find indeed. Collectors are willing to pay a great deal of money for unusual items of historic and artistic interest. At the very least, an exposed plate would show the exact image that Curtis had captured. Depending upon the image, a glass plate might command thousands of dollars. The more significant the image, the more valuable the plate would be. None of the details would have been changed or manipulated, which can happen in the developing process. Are you saying that you've come across Curtis plates? We'd certainly be interested in representing you, if you wish to sell."

"I'm afraid they're not mine to sell," Father John said. Then he added, "If they exist." He thanked the woman, hung up, and stared at the phone. Dear Lord. What had Christine stumbled into? Tracking vintage photographs, coming upon exposed glass plates? Where? In T.J.'s and Denise's shed? Stored for a century?

And all the time running from Eric Loftus, a man who owned an art gallery. A man who would know the value of glass plates exposed by Edward S. Curtis.

From outside came the hum of an engine, the sound of gravel crunching under tires. The engine cut off. A moment later, cool air swooshed across the office and the front door slammed shut. There was the tap of footsteps on the floor. Father John looked up as Vicky walked into the office.

28

"WHAT HAVE YOU found?" Father John asked, nodding toward the brown envelope in Vicky's hand.

She pulled out a thin stack of papers and arranged them in some kind of order. "Take a look," she said, laying one sheet on the desk in front of him.

Father John took in the words at the top of the page: *Allotment of Bashful Woman.*

"Read the legal description," Vicky said with so much urgency in her voice that he lifted his eyes and looked at her a moment before he skimmed through the lines of black text.

"Here's a legal description of the adjacent forty acres that Sharp Nose left to his daughter. He left more land to his daughter than to his sons because, he said, a woman would need it more." Vicky set another sheet on top of the first. "I got the first description from the agency. And I got the legal description of the Evans Ranch from the county clerk's office. The descriptions are identical."

Father John was still reading through the text, comparing one to the other. A perfect match. After a moment, he glanced up. "You think Evans was responsible for his wife's death?"

"I think that two hundred acres of the best ranchland

in the area is a very big motive."

"He was already running a successful ranch on her land, Vicky. Why would he want her dead?"

"He married a white woman after Bashful's death, didn't he? He went on to establish a prominent Wyoming family—a white family. His grandson is a United States senator who intends to become the next president. Do you think Carston Evans could have made that possible with an Indian wife? She would have held him back at every step. What doors do you think would have opened to half-breed children?"

Vicky had crossed her arms and was hugging herself. He could see that beneath her tan jacket, she was trembling. "Carston Evans saw his chance, John. Curtis was on the reservation, taking photographs, trying to capture the old ways, such as enemy warriors attacking an Arapaho village. The only problem was, there weren't any more enemy warriors. And there weren't any more villages. Curtis created the warriors, the village, and the attack. The perfect opportunity for Bashful to die, except that he knew there wasn't enough money to pay an Arapaho to kill a chief's daughter. Evans had to do it himself, then he testified against Thunder and the others." Vicky threw her head back and appealed to the ceiling. "The word of a white man against the word of three Indians? Who do you think the magistrate believed?"

She walked over to the window and back, then retraced her steps. He followed her with his eyes. Outside, the cottonwoods, lined in frost, were dancing in the breeze.

"He probably killed their child," Vicky said, facing him again. "What did the newspapers say about the child?"

Father John shook his head.

"A half-breed child." Vicky traced the circle again. "Anything might have happened to the child on the ranch, and no one would have known. Carston Evans committed murder and got away with it." She shook her head in wonder. "He's still getting away with it."

Father John walked around the desk and perched on the edge. "Maybe not," he said, trying to fit the jumble of disconnected pieces into a coherent, logical sequence.

"What are you saying?"

It was clear now, the images chasing through his mind. "The three warriors rode toward the village, and Curtis snapped a picture. The warriors swooped down into the village, and Curtis took another picture, then another as fast as he could insert new plates. He had an assistant, which means he probably worked pretty fast. He could have taken several pictures in a few seconds. But the only photo that survived is 'Before the Attack.' What happened to the others?"

Vicky was staring at him, her lips parted as if she'd exhaled her last breath and couldn't take another.

"Curtis left after the attack," Father John hurried on. "Suppose he only took the first plates he'd exposed and left the others behind as evidence of what had really happened. Suppose the Sharp Nose family found the other plates."

Vicky shook her head. "If that were true, they would

have taken them to the magistrate. The warriors wouldn't have been hanged."

She had a point. Father John kneaded his fingers into his forehead. "Okay," he said. "What if the family didn't find the negatives in time to save the warriors?"

"They would have killed Evans themselves," Vicky said. "They would have avenged Bashful's death."

"Maybe they chose not to seek revenge, Vicky. Maybe there was some reason they chose to let the man get away with murder."

Father John waited a moment, giving her time to absorb this new idea before he said, "Christine could have found a glass plate with the image of Carston Evans shooting his wife."

"What difference would it make?" Vicky asked, not taking her eyes from his. "The past is dead, John. It's forgotten."

"Look," he began, and he told her what he'd learned from the Curtis expert at the West Wind Gallery. "Any Curtis glass plate negative might be valuable," he said, "but a Curtis negative that captured the image of a senator's grandfather shooting his Arapaho wife would be very valuable. Christine would know the value. So would Eric Loftus." He paused, another image forming in his mind. "Loftus might have found his wife here and seen her with T.J. He might have figured out that she'd located vintage photos. Maybe he even talked to Denise or T.J. and found out about the negatives."

"You're saying that the man might have killed his own wife? Just like Evans?" Vicky gave a little laugh, edged with bitterness. "Wife has something that husband wants. Wife has to die."

"No," Father John heard himself say. That wasn't it. "I think Christine is still running." He could still see the hunter's gleam in Loftus's eyes. "Loftus is looking for her," he said.

Vicky swung around and started pacing again. "It makes sense that the glass plates were passed down to Denise," she said. Pacing, glancing back at him over one shoulder. "Denise loved history. The shed in back of the house was crammed with old things. The glass plates could have been in the shed. T.J. said he knew who had killed his wife. He said *they* had killed her. It all makes sense, except . . ."

"Except?"

Vicky was looking beyond him, as if she were trying to pluck something out of her memory. "He said he didn't have the evidence. That means the plates were no longer in the shed. Loftus and whatever goon he had brought with him must have taken them when they killed Denise."

Father John got to his feet and came around the desk. He punched one fist into the palm of his other hand. "No," he said. "If Loftus had the plates, he wouldn't have gone to Christine's place and torn everything apart. No," he said again, willing the pieces to fit into a coherent image in his head. "He could've gone to T.J.'s intending to find the plates, but instead he found Denise at home, and Denise would have done anything to protect the images of the ancestors."

"She would have died . . ." Vicky said, her voice

low, trailing off into a whisper.

"Somehow she must have managed to convince Loftus that T.J. had put the plates in a safe place. Maybe she even showed him the vacant spot in the shed where the plates had been stored. Whatever happened, he believed her. He could have forced her into the bedroom and shot her, making it look like suicide. Then he would have gone to Christine's, figuring that T.J. had given the plates to the curator."

Vicky had stopped pacing. She was staring at him again. "My God, John. Suppose you're right. Suppose T.J. did give the plates to Christine, but she didn't keep them at the house. She kept them with her."

Other images now: Christine picking up the briefcase at the mission, holding it close, as if whatever it contained was precious. And Loftus, determined to find his wife, willing to do anything, even torture and kill a man, to find her.

"If Christine has the plates," he said, "she's in serious danger. Loftus won't stop until he finds her."

Vicky began gathering up the sheets of paper and stuffing them back into the envelope. "I have to take this to Gianelli," she said.

"Call me after you talk to him," Father John said, but she was already across the office and through the door, her footsteps receding in the corridor.

29

JESSE WHITE OWL left Fort Washakie and rode hard cross-country to Arapaho, detouring past the fences that Arapahos had put up around their allotments, in the way of white men. Ahead, in the far distance, the Mercantile store sprawled over the rise, white walls gleaming in the sun.

Jesse slowed uphill past a child leading a pony toward the water pooled in the gully. He dismounted and walked up the steps to the men standing on the porch, working at cigarettes cupped in their hands, dressed in canvas trousers, brown leather vests, and long-sleeved white shirts with black bands above the elbows. They wore gray hats with rounded crowns and wide brims that threw a line of shade over the top half of their faces. Thick black braids hung over their chests.

Jesse had known the men all his life: Joe Yellow Plume, William Red Horn, Sumner Bull, Old Man Scarface. Jesse was the one who'd stood on the porch and told them how Curtis was going to photograph a real Arapaho village. They'd thrown their heads back and shouted with laughter. "Where's he gonna find this village?" they'd asked.

Well, that was the thing, he'd explained. Curtis was gonna create the village and he was gonna pay good money to anyone who brought his family and tipis out to Black Mountain.

That had caught their attention, and two days later, all four men had shown up, wagons humped with canvas tipis, feathered headdresses and elk-tooth shirts and breastplates dragged out of sheds.

Now they stared at him, the cigarettes burning down between their fingers, smoke curling around the cuffs of their shirts, wariness and alertness in their eyes.

"I been at the agency," he said.

"They're gonna hang 'em soon's the executioner gets here day after tomorrow." Old Man Scarface tossed his head toward the railroad tracks that ran behind the Mercantile.

"They aren't guilty," Jesse said.

"There was witnesses." This from Sumner Bull, the youngest man there, not out of his teens yet, still on the first hill of life. What he saw from the first hill was small. He'd see farther as he climbed the next three hills.

Jesse moved in front of the young man. "You one of the witnesses?"

Sumner backed away until he was wedged against the porch railing. "There was lots of witnesses. The white man was the most important."

"What're you after?" Old Man Scarface said.

"I want the truth."

"We said the truth to the agent, and we said the same truth to the magistrate. We said what we seen." Scarface glanced at the closed door to the Mercantile. "You can ask anybody inside. We were running around the village, shouting like the photographer said we was to do, shooting off the blanks in our rifles. People started screaming and crying, like the Crow was really attacking. Thunder rode straight to Bashful's tipi, them other two right behind him, all of 'em shooting off their rifles. We seen the truth, Jesse."

"Your eyes seen something else."

"You was there." Yellow Plume spoke up for the first time.

"I was taking plates out of the camera and handing new ones to the photographer so he could keep shooting his images." Jesse stopped. He felt as if a bolt of lightning had crashed into him and knocked out his air. It was a moment before he could speak. "The photographer was looking through that big, black eye of his," Jesse managed. "He must've seen what happened. What did he tell the magistrate?"

"You ain't heard?" Scarface shook his head. "Mr. Curtis packed up his belongings in that wagon of his and pulled out of here before the agent come out to the village and started asking questions. Said he wasn't gonna have no part of murder. Said he was going up to the Sioux 'cause they was civilized." The old man gave a bark of laughter. "Mr. Curtis didn't know the Sioux in the Old Time. You ask me, Curtis was scared he was gonna get blamed and Bashful's people was gonna punish him 'cause he's the one who set up the village."

"He took everything?" Jesse could barely form the question. The black eye on the photographer's box had seen what happened. It had captured the truth.

"Everything he could pile into the wagons. Sumner here helped him." Scarface nodded at the young man over by the railing. "Ain't that right?"

250

Sumner took a long pull on the cigarette and let his shoulders relax. "Loaded stuff out of the cabin and packed up his tent and loaded it into the wagon with the cartons of bottles and paper, all that would fit. Some of it he left behind."

"What about the glass plates?" Jesse felt his jaw muscles tighten.

"He was sitting in the middle of the floor, packing things up." The young man shrugged. "I took the cartons he gave me and put 'em in the middle of the wagon and wrapped the tent around 'em. There was some cartons still in the cabin, but when I went to get 'em, the photographer says, 'Leave 'em.' Guess he didn't want 'em any more."

The Indian was still talking when Jesse swung over the porch railing. He placed two fingers in his mouth and whistled for the pony, which started trotting up from the water. Jesse ran to meet it, swung up into the saddle, and, leaning along the pony's neck, galloped north.

BLACK MOUNTAIN HAD turned gun-metal gray in the afternoon shadows when Jesse turned the pony loose at the stream that ran crooked in the flats below. He made his way through the brush crackling under his boots, trying not to look at the stretch of bare ground where the village had stood. The place of death. He walked on, following the little creek that was no more than a thread of water angling off the stream, until he came to the log cabin with the sloping roof that looked as if it might fall onto the ground and the porch that shifted to one side, broken planks like the teeth of a monster animal jutting out of the wood floor.

The cabin had stood there since the Old Time, the elders said, when whites came to Indian lands to trap beaver and trade their white goods. "It will work just fine for my lodging," Curtis had told him that first day they'd ridden out to Black Mountain. "I can set up my tents nearby."

The door was open, moving back and forth with the gusts of wind that blew across the porch, hinges squealing like a trapped animal. Jesse stood in the doorway a moment and let his eyes adjust to the dim light glowing in the small window in the opposite wall. The place looked as if a tornado had blown through. Pieces of paper and bundles of cloth scattered over the floor; cardboard cartons that looked as if they had been tossed aside. For a moment, Jesse wondered if a bear had gotten in and rummaged about for food. Then he understood. The photographer had left in a hurry. Sat in the middle of the floor, Sumner said, packing things up, setting other things aside.

Jesse dug in the pocket of his trousers, past the bag of tobacco and little envelope of cigarette papers, and pulled out a stick match. Then he stepped inside, struck the match against the wall, and lit the wick of the candle on a wooden bench. The light flared blue and danced about over the log wall behind, then settled into a low, steady yellow flame.

He stepped over the debris, glancing around the cabin. In the far corner, a carton that had once held glass plates, wrapped in foil, tidy, ready for use. The carton was empty. Jesse turned slowly, his eyes scanning the other cartons. Under the bench, he spotted an over-turned box—also empty, he saw. But sitting beside the box, almost hidden in shadow, was a stack of three blue and white enameled developing tanks. There was a bulge in the center of the top tank, as if a boot had stomped on it.

Jesse swung around and, picking up the candle, sur-veyed the piles of grayish rags. He poked the tip of his boot at one pile, then another, until he uncovered a twisted jumble of red cloth. Something caught his atten-tion—the smallest outline of an object. He stooped down and began patting the cloth until his fingers gripped the smooth edge of wood. He dropped to his knees, pushed the base of the candle into a crack in the plank floor until the candle seemed steady. He tugged at the cloth pulling out three wooden plate holders, with glass plates still secured in place, protected by dark slides. The plates had been exposed, he could tell. After the photographer had snapped each picture, Jesse had been careful to insert the slide with the dark rim visible, so that the photographer would know not to use the plate again and make a double exposure.

For the briefest moment, Jesse had the sense that the photographer had meant for him to find the three plates. And yet—his heart was hammering now—the plates were no good without chemicals to develop them and paper on which to print the images.

Jesse picked up the candle and got to his feet, squinting into the flickering light. Some of the cartons left behind had remnants of cloth and paper inside. In the corner next to the stone fireplace was a wood box with the tops of glass jugs poking over the edges. He walked over and pulled out a clear glass jug, half-full of yellowish-brown liquid developer, sparkling in the candlelight. In another jug, he realized, were the white crystals of sodium thiosulfate. He lifted out two small bottles wedged among the jugs, next to a box of thumb tacks and a glass ramekin holding a thin, glass rod. Still squinting, he read the tiny print on the labels pasted to the bottles: FERRIC AMMONIUM CITRATE and POTASSIUM BICHROMATE.

He set the bottles back into the carton, his heart crashing against his ribs. The photographer had also left him the chemicals, and enough paper in the cartons—it was possible—to print the images. He would make the blue pictures first, he decided. The cyanotypes, Curtis called them. Working pictures that showed blue-gray images on paper and were quick to make. If the cyanotypes showed what he expected, then Jesse could make the black-and-white prints. He had one more day before Thunder and the others would die.

Jesse pushed the base of the candle hard into the plank floor again, then he gathered up the red cloth and began tucking it around the edges of the window. Now the light coming through the window glowed a dim red—a safe light for developing the exposed plates, the photographer had said. Jesse lifted the enameled tank with the bulge in the middle, went outside and, after pounding out the bulge with his fist, filled the tank with creek water. He would have to hurry. The day was wearing on; the sun already fading into a pale white glow.

Back in the cabin, he set the tank on the bench and arranged the other tanks on either side. After shutting the door, he ripped up pieces of paper and cardboard and stuffed them into the cracks until the rim of light around the edges had disappeared. Then he blew out the candle, allowing the dull red light from the window to float around him. He was ready.

In one of the cartons, he found three pieces of smooth paper, which he laid out on the end of the bench. Then he took out the two small bottles and poured the chemicals into the ramekin. Using the glass rod, he spread the mixture over the sheets of paper and thumb-tacked them to the log wall to dry.

Working as fast as he could, he lifted out the jug with the yellowish-brown developer and poured the chemical into the tank to the left of the tank of water. He poured the white crystals into the tank on the right. Carefully, the way the photographer had shown him, he removed one of the glass plates from the holder and slipped the plate into the developing tank. The image began to take shape before his eyes: the village spread at the base of Black Mountain, the warriors galloping around the tipis. When the image was clear, Jesse moved the plate into the water tank to stop the developing, then into the tank of crystals to fix the image. He rinsed the plate in water again and propped it upright against a carton so that the water could drip free.

He went through the same motions with the second glass plate, then the third. Finally he opened the door, dislodging the wads of papers and cardboard that fluttered over his trousers and boots. Outside on the porch, he lit a cigarette, the match shaking between his fingers, the flame closing down, then flaring again. He had seen the images. They were what he had expected.

After a few moments, Jesse ground out the cigarette butt under his boot and went back inside. He rummaged through the piles of rags until he'd found three wooden printing frames, never doubting that Curtis had left them behind with the rest of materials and that he had only to find them. He fitted one of the coated sheets of paper—which had turned yellowish—against each of the glass plates, then fastened them into the frames, took them outside, and set them upright in the thin column of sunshine still falling over the porch. It took several moments before the shadows of the images printed themselves onto the sheets of paper in bluish-gray tones.

Back in the cabin, he rinsed the cyanotypes in the tray of water to remove the last of the yellow tinges. Now the images were a deep blue color, highlighted in white. No one would believe blue images. *What are these strange images?* He could hear the agent's voice in his head. He would have to turn the images into black-and-white photographs.

Rummaging through the cartons, hurrying against the fading sun, Jesse found several sheets of printing-out paper, coated with silver chloride. He could fasten the sheets against the glass plates in the printing frames and let the sun develop the black-and-white prints, but it would take longer than it had taken to develop the cyanotypes. He would have to fix and tone the black-and-white images in the chemicals. It would take time. He stared out the door at the pencil-thin column of sunshine evaporating like water off the plank floor of the porch and the blue shadows moving over the ground. It was too late.

He would have to sleep here in the cabin with the blue-and-white images, and tomorrow he would make the photographs. If he started early, in the first strength of the sun, he could bring the images to light. Tomorrow he would watch the village take shape. He would see Bashful again.

30

"FATHER, YOU'D BETTER get over to the museum right away." Catherine's voice stuttered down the line.

"I'm on my way," Father John said. He slammed down the receiver and headed out the door, grabbing his jacket as he went, bunching it under his arm. He jogged around Circle Drive and mounted the steps to the porch. The wood creaked beneath his boots. The moment he opened the wood door, the warm air and vacant silence came at him like an invisible force.

"Catherine," he called, heading into the office. He tossed the jacket onto a chair. No sign of the woman, apart from the impression she'd left in the worn leather chair behind the desk. He went back into the entry, his eyes searching the gallery ahead and the halls that ran to the left and to the right. No one. Two or three minutes ago, Catherine had been here. She couldn't have disappeared. And yet . . .

Christine had been here, standing in the entry, talking

to him, and in a *few minutes,* she'd disappeared.

Father John started down the hall past the office, opening the doors, looking inside: a lecture room, vacant except for the chairs in haphazard rows in front of a podium; a small gallery with exhibit cases pushed like coffins against the walls. Behind the glass fronts were displays of breastplates and headgear, parfleches, moccasins and leggings beaded and painted by Arapahos in the Old Time, silent images of the past.

He closed the door and reversed his steps past the main gallery, the Curtis photos mute under the wash of fluorescent light. Across the hallway the bathroom door was shut. He rapped lightly. "Catherine?" he called.

There was no answer. He tried the knob. It turned in his grip, and he moved the door inward about an inch. "Catherine," he said again, leaning into the narrow opening. Silence, except for the *drip drip* of a faucet. He flung the door back. There was no one inside.

He'd started for the library at the far end of the hall when he heard a scuffing noise, like that of a heavy object being dragged across a rough surface. Through the opaque glass in the door he could see the shadow of someone moving about the room. He flung open the door.

Catherine was pushing a carton onto a shelf, and for a moment he thought she might drop it. He hurried over, took hold of the box, and shoved it into place.

"He was here, Father!" The woman exhaled the words.

"Who?"

"Christine's husband."

"Eric Loftus was here?"

"Twenty minutes ago. I thought he was still here looking at maps, but when I came to check . . ."

"Whoa, Catherine." Father John held up one hand and walked over to the table. He pushed one of the round-back wood chairs toward the woman. "Sit down and start at the beginning." He waited until she'd folded herself onto the seat before he dragged another chair over and sat down beside her.

Little beads of perspiration glistened in the furrows of the woman's forehead. She pulled a wad of tissue from the pocket of the sweater she wore over a dark dress and began patting at the moisture. Finally she clasped both hands in her lap, the white tissue poking between her fingers. "I'm not good at this job, Father," she said. "Being in charge of the museum isn't what I thought I was gonna be doing at the mission."

"You've been doing a fine job, Catherine."

"I don't want nothing to disappear. I been trying to watch everything."

Father John set his hand on top of her clenched hands. They were like chunks of ice. "Tell me about Loftus," he said.

The woman lifted her head and stared at the shelves, as if the cartons and rows of books might contain the image she was trying to conjure. "I was in the office when he showed up in the doorway. I never heard him come in. It was like he wasn't a true person. 'Did I startle you?' he says, like he was hoping he did. I don't mind telling you, Father, he almost startled me into my grave. He's got them blue eyes that shoot into you like bullets. 'Can I help you?' I say, and I was wishing there was some visitors in the museum right then. How a smart woman like Christine could've ever married . . ."

Father John gently squeezed the woman's hands. "What did he want?"

"He wants his wife back, Father. First thing he asks is have we heard from his wife. No, I tell him, and I'm thinking I hope she got so far away that you can't ever find her and I hope . . ." Catherine drew in her lips and lowered her gaze to the table. "Oh, God, Father. I been hoping all along that Christine is still alive. So I told him that."

"You told him that you hoped his wife was still alive?" Father John smiled at the woman. She'd had the courage to say what he and Vicky had been thinking. And she'd said it to the man who might know the truth. "What did Loftus say?"

"Oh, she's alive all right. We shouldn't be worrying ourselves, he says. He knows his wife . . ." Catherine shifted sideways and looked at him, her eyes darkening with a new resolve. "He says, soon as things got hot, Christine went into hiding, just like he taught her. I remember him laughing and me thinking, what's so funny? And he says she was the damned best student he ever had, but she wasn't as good as her teacher. He'd talked to people on the rez, he said, and I'm wondering how many people was willing to talk to him. He says Christine was looking for old photographs, and the only thing she knew about the rez was the Curtis photographs, she being a stranger here."

Catherine pulled her hands free and mopped at her

brow again. "I don't mind telling you, I was getting real jumpy all the time he was talking. Next thing I know, he stomps into the gallery, and I hurried right behind him because, you know, I didn't know what he might do to the photographs. I mean, he might blame the photographs for making his wife go away, and I was thinking, if he so much as touches the glass on one of the photographs, I was gonna pick up a chair and hit him in the head."

Oh, my God, Father John thought. He blinked back the image. Loftus, a killer trained to react out of instinct. The woman could have been dead before the man stopped to think.

"He marched right over to the photograph of the village," Catherine went on. " 'This is the photograph my wife was trying to identify, right?' When he looked at me with them blue eyes of his, Father, I started shaking. I told him it wasn't none of my business what Christine was doing. 'Oh, I got it right,' he says. 'My dear wife starts thinking that if anyone has Curtis photos of their ancestors, she can buy them on the cheap, sell them to a dealer, and get herself a plane ticket far away. Only problem, it could take a lot of photos to get some real money. Then I got to thinking. What if she happened on a few Curtis glass negatives? Well, that's a different ball game. She would've looked everywhere for negatives. Would've gone out to the village site. It would've been like a treasure hunt. Looking in the brush and caves, hoping Curtis might've left something behind that nobody ever found.' "

The woman started laughing, a slow chuckle that gurgled out of her throat. "I don't mind telling you, Father, I laughed good at that, and he got real mad. 'You think that can't happen?' he says. 'You think there wasn't a trash pile at the site where Curtis tossed stuff he didn't want?' Then he says that somebody told him the village was out by Black Mountain, and he wants to know where that is."

Catherine leaned so far forward that Father John thought she might slip off the chair. "I told him we got hundreds of acres of space here. You think I know every square inch? You think I know where things was a hundred years ago? But I been out there plenty of times, Father. My uncle ranched out there, and I rode all over that scrub brush land. Next thing he wants to know is if we have any old maps."

"You did fine to bring him to the library," Father John said. "You should have called me then."

The woman was nodding. "I went back to the office thinking I was gonna call you, 'cause I didn't want to be alone with that man. That was when the people from Idaho came in and started asking questions, and I had to take them into the gallery and tell them about the photographs. Soon's they left, I went to check on Loftus, and he was gone. Up and gone, Father! It's like the man can walk through walls."

Catherine gripped the edge of the table and pushed to her feet. "I been checking the map boxes. There's no way I can be sure he didn't take something. I shouldn't've left him . . ."

"It's okay, Catherine." Father John stopped the woman. "You handled things very well. What about

Black Mountain?" he asked, trying to get hold of a memory moving in the shadows of his mind. "Any old buildings or caves or shelter?"

Catherine was shaking her head. "Nothing but the land. We could ride forever and never come across anything." She drew in a breath and closed her eyes a moment.

"What about the old cabin?" he asked, bringing the memory into clearer focus now. What was it she had said—tossed off—three days ago about the cabin that Curtis had stayed in?

"Couple miles from my uncle's ranch was this old cabin, the one that's in the photograph. Still there, far as I know."

"Who owns it now?"

The woman contemplated the top of the table for a moment, as if she were studying a picture of the site and the cabin. "That's all tribal land, Father. I guess anybody can go out there and use that cabin to hunt and fish. I expect lots of people working at the tribal offices go there."

"Christine could be hiding there," Father John said. He was thinking out loud. He could see by the expression on Catherine's face that she was making her own connections.

"I guess her husband could be right," she said, her head bobbing up and down. "Maybe Christine went out to Black Mountain and walked around until she found the old cabin."

Or maybe, Father John thought, T.J. told her about it. "How do I get there?" he asked.

The woman pushed herself to her feet, walked over to the desk near the door, and, leaning down, jotted something on a sheet of paper. Stepping back, she held out the paper. "You gotta keep watching for the turnoff soon's you cross Sound Draw. Take the bridge over the Wind River and keep driving north. Don't pay attention to the dirt roads going off in all directions, just stay close to the draw even after the road wears out. Keep going, and when you find a flat spot between the bluffs, bear east. You'll see the cabin."

He stood up and headed back down the hallway. He'd grabbed his jacket in the office and was already in the entry, about to open the front door, when Catherine called out from the library, "What'll I do if Loftus comes back?"

"He won't be back," Father John called before letting himself outside. Pulling on his jacket, he plunged across the grounds for the pickup.

31

FATHER JOHN HAD no idea of how far he'd driven. The odometer, like the speedometer, hadn't worked in years. He'd gotten pretty good at gauging distances by guessing at his speed—hard shimmying meant he was pushing sixty-five miles per hour—and counting the telephone poles flashing past the window. He'd run out of telephone poles ten minutes ago.

He'd never been to Black Mountain, but he'd driven Highway 287 many times. A spider web of dirt roads intersected the highway, and he squinted into the sun setting like fire over the mountains for the turnoff.

Outside the passenger window, a dark line of trees trailed the Wind River, but ahead, another line veered north away from the river. He let up on the accelerator, hunting for Sound Draw, the engine grinding to a slower pace. It was another five minutes before he spotted the draw, like a dark cut in the earth. He eased on the brakes and bumped into a narrow two-track that lengthened into a rickety wooden bridge spanning the river. He bounced over the bridge, then back onto the two track, staying with the trees, avoiding the temptation to turn onto another road that emptied into the two-track.

Two or three miles passed—he wasn't sure—and what passed for a trail had run itself out. He kept his boot steady on the accelerator and kept going, crawling over rocks, bouncing through the hard depressions that ripped the ground. Darkness was coming on, bringing a mix of shadows and light under a blue sky that had started to change into silver, the full moon shining in the east, bathing the slopes of Black Mountain in a pale, white light.

He kept going. Then he saw the cabin—nothing more than a shadow, an anomaly in the landscape, brown and small, hunkered down in a clump of junipers. He slid to a stop at the edge of the trees and got out. There was no sound apart from the wind rustling the branches and the crunch of evergreen needles and dried brush under his boots. The trees obscured the last daylight clinging to the mountain ridge on the west. At first he thought the faint odor of smoke in the air was the smell of the over-heated engine, but the odor was stronger as he neared the cabin, and he saw the thin trail of gray smoke winding over the treetops.

The cabin was a small rectangular structure of logs fitted together and chinked with mortar. Built a hundred and fifty years ago, smoke floating out of the rock chimney that ran up the side wall. The roof sloped forward over a narrow porch where the wind had blown sprays of twigs and pine needles. A path had been worked through the needles.

As he started around the porch toward the step, a woman emerged from the trees, a small figure in dark waterproof jacket and pants and thick-soled lace-up boots, the kind of gear that people hereabouts carried in the back of their pickups for emergencies. She wore a knitted cap pulled down around her face, which made it difficult to make out her features. Her hands were encased in outsized gloves that gripped the piles of logs she cradled in her arms.

"Christine," he said.

Her head jerked up, as if she'd been yanked backward. The logs rolled out of her arms and thudded onto the ground. She let out a high-pitched noise like the howl of a wild animal caught in a trap, then wheeled about, ran past him across the porch and into the cabin. The door slammed shut.

Father John picked up the logs and went to the door. "Christine," he shouted. "I'm here to help you. Let me in."

He waited. Nothing but the swoosh of the wind. He had to stoop over to brace the pile of logs against the door while he grappled with the metal latch, half-expecting it to be locked. There was a clicking noise and the latch shot upward. Something gave, and the tension fell away. He gripped the logs again, kicked the door open, and stepped inside.

The cabin was small; the air stuffy and hot. Gray light seeped through the window across from the door. A fire burning in the stone fireplace on the left cast fingers of light across the log walls and the plank floor.

Christine sat on an old wood bench pushed under the window, the butt of a rifle wedged against one shoulder, the barrel pointed at his chest. He could see down the barrel—a black tunnel that looked as though it went on forever.

"Go back to the mission, Father O'Malley," she said, drawing out the words in a monotone, like the simulated voice of a machine. He felt a wave of shock at the change in the woman. She'd removed the cap, and her dark hair was matted against the curve of her head, stringy around her neck. Her face was pale and sunken, her lips tightly drawn, almost white.

"Are you planning to shoot me?" He tried to keep his own voice calm. He could feel his heart pumping.

"This has nothing to do with you. It isn't your business."

"You worked for the mission. That makes it my business."

"This is between me and T.J." Exhaustion pulled at the woman's voice. "Everything will be over in a few more days, and you'll never see me again. Please leave."

"T.J.'s dead, Christine."

The white lips parted, but she didn't make a sound. The rifle was bucking in her hands, and Father John could see that she had to tighten her grip to hang onto the barrel.

"Dead." It was barely a whisper. "What happened?"

"I think you know what happened." Father John was still holding onto the logs, his eyes locked on the rifle. "Put the gun down," he said.

The woman leaned back against the log wall and allowed the rifle to drop slowly until it lay on the floor at her feet, the barrel still pointed at the door.

Father John waited a moment, his heart still thumping. Finally he walked over and set the logs down at the side of the fireplace. He backed away from the heat pouring out of the grate toward the draft of cool air that blew through the opened door. The cabin contained a couple of weathered benches that looked as if they had once been joined, a sleeping bag rolled up against the wall opposite the fireplace, and a cardboard carton stuffed with packages of food that looked like dried noodles and crackers. Next to the carton was a plastic case of bottled water.

He lifted one of the benches, carried it across the cabin, and sat down facing the woman. "I know who you are, Christine," he said. "Why don't you tell me what's going on."

"I never meant for this to happen." Her voice was shaky. She drew in a series of quick breaths, her eyes darting about the cabin as if she expected someone to materialize at any moment. It was a while before she said, "It was supposed to be simple. I could get some money and get the hell out of here, make a new start where my husband would never find me." She turned her head and stared at whatever images leaped at her in the fire. "You don't know what it's like to be married to Eric Loftus. I'm nothing to him, nothing more than his own shadow. I've tried to leave him, but he wouldn't let me go. He always found me. One day, I offered to run an errand for him. He was busy in the gallery with an important client, and he let his guard down. I walked out, got in the car, and drove away. I had twelve hundred dollars hidden in the lining of my bag—money I'd been squirreling away for two years. A week later I had a little furnished apartment and a job at an Indian museum."

She gave a tight, strangled laugh and turned her head back to Father John, as if she'd sensed him studying her. "Eric would never suspect that I'd gone only a hundred and sixty miles over the mountain to an Indian mission. Funny thing, I liked working in the museum. I liked arranging the Curtis exhibit. I could have gone on for a long time, but I knew I didn't have a long time. Sometimes I'd wake up at night and sense his presence, as if he was in the bedroom watching me. Then I found out that people on the reservation had original Curtis photographs. No telling how many vintage photographs were here. It was my way out. I could sell the photographs, pay off the owners, and have enough for a plane ticket to the east coast. But nobody wanted to sell me the photographs. Then T.J. pulled me aside after a meeting and said, "My wife's a descendant of Sharp Nose. She has something you might find interesting."

"Photographs of a woman's murder."

Christine blinked, then gave him a half smile. "Not only photographs, but glass negatives. The murdered woman was Arapaho, and she was the wife of Senator Evans's grandfather. How did you know?"

Father John shook his head. "It doesn't matter. You should know that your husband is looking for you."

"Eric? Here?" She jumped to her feet. "Oh, God. T.J. said the cabin would be safe."

"Eric might find it."

"He'll find me. I have to get out of here." She was lunging for the black bag wedged between the log wall and the cardboard carton of foods.

Father John stood up. "I'll take you to the FBI agent. You can tell him what you know about Denise and T.J.'s murders."

"FBI?" She moved toward the door, hugging the bag to her like an infant. "Are you crazy? The minute I walk into an FBI office, Eric will know where I am. Don't you understand? He has contacts everywhere."

She threw herself past him and headed outside. He went after her. It was getting darker, the moonlight striking through the branches. "I'm parked beyond the trees," he said, trying to take her arm.

She shook herself out of his grasp and veered in the opposite direction. "I have to get the Range Rover. I have to get away."

He grabbed her arm and turned her toward him. "Listen to me, Christine. You could be facing serious charges. The best thing you can do for yourself is come with me to see the FBI agent."

She stared up at him, a flicker of comprehension in her eyes. He could feel her muscles relax beneath his grip, and he began guiding her—half pulling her—through the trees to the pickup. There was a mixture of reluctance and resignation in the way she slid onto the passenger seat. He shut the door behind her, then walked around and got in behind the wheel. Leaning sideways, his shoulder crammed against the window, he pulled the keys from his jacket pocket and jiggled the ignition a couple of times before the engine coughed into life. Then he reached past her and dragged his cell out from beneath the piles of papers in the glove compartment. He pressed in the number for Gianelli's office. It took a moment before the buzzing noise started in his ears.

"No," she said, grappling for the door handle. "I can't go to the FBI."

"You've reached the offices of . . ."

"Two people are dead, Christine," he said over the recorded message. "I don't see that you have a choice."

The woman pushed down on the handle and spilled outside. A burst of cool air filled up the cab. "I'm with Christine Loftus," Father John told the answering machine. "She's at an old log cabin west of Black Mountain." The cell was clicking in and out. He wasn't sure if he'd gotten through.

He hit the off button, tossed the phone onto the dashboard, and went after the woman. She was about a dozen yards ahead, weaving like a drunk down the tracks left by the pickup. He sprinted to catch up. When he tried to take her arm, she jerked away and turned on him. "That was a rotten thing to do."

"What did you do, Christine? Try to sell the photographs of a murder?"

She gave a shout of laughter, the sound cutting through the wind. "For a few thousand dollars? What good would that do me?" She swung around and took off running into the trees.

Father John stared after her, feeling as if the images were flashing across a screen dropped in front of him. Images of glass plates made by Curtis were worth more than a few thousand dollars.

He cut a diagonal path through the trees and came out ahead of her. When she tried to duck past, he took hold of her shoulders, surprised at how small and fragile she was. He loosened his grip. It took so little to hold on to her. "You tried to sell the glass plates to Senator Evans," he said. "You wanted to blackmail him."

"Why don't you talk to the FBI if you know everything?"

"Who did you go to? Quinn? Russell? Which one of the senator's people?"

"The senator's people? We went to the great man himself." She looked away, as if the realization had hit her that she'd said too much. She started tossing her head about, like a wild animal looking for an escape route. A couple of seconds passed before she looked back at him, her face glowing white in the moonlight. "What difference does it make?" she asked.

He could feel her beginning to fold, as if she might fall to the ground. He kept hold of one shoulder and threw his other arm around her to hold her upright. "Take it easy," he said.

She drew in a stuttering breath. Then she said, "T.J. called the senator's office and left a message that there was material on the reservation he might be interested in. The senator understood. He called back within the hour. Said he'd be at the ranch the next day. T.J. made copies of the photos, and we gave them to the senator, but it wasn't necessary. The senator knew about the photos. The family has been trying to get them for a hundred years. Well, we gave him the opportunity. One million dollars. A fair price, don't you think?"

"He agreed to pay you?"

"For the photographs and the glass negatives. He didn't want any more Indians trying to get money out of his family. He said he wanted to be done with it. We set up the exchange with Evans's people for Monday night, behind Great Plains Hall. The place will be deserted, T.J. said. I waited fifteen minutes, but no one came. So I went to T.J.'s He was there. He was a wreck. Disoriented almost incoherent. It took me a while to get it out of him that Denise was in the bedroom. Dead."

Christine lifted her head, her nostrils flaring for air. "T.J. said he'd gone home to get the photographs and negatives, but they weren't there. He said that Evans must have sent his people to find the evidence, so he wouldn't have to part with any of his precious money. Evans was ruthless, and whoever he'd sent had left us a message by killing Denise. T.J. said I should go and stay at the log cabin until he figured out what to do."

"They didn't find the photos and plates," Father John

said. "They ransacked your apartment looking for them."

"I never had them."

"Where are they?"

"Don't you understand?" She lifted a fist and hammered against his chest. "They belonged to her. Denise! She'd kept them in the shed behind the house for years. T.J. showed them to me. If Evans didn't get them, then she must've taken them. She must have put them somewhere else."

They didn't know, he was thinking. Quinn and Russell didn't know where the evidence was. They had tortured and killed T.J. and searched the house. They were still looking.

Dear God. They were looking for Christine.

"Look." He nodded toward the headlights jumping across the ground in the distance.

Everything about her seemed to freeze. She stared at the lights. "Eric!" she said in a whisper, dry and breathless.

32

CHRISTINE TURNED ABRUPTLY and started running toward the pickup. Her boots kicked up little dust clouds that hung in the air behind her before settling onto the ground.

Father John glanced around at the shafts of light bearing down on him, riding high. The pickup could never outdistance an SUV.

He darted through the lights. "Wait," he shouted. The SUV's engine thrummed behind, the tires scraping the ground. "We can't outrun them." He came up beside her and reached for her arm.

"Let me go." She slapped his hand away and kept going.

He threw another glance over his shoulder. Still coming on. Not more than thirty yards away now, the headlights sweeping the ground between them. He caught up to Christine again, and this time he threw both arms around her shoulders, pulling her to him. "Listen to me," he said. "Go to the cabin and lock yourself in. I'm going to get the cell and try to call the police. Do you understand?"

"Eric's here." It came in a quick expulsion of breath. "He'll make me come with him." In the moonlight splashing across her face, he could see the raw, animal terror. She was breaking into pieces in his hands. "I'll kill myself first," she said.

"Try to hold yourself together." He gripped her shoulders hard and shook her a little in an effort to bring her back into one piece. "Run through the trees. I'll meet you at the cabin. We can bolt the door. We'll be safe there."

He had to move her sideways to steer her into the direction of the cabin. "Go," he shouted, nudging her forward. He followed her with his eyes for a second to make sure she was on course. Something must have snapped together in her, because she started running full out, dodging through the trees, until she was nothing more than a dark, moving shadow.

The headlights splaying around him were brighter, the engine revving up as the SUV plunged forward. The gap between them was closing. He started zigzagging toward the pickup's taillights shining red through the trees, the headlights still behind, tracking his shadow. Left. Right. He yanked open the door and swept his hand over the dashboard for the hard plastic of the cell, then spotted the glint of metal on the floor. The SUV's headlights swept over the pickup again as he grabbed the phone and pushed it into his jacket pocket.

He could hear the vehicle grind to a halt behind him as he headed into the trees, picking his way by the moonlight falling through the branches. A car door slammed, then another. Sharp cracks in the brittle air. As he veered left, he caught sight of the waving light of a flashlight skimming across the ground and, behind the light, two dark shadows.

God! Whoever they were, they would follow his tracks straight to the cabin.

He kept moving, his eyes searching for a fallen branch. There was nothing except the little mounds of underbrush. Then, blue-tinged in the moonlight ahead, a broken branch dipping to the ground, sprays of smaller branches on the end. He plunged forward, grabbed the branch and started twisting. The bark tore into his hands. He kept twisting until, finally, the stalk broke free, almost throwing him off balance. He turned and ran back the way he'd come, a good twenty feet, then started forward again, dragging the branch behind until his tracks disappeared into a smooth carpet of pine needles, twigs, and brush.

The flashlight was bobbing to his left now but it would turn right any minute, following his own back-

and-forth trail until it ended. But the smoke—God, the smoke wafted like a cloud through the trees. They would follow the smoke.

The gunshot, when it came, was like a burst of thunder, echoing through the trees, shaking the earth.

Father John dropped the branch. There was a rifle in the cabin. A rifle and Christine. He sprinted for the cabin, his heart beating in his ears. No. No. No. Dear Lord, no. Don't let it be.

He burst into the small clearing, mounted the step to the porch, and grabbed for the latch. It held fast. "Christine," he shouted. Then he was pounding the door with both fists, muffled thuds that reverberated around him. "Christine. Christine."

Another gunshot cracked the air, and this time he realized that it came from the trees. Father John started moving across the porch toward the sound, staying close to the wall, the logs scraping the sleeve of his jacket. He reached the corner and stopped, straining to hear the sound of footsteps, the snap of a branch under boots.

Silence.

He leaned out a couple of inches and peered around the stone chimney. Nothing but gray layers of moonlight on the ground, and beyond, the black line of the trees positioned like guards.

"Turn around, Father O'Malley."

They were behind him. They'd come around the far side of the cabin while he'd been inching toward the chimney. He gripped the porch railing.

"It looks like I was correct in assuming that the sound

of gunshots would bring you to us." The voice was closer.

Father John pushed himself off the railing and turned around. Planted in front of the porch step, in black overcoats, were two men: Martin Quinn, with the short, narrow build of a boy; and Paul Russell, tall and beefy, looming over his boss. It was Russell who held the gun, and in Quinn's hands, a flashlight the size of a truncheon.

"Haven't you done enough for the senator?" Father John said, surprised by the calm confidence in his voice. His muscles were tense, his hands curled into fists.

"There is one more task that must be completed," Quinn said. "And you, Father O'Malley, have lent your assistance and led us to the woman."

"You followed me here?"

"One might say that." A laugh gurgled out of the man. "Your assistant insisted we go to the museum and have another look at the Curtis exhibit. The woman whom you'd placed in charge after Christine Loftus made her unfortunate disappearance informed us that we had just missed you. She said you'd gone to an old log cabin looking for Christine. Naturally, we said we would like to be of help, and she was kind enough to give us the directions."

"Christine doesn't have the photographs." Father John didn't move.

"Is that what she tells you?" Quinn shook his head, as if he were sadly disappointed. "I suspect the photographs and negatives are hidden here—in a log cabin in no man's land." Now the man emitted a shout of laughter, and the bulky man behind him laughed, too, mimicking his boss. The gun jumped in his hand.

"Very clever, I must admit. No one would think to look here. I'm sure that T.J. Painted Horse and Christine Loftus"—another laugh, like a grunt—"an unlikely pair of criminals, wouldn't you agree? I'm sure they convinced themselves they had found the perfect hiding place."

"How many people are you willing to kill, Quinn?"

"The saga ends here," the man said. "Senator Evans has lived long enough with this Damocles sword hanging over his head, never knowing when some crazy Indian will try to blackmail him and threaten to publish photographs that would do nothing except damage the name of a very fine family and stop a good man from becoming the next president."

"You killed Denise, didn't you? Then you waited for T.J. and killed him."

The man shrugged and jammed his hands into his coat pockets. "Regrettable incidences, I'm afraid. There's no end of fools on the reservation. Whenever Jaime Evans decides to run for another office, Indians start thinking the Evans family owes them." He pulled his lips back into a sneer. "Now this white woman sticks her nose into this, and we have a new equation, do we not? Now we have a white woman with connections. If the senator refuses to pay her, she would know how to do the maximum amount of damage. We can't let that happen, can we? Tell the woman inside to let you in."

"And if I refuse?"

"Merely delaying the inevitable." Quinn motioned to

the man behind him, waving him forward. "Shoot the latch," he said.

Russell stepped onto the porch, moved close to the door, and pointed the gun at the latch. The shock of the bullet slamming into metal and wood ran along the floorboards. The door seemed to come unhinged, swinging inward, like a gate blowing in the wind.

"Ah . . ." Quinn began, the look of satisfaction moving across the thin face.

The blast sounded like a cannon. It burst through the swinging door, splintering the wood that dropped in shards onto the floor. Then another blast, and another. Everything was moving in slow motion—an old black-and-white film reeling itself out at half speed. The bulky man lifted off his feet, blown back across the step, his head pushed into the ground. And Quinn, behind him, staring down at the other man's prone body, shock and horror replacing the satisfaction on his face.

Still another blast, this one lifting the small man into the air where he seemed to hang a moment before crumpling backward. Blood, pooling around the bodies, ran black on the ground.

It was a moment before Christine appeared, still gripping the rifle, caressing it almost, like something that made her safe and secure.

"Eric?" She pivoted toward Father John.

"He's not here, Christine." He had to force his gaze away from the barrel pointing at him and meet the woman's eyes. "There's no one else here."

It took a moment for this to register, for the frozen fear in her eyes to begin to melt into comprehension. She turned toward the men at her feet, lined up one after the other, like a path leading from the porch toward the trees. "They shouldn't have come here," she said.

Father John started toward her, his eyes riveted to the gun. His muscles felt glued together. "They were the ones in the SUV," he said. The voice of a priest, a counselor. "Eric isn't here. You're okay." Calm. Calm. "I'm going to take the rifle now, because you don't need it anymore."

She seemed to tighten her grasp on the barrel, pulling it into her chest.

"You don't need the gun anymore," he repeated. "Not anymore." A mantra that he hoped would sound in her head. *Not anymore. Not anymore.*

Was the muzzle dipping toward the floor, or was he only imagining that it was true? He waited another moment, then reached out and grabbed hold of the barrel. A second passed, two seconds—a lifetime—before he felt the barrel start to give.

He lifted the gun out of her hands. "Let's go inside."

She stared at him a moment, then turned and walked into the cabin. He stayed behind her. Dropping onto the bench across from the door, she said, "Are they dead?"

"I think so." Past the shattered door, across the porch, he could see the black holes gaping in the men's chests, the pools of blood widening on the ground.

"I'll be right back," he told her. Then he went back out and walked across the porch. He leaned around and set the rifle in the dark corner between the log wall and the stone chimney.

He pulled his cell out of his jacket pocket as he came

back inside. Christine was bent over, arms crossed, hugging herself and bobbing up and down. "What have I done, Father. God, what have I done?"

He straddled the bench he'd pulled out into the center of the room earlier and punched in 911, keeping his gaze on the bobbing woman. The operator—a female voice—picked up on the second ring, and he told her that he was Father O'Malley, from St. Francis Mission. Two men named Martin Quinn and Paul Russell had been shot at the old log cabin near Black Mountain. They should send cars right away.

"There's a car in the vicinity. Do you need an ambulance?"

"Yes," he said, his eyes still on Christine. Then he told the operator to notify Gianelli.

Before he'd hit the off key, he heard the scratching noise outside. Christine had heard it, too, because she shrank backward and stiffened against the walls, as if she could disappear into the logs.

The noise stopped. The quiet seemed more intense, a noise unto itself. Then the scratching again, footsteps coming closer.

An animal, Father John thought, then dismissed the idea. The footsteps of an animal lacked the purpose, the *willed* deliberation, of the noise outside. He got up, leaned toward the woman, and whispered: "Wait here. I'll see who it is." Then he stepped over to the shattered door and peered out into the moonlight streaming like a banner across the porch and over the prone bodies. At the end of the light, a bulky shadow bent over the lifeless head of Martin Quinn, then, coming closer, stooped to look into the face of Paul Russell.

"Well, what do we have here, Father O'Malley?" Eric Loftus stepped around the bodies and came up onto the porch.

33

VICKY LOOKED DOWN at the headlights streaming through the gray light of Main Street, struggling to rein in the surge of impatience as Gianelli, stationed at his desk behind her, delivered a summation of what she'd spent the last thirty minutes laying out. Photographs of a hundred-year-old murder committed by Senator Evans's grandfather, which proved how the Evans family had obtained a ranch floating on a lake of oil.

Vicky heard the skepticism running through the summation and steeled herself for what was bound to come next: Granted, Senator Evans wouldn't like the scandal if the photos became public. It would be embarrassing, but it would hardly derail his career. Face it, Vicky, nobody cares about a hundred-year-old murder.

She turned and faced the man leaning back in a swivel chair, gaze fastened at the stacks of papers covering his desk, feet propped between the stacks. "What about the murder of Denise's cousin twelve years ago?" she said.

"Okay. Okay." Gianelli swung his feet to the floor, lifted his bulky frame out of the chair, and walked over to the file cabinets. After thumbing through the files in the top drawer, he yanked one free, then sat back down. He opened the folder and stared at the top page. "October twenty-three, nineteen-ninety-two, the body of Lester Brave Wolf was found on the banks of the Little Wind River. Homicide victim. Shot in the head . . ."

"He was executed," Vicky said. The moccasin telegraph had reached all the way to the Denver law firm where she had just started working, and with the gossip had come the current of fear pulsating through the reservation. "The murder was never solved."

"Not for lack of trying." The fed studied another page, then snapped the folder shut. "We just didn't have the evidence, Vicky."

"Lester was part of the Sharp Nose family," Vicky said, fighting back another surge of impatience. "Evans was elected to the Senate that November. If the photographs had been made public, Indians in Wyoming would have turned out to vote against him. He would have been defeated."

"Photographs," Gianelli said, tapping the folder. "Where the hell are these photographs? All you're giving me is a grandiose theory."

Vicky turned back to the window a moment. For an instant, headlights refracted in the black glass like a burst of fireworks.

"I don't know where they are," she said, locking eyes again with Gianelli.

"Maybe they don't exist, Vicky. Maybe they're just figments of the imagination, black-and-white pictures in your head. Maybe they're part of an Arapaho legend about how the Evans family got the ranch."

The fed leaned forward and thumped the folder with his fist. "I have to see the photographs. Otherwise they aren't real. None of this is real. Do you know what would happen if I involved Senator Evans in a murder investigation? In five minutes, I'd be packing my bag for a new assignment on the Bering Strait, and you know how long the nights are up there?"

"The photographs exist, Ted. They belonged to Denise." She could feel the truth of it. She could almost see the black-and-white images of Carston Evans, rifle lowered, and Bashful Woman crumpled onto the ground. She walked over and sat down on the other side of the desk. "Christine Loftus must have taken them. It would explain why she disappeared, wouldn't it?"

The phone had started ringing, but the fed kept his eyes on hers a long moment, as if he were allowing for the possibility. Finally he stretched his hand across the stacks of papers and picked up the receiver.

"Special Agent Ted Gianelli," he said, turning his gaze toward the window.

There was a long pause before he blurted out, "I'm leaving now." He hung up and got to his feet. "Seems that Father John found Christine at Black Mountain. Police just got a call that two people were shot . . ."

"Shot!" Vicky jumped up. She clasped the edge of the desk, trying to stop the room from closing around her, choking off the air.

"Take it easy, Vicky," Gianelli came around the desk and took her arm. She felt a wave of gratitude for the strength in his hand. "John reported the shootings," he said.

She heard the sharp exhalation of her own breath, like the sound of air escaping from a punctured tire.

God, what was wrong with her?

She made herself turn toward the man beside her. He knew, she thought. Everyone knew. "Who, then?" she asked, summoning the most lawyerly tone she could manage.

"The coroner hasn't identified . . ."

"Tell me, Ted."

"Martin Quinn and Paul Russell."

Vicky swallowed hard against the shout of triumph erupting inside her. "There's an old cabin at Black Mountain. Christine must have been hiding there, and Evans's men came after the photographs."

"I have to go," Gianelli said.

"I'm going, too."

The agent was already pulling on the leather jacket that had been draped over a hanger on the back of the door. "I'll call you tomorrow and give you an update."

"T.J. was my client, Ted. He was killed for the photographs. I want to know what happened out there." Vicky grabbed her coat from the back of the chair and followed the agent through the door and across the dimly lit entry to the stairway down to the street.

"THIS ISN'T YOUR business, Loftus." Father John stepped out onto the porch. "The police are on the way. Unless you want to be part of an investigation into a double shooting, I'd suggest you leave."

"Who pulled the trigger, Padre? You or my wife?" The man tossed his head forward like a bronco coming out of a chute, and for an instant, Father John thought that the man intended to crash past him into the cabin.

Father John didn't move, and this seemed to cause the other man to reconsider. He glanced around at the bodies. "Who are they?"

"They worked for Senator Evans."

Loftus threw his head back and let out a shout of glee. "Ah," he said. "The picture is clear. My wife got herself mixed up with the Indian councilman who didn't like the idea of the senator and his good buddies drilling for methane gas on the rez. T.J. Painted Horse threatened to make trouble when the senator paid his visit, so the senator invoked the old code of the West: Shoot your enemy and ask questions later." He stopped, his gaze still running over the prone bodies. "What was Christine? A witness when they shot the councilman's wife? Oh, it's making sense now. She's been hiding out, just like I taught her. 'Go to ground when things get hot,' I said. 'Get yourself supplies and hole up where nobody's gonna come looking for you.' I got it right, don't I, Padre," he said, looking back.

"Part of it." Coming through the night from far away was the faint wailing of a siren.

"Well, here's the rest," Loftus said. "My wife's not mixed up with the deaths of anybody connected to Senator Evans. She wasn't here, you understand? You can tell the police what you want, but Christine's coming with me. Maybe she was staying at the cabin for a few days, but she left before this happened, and I'm gonna swear to it. You see, she was with me all evening."

"How are you going to explain her fingerprints on the rifle?"

Loftus ran a tongue along the inside of one cheek, so

that the skin poked out like a sudden swelling. "Well, I'm gonna have to dump the rifle where it's never gonna be found." He tossed his head back, as if he'd finally heard the sirens swelling behind the line of trees. "Maybe you don't understand," he went on, a conciliatory tone now. "My wife is bipolar. That means days of extreme euphoria where she believes herself all powerful, capable of hanging the moon. Then she crashes and spends weeks in bed curled in a fetal position. Do you hear what I'm saying? She's not responsible for what happened here. She could not stand up to a trial. It would destroy her."

"Your wife won't stand trial. She shot both men in self-defense."

"Ah, self-defense. Of course. She'd been hiding from them, and when they arrived . . ."

"She thought it was you."

This stopped the man, as if he'd taken a punch in the solar plexus. He rocked back on his heels and tossed his head sideways. The sirens were loud and distinct now, arrows of noise piercing the darkness.

Loftus steadied himself. "You're as crazy as she is," he said. "Get out of the way."

"You won't get more than thirty yards before you're stopped. Then Christine will have to explain why she left."

"I'm taking my wife."

"She doesn't want to go with you." The sirens were filling the air around them, and headlights jittered over the ground.

"You gonna stop me?"

Father John tightened his hands into fists. "Maybe we'll have to find out."

The sirens cut off, leaving a vacuum that absorbed all sound, apart from the short, quick, gasps of the man standing a few feet away, his face contorted by shadows and rage. Then, car doors slammed shut, and footsteps scraped the ground. "Over here," a man's voice shouted.

"Your wife's in shock," Father John said. "If you care about her, you'll let the medics look after her."

A second passed before the rage in the other man's face began to give way to something that was even more disturbing. "Okay," he said finally. "I'm gonna let you have this one, but only because I'm thinking about Christine. She'll get better again, then she'll want to come home where she belongs."

VICKY KEPT HER eyes on the headlights bouncing over the tire tracks that flared across the asphalt ahead. Gianelli was ahead in the darkness somewhere. The sky was cloudless, suffused with the pale-gray light of a moon that looked as if it were plunging toward the line of trees that ran alongside the road. *Look at the moon sideways,* grandmother said. *You can see the face of a white man.*

Vicky eased on the brake, watching for the turn-off ahead. A half mile, and she pulled onto the two-track and bounced across the hard ground toward the glow of light swelling through the trees. When the two-track disappeared into clumps of grass, she kept going. Ahead was a cluster of vehicles—red, blue, and yellow lights flashing in the trees like bursting firecrackers. She pulled in behind one of the police cars, threw herself out the door, and started past the vehicles toward the log cabin.

Dark figures were milling about the porch, ducking in and out, merging into little groups before dissolving back into the shadows. Two of the figures were bent over humps that trailed down the porch step and out onto the ground. One of the figures straightened up and started toward the ambulance parked halfway between the cabin and the trees. She recognized Gianelli.

John O'Malley was nowhere.

Then she spotted him, the tall man in the cowboy hat standing at the back of the ambulance. Through the opened doors she could see two medics hovering over someone on the gurney. She felt John O'Malley's eyes on her as she walked over.

"Are you all right?" she asked when she was still a few feet away.

He nodded. "They're looking after Christine."

Vicky was aware of the enormous sense of relief, like a warm wind wafting over her, at the sight of him and the sound of his voice. She did not want to imagine a world without John O'Malley.

It was a moment before she noticed the bulky figure of another man on the other side of the ambulance. He raised one hand and bent into the cigarette clasped in his fingers. A red bullet of light flared and faded, then flared again.

"Loftus found her?" Vicky could barely expel the words. She kept hoping the answer was no, even when

Father John gave her a quick nod yes.

"What happened?" she asked.

"Suppose you tell me, John." Gianelli's voice came from the right, and Vicky realized that the fed had planted himself beside her with hardly a disturbance in the air.

Father John was quiet a moment, then—his voice low—he began explaining that Russell had fired at the door. Christine was inside, and she'd fired back, hitting both men. And as he explained, Vicky struggled to fight back the panic crashing over her like the wind and blotting out the scream in her mind: *You could have been killed!*

"So all this over some old photos." Gianelli sounded resigned, as if he already knew and only needed the confirmation.

Vicky tried again to focus on what John O'Malley was saying: How T.J. and Christine had offered not only photographs but original glass plates to the senator for a million dollars, how the exchange was supposed to take place Monday night, and how Quinn and Russell had gone to T.J.'s house intending to take the photographs and plates.

"Denise happened to be there." The agent was shaking his head. "It probably went down the way you'd guessed, John. The poor woman had convinced them that T.J. had removed the photos and plates to keep them safe. They believed her. After all, she was pleading for her life. After they shot her, they decided T.J. must have given them to Christine."

One of the medics jumped out of the ambulance and

righted himself against the door. "We've got to take her to Riverton Memorial," he said.

Looming behind the medic was Eric Loftus, smoke pouring from his nostrils and a cigarette glowing in his fingers. "I'll take custody of my wife now," he said. "I know what's best for her when she hits bottom."

Gianelli stepped forward, and as he did so, the medic dodged to the side. "I can arrest your wife," he said, moving in until he was in Loftus's face. "I can arrest her on charges of double homicide and take her into the custody of the federal government."

"She's guilty of nothing other than protecting her own life." Loftus gestured with his head toward Father John. "Here's your witness."

Gianelli didn't move. "Your choice, man."

Loftus didn't say anything. The ambulance doors snapped shut. The engine kicked over and the vehicle began inching forward, then made a tight turn through the scrub brush and trees and headed toward the two-track.

"I intend to interview your wife as soon as she's able," Gianelli said.

"Not without my lawyer, Howie Forman. Heard of him? He'll be in touch." Loftus took another drag of his cigarette, then turned around and started toward the pickup wedged between two police cars.

Gianelli kept his gaze on the man lumbering through the shadows. "So he's going to lawyer-up with Howie Forman," he said, under his breath. "Celebrity gun-for-hire. Specializes in keeping the rich and famous out of prison."

Vicky glanced away. When she was in law school, she'd gone to the courthouse to watch Forman at work. Short and bald with the round face and tortoiseshell glasses of a professor and a pleasant, unassuming demeanor. But in the courtroom he turned into something else—a rattlesnake, she remembered thinking at the time, with a pink tongue darting at the opponents, inflicting its fatal poison. He was good. God, he was a good lawyer.

"No telling what big guns the senator's going to bring in now that his campaign people have been killed," Gianelli was saying. He shifted toward Father John. "Christine Loftus tell you about the Curtis photos and plates?"

"She doesn't have them."

"Ah, that's what the wife of Eric Loftus told you, is it? Photographs and glass plates that might bring her a million dollars, if she plays her cards right and avoids whatever mistakes she and T.J. made on the first attempt at extortion. Maybe she hid them. Biding her time until the senator might be more receptive, perhaps after he gets the party's nomination. When Russell fired at the door, she let them have it, rather than take a chance on their finding her hiding place."

"I don't think so," Father John said.

"No? Well, indulge me, John. We're going to tear up every floorboard in that old cabin. We're going to look in all the nooks and crannies and check the ground for any signs of disturbance, in case she decided to bury them. Christine Loftus came this far, and for the moment, I'm going to assume that she might be willing to go a lot further." He stared after the ambulance threading its way through the trees, headlights jumping ahead. "Tomorrow morning, my office, John. I'm going to need all the details. Go home now, both of you," he said, shifting his glance between Father John and Vicky. "There's nothing you can do here."

"Come on," Father John said, and Vicky felt the weight of his arm around her shoulders. "I'll walk you to the Jeep."

They'd cut through a clump of trees and emerged in the clearing where the vehicles were parked when she glanced up at him. "Evans will claim total ignorance of everything that happened, you know," she said. "He'll say that Quinn and Russell feared for his safety on the rez after T.J. denounced the senator's drilling plans."

Father John didn't say anything, and she pushed on, reeling out the story: "He'll say they must have gone to T.J.'s house to discuss their concerns over the senator's safety. He'll say they were worried—and rightly so—that T.J. blamed the senator for Denise's death. After all, T.J.'s people wouldn't have turned against him if it hadn't been for the senator's determination to open the rez to the drilling. He'll say that an argument must have broken out with T.J. and somehow—oh, Evans will regret it very much—his campaign advisers lost their heads and committed a heinous crime. He'll be shocked by the brutality. He won't have any idea of why Quinn and Russell had later gone to the cabin unless, again, it was out of concern for the senator's safety. After all, Christine Loftus was T.J.'s mistress and might have been in on any plans to harm the senator."

294

"They came to the cabin with a gun, Vicky," Father John said. His hand tightened on her shoulder.

"They were overzealous, loyal to a fault. The senator will very much regret the unnecessary deaths, but he won't be able to duck the fact that he'd hired psychopaths to manage his campaign. There'll probably be a Senate investigation that will embarrass Evans. It will probably stop his bid for the presidency, but he'll come back to his ranch and live like the local baron. He'll go on, John, just like Carston Evans went on."

When they reached the Jeep, Father John opened the door and she slid behind the wheel. "The plates and photos could still be found," he said. "And if they are, Bashful's murder will be brought to light."

Vicky jabbed the key into the ignition and listened to the motor whir for a moment. "You're wrong, John," she said. "They'll sink back into the reservation until somebody else in the Sharp Nose clan decides he can force the Evans family to repay a small part of what they stole. He'll approach the senator, and another body will turn up on the riverbank with a gunshot to the head."

Vicky started to close the door, but it remained rigid. She looked up at John O'Malley. He was staring out across the top of the Jeep into the moonlight and the darkness beyond. "You know where they are, don't you?"

"I have an idea," he said.

34

October 1907

JESSE GALLOPED DOWN the dirt road, his eyes on the cluster of squat buildings that interrupted the horizon ahead. The pony's hooves kicked up clouds of dust that rose around him and pricked his hands and clung to the sweat on his face. His mouth was gritty with dust. He turned the pony into the dirt yard and rode past the big house, past the cabin where Bashful had lived with Auntie Sara, past the storage shed. He reined in at the barn, jumped down, and unbuckled the saddle bag.

Stands-Alone appeared in the doorway, a pitchfork in one hand. He wore a brown shirt that hung over denim trousers. His hair was caught in braids wrapped with red ribbon and tiny feathers. He had on tiny, wireless spectacles that, on his broad face, looked like glass coins set over his eyes.

"Why do you ride in here like the whirlwind?" he asked.

"I got the proof of Bashful's murder." Jesse held up the saddlebag like an offering.

"What are you talking about."

Jesse lifted the leather flap, yanked out the sheets with the blue images, and thrust them at Stands-Alone. "I made the cyanotypes first," he said.

Inside the barn, Jesse saw a shadow move. Then Thomas stepped into the light. Almost as large as his father, but with a narrower face and a receding jaw that made him look weak and untrustworthy despite his broad shoulders and thick hands. "What is this?" He nodded at the cyanotypes.

Stands-Alone gripped the sheets in both hands, his gaze frozen on the top image. "It is as we suspected," he said. "The white man killed Bashful." He slipped the top sheet behind the stack and stared at the next, then the next.

"These are blue images." Thomas bent his head around his father's shoulder. "They are not clear."

"These are clear." Jesse took three white sheets of paper from the saddlebag. "The agent will not trust the blue pictures, but he will have to trust these images." He handed Stands-Alone the three black-and-white photographs that he had made after he'd realized what was in the cyanotypes. In the first image, the white man held his rifle close to Bashful. The next image showed Bashful falling backward. In the last image, Bashful lay in a heap on the ground, Carston Evans looming over her.

"The photographer captured the moment Bashful died," Jesse said, freeing the plates from the saddlebag. "The moment is here . . ." He held up the plates, struck by the sorrow moving through Stands-Alone's eyes. The sorrow would be there forever, he knew, like the images on the plates.

"Where did you find these things?" Stands-Alone dropped his eyes back to the photographs and cyanotypes in his hands.

"The photographer left the glass plates in the cabin with some of his chemicals and papers. I figured he left them for her people. He meant for me to find them and make the pictures, so we'd know the truth. I made the cyanotypes yesterday. This morning I printed the photographs to show the agent." He drew in a stream of air. "We must gather the men. There must be many of us to take this proof to the agent. Otherwise he will say that he does not believe the truth that his own eyes can see. We must ride to Fort Washakie with our weapons and demand that the agent allow Thunder and the others to return to their families."

Thomas let out a loud guffaw. "You come too late."

Jesse felt the moment freeze, as if the sun had stopped in the sky and the air had turned into a solid mass that he could not breathe in. "What do you say?" he managed.

Stands-Alone lifted his eyes blurred with grief. "Last night the train brought the executioner. Thunder, Pretty Lodge, and Franklin—they were all hanged this morning."

"No!" Jesse shouted. "The hanging is tomorrow. Tomorrow. Tomorrow."

"I tell you," Stands-Alone said, "the moment of the execution has come and gone. It is no more."

Thomas moved forward. "What makes you think the agent would've believed these pictures? Against the word of a white man?" He let out a loud guffaw. "The agent would've sicced the soldiers on us if we rode into Fort Washakie with these pictures."

Jesse swung around, walked back to the pony, and leaned his head into the warmth of the animal's neck. What Thomas said was true. The photographs and the images on the glass plates—what were they? Nothing next to the word of the white man.

He turned back to the men in the doorway, the shadows dropping over their faces. "I must kill the white man," he said.

"So you can also hang at Fort Washakie?" It took Jesse by surprise—the calmness in Stands-Alone's voice. It pulled the air out of him.

"She was your sister," he said. "You should come with me to revenge her."

"I will come," Thomas said. "The white man has taken Bashful's land. We will take it back."

"There will be many hangings." Stands-Alone faced his son. "You are hotheaded, and you have much to learn. Let the white man keep the land." He waved the photographs in Thomas's face, then turned to Jesse. "She is dead, Jesse. Killing the white man will not bring her back to us, but part of Bashful lives. We will use this evidence to make an agreement with the white man. We will take what is important."

FROM THE GATE at the road to the ranch house, Jesse could see Carston Evans on the porch of the two-story house, rifle raised, head bent alongside the stock. Jesse spurred the pony forward, his eye on the rifle barrel. It held steady in the white man's hands. Stands-Alone rode to the right, and out of the corner of his eye Jesse could see the head of Thomas's horse coming up on the far side of his father.

As they neared the house, Stands-Alone began to rein in, stopping in front of the white man. "We come in peace," he shouted.

"Turn around and ride out of here." Now the rifle was waving back and forth, moving from Stands-Alone to Thomas to Jesse. The white man was smaller than he remembered, Jesse thought, not much larger than a branch that he could snap in two. Jesse swallowed hard at the rage welling inside him. He could kill the white man with his hands.

"We came to talk," Stands-Alone said.

"Nothing to talk about. The woman's dead, and her killers gone with her. There's no more business between us."

"Put down your rifle. We bring you images of Bashful."

"Images?" The white man looked up. "You talking about photographs?"

Stands-Alone sat like a statute and waited. A moment passed before the white man stepped back and set the rifle against the log wall of the house.

"Let me have them," Evans said.

Jesse felt hot inside, the rage burning through him. He made himself look away from the white man. He was a warrior, and Stands-Alone was the leading man. He would do as Stands-Alone said. The signal came in the almost imperceptible nod—the nod of a chief to the men who rode with him.

Jesse slid from the pony and pried the cyanotypes from his saddlebag. He walked past Stands-Alone's pony and handed the blue-and-white images to the white man.

It was a moment before the white man let his eyes

fasten on them. His face was unreadable, like a sheet of blank paper, as he studied the images. "This ain't nothing," he said. "Nobody's gonna believe ghost images."

"Everyone will believe these." Jesse pulled out the black-and-white photos and handed them to Evans.

The man looked at them for a long moment, then he raised his head and threw a glance back at the rifle. "What would stop me from shooting you and taking these photographs?"

Jesse could hear his heart thumping in his ears. They should have brought their own weapons, but Stands-Alone had said that they would go unarmed. They had the weapons they needed, he'd said.

"You could shoot us," Stands-Alone's voice again, calm and confident, "but it is not necessary. We bring you the photographs as a gift."

"What about the glass plates."

"They are also yours."

The white man tilted his head and stared at Stands-Alone out of the corners of his eyes, as if he might get a clearer, better image. Finally he said, "I never knew any Indians to come bearing gifts for nothing. You want the land back, ain't that so? Well, you ain't getting my land. It's my land, the way it oughtta be. Bashful never worked this land. She was nothing but a woman, and what's a woman gonna do with land like this? I'm the one who fixed up this house with my own hands. I got the herd together. Got the best bull in the county. Got the ranch up and going, and all the time I was nothing but a hired hand. It was Bashful who owned the place, and when she told me she didn't want me for her husband no more, that she wanted to go back to her people, oh, I knew the truth. She was still pining over Jesse here. Would've gone running to him, taking her land to him. And where was that gonna leave me? All my work, and for what?" He gathered up a wad of phlegm and spit it onto the ground. "For nothing, that's what."

He stepped back and, still watching Stands-Alone, reached for the rifle.

"You can keep the land," Stands-Alone said.

"Don't think I don't know what you're up to." The white man lifted the rifle, crumpled the cyanotypes and photos in the fist of his other hand and stuffed them into his trouser pocket. "You come here to kill me. You're gonna take your Indian revenge. Well, I got myself the perfect excuse for shooting first."

"I tell you, you can keep the land," Stands-Alone said. "You will have the plates. All of the proof of your shame is yours. We have come for Bashful's child. Where is she?"

The white man blinked up at Stands-Alone, who sat tall and dignified on his mount. A long moment passed before the white man set the rifle back against the wall. "You gotta be crazy," he said. Then he pushed the door open and yelled inside the house. "Pauline, get out here. Bring the girl."

A gust of wind blew across the porch and caught at the white man's hat so that he had to grab the brim and pull it down. From inside came the soft scrape of moccasins on wood, and then an Arapaho girl no more than ten years old appeared in the doorway. The daughter of

Shavehead, Jesse thought, one of the Arapahos who worked on the ranch. The girl must work in the house. She pulled a small child forward, then stooped over and lifted the child onto one hip, swaying with the weight.

The little girl blinked into the light before looking from the white man to Stands-Alone. She had the shiny black hair and oval face that made Jesse close his own eyes a moment. She was an image of Bashful. Except that she had light eyes, the color of finely tanned leather. The eyes of the white man. There was a mixture of confusion and fear in the child's eyes now, a glimmer of recognition and something else—longing?—as she stared at her uncle.

"You want her, do you?" Evans seemed to find the situation amusing. "A half-breed girl. What good's she gonna be to you?"

Stands-Alone leaned forward over the horse. "What good is she to you, white man? Will another wife—a white wife—want a half-breed daughter? You can have your own white children. Bashful's child belongs with her people."

Evans turned his head and gazed out into the distance, as if he were considering the images in his mind. White wife. White children.

He looked back. "I want everything. All the photographs and glass plates and anything else that you got. There will be no more about this matter, you hear me?"

Jesse waited again for Stands-Alone's nod before he walked back to the saddlebag. He began withdrawing the glass plates.

"Leave them," Evans barked. "I'll take the whole bag."

Jesse unbuckled the bag and clasped it against his chest a moment. The plates were all they had. They were the truth. They were everything.

He watched Stands-Alone slip off his pony and walk across the porch past the white man. He put out his arms and the child lunged into them. She wrapped small brown arms around the man's neck and nestled against his chest.

"The saddlebag." The white man stepped forward holding out his own arms.

Jesse held out the bag, the edge of the glass plates inside the leather hard against his palms. He waited until Stands-Alone had settled the child in the front of the saddle and swung up behind her before he let the white man take the bag. Starting to turn the pony now, Thomas turning his pony behind, shielding his father and the child. The ponies breaking into a gallop.

The white man had already turned back to the porch when Jesse brought his fist crashing against the man's head. He stumbled forward, and Jesse reached around and yanked the saddlebag free of the man's grasp.

He threw himself onto the pony and started galloping after the others, the images blurred in the whirlwinds of dust. From behind came the shrill shouts, like a wail of grief, followed by the thud of a rifle shot. Another shot and another, the bullets spitting into the ground around him.

He leaned down along the pony's head and grasped the saddle bag to his chest. He rode on.

They didn't stop until they reached Stands-Alone's place. Jesse dismounted, still clutching the saddle bag as

Stands-Alone carried the child to the house and handed her to the woman standing on the porch. Several other children clustered about, wide-eyed, giggling, small brown hands reaching for the new child.

Then Stands-Alone walked back and Jesse handed him the saddle bag. "I can make other photographs," he said.

"Yes, in time you will do so. Now we must hide this evidence. It must stay hidden until the time is right for the truth."

"The white man will come with the soldiers." Thomas was looking over at the porch. The woman had set down the child, and the other children had closed her within their circle, laughing and cooing, patting at the black head that bobbed among them. "He will say we stole his child. She is not worth the danger to us. We should have taken back the land."

Stands-Alone moved close to his son. "Do not be a fool. You must think like white men if you are to keep ahead of them. The white man has what he wants. He does not want the half-breed girl. If he comes with the soldiers, he knows that we will show them the evidence. He cannot take the chance that an officer would not believe the evidence." Stands-Alone paused. "Do you understand now? It is over."

35

ST. FRANCIS CEMETERY SPRAWLED across the top of a rise between the mission and Seventeen-Mile Road. It was a short walk up the bulge in the earth, but most of the people who had filled the church for the funeral Mass had piled into pickups and sedans and made the loop out of the mission and back into the cemetery. The vehicles were parked on the narrow dirt road that wound around the perimeter, and the crowd gathered together in a circle around the two coffins poised on gray straps over the open gravesites.

Last night, the people had filled Blue Sky Hall for the wake, crowding into the rows of folding metal chairs, standing along the walls, blocking the doors, and flowing outside into the parking lot. They had come from across the reservation, from Lander and Riverton—whites along with Arapahos—to pay respect to the councilman who had stood up to Senator Evans in the methane gas controversy. Even if they hadn't agreed with T.J. Painted Horse, they'd admired his courage. The courage that had gotten both the councilman and his wife killed.

Father John had led the prayers of the rosary, voices murmuring the responses in waves of sorrow flowing over the hall. Afterward, Max Oldman had blessed Denise's and T.J.'s bodies in the caskets. He placed the sacred red paint on their foreheads, cheeks, and hands. *"Go with the ancestors,"* he'd prayed. *"They will welcome you to the sky world. But we know that your spirits*

306

will always be with your people to help us."

Then Max had lifted the pan with the smoldering cottonwood chips and cedar and walked down the center aisle, allowing the smoke to waft across the hall, touching the faces turned toward him. Father John had felt the sense of peace that had moved through the hall.

Now he stood at the head of T.J.'s coffin, Father Damien beside him at the head of Denise's. They waited until the last knots of people had worked their way around the mounds of other graves and flowed into the rest of the crowd. The wind blew cold and sharp across the cemetery, flapping at the yellow, red, and purple plastic flowers that rose around the white wooden crosses on the dirt mounds. People shuffled about, moving in closer, tightening the circle around the coffins.

Father John opened the prayer book and began reciting the burial prayers: *"God, by Whose mercy rest is given to the souls of the faithful, in your kindness, bless these graves."* As he read, the other priest began sprinkling holy water over the coffins: first for Denise, then for T.J.

Father John glanced around the circle of brown faces pressing toward him, then went on: "Almighty and merciful God, take pity upon your people who carry a heavy burden of sorrow. Remove the anger and despair from our hearts, and let us not be consumed by grief and sorrow, as those who have no hope. Let us believe in You and in Your love for us."

Closing the prayer book, Father John turned to Max Oldman, standing gray-haired and stoop-shouldered beside Denise's coffin. The elder nodded, then made a slow circle, letting his gaze fall over the crowd. He cleared his throat and began speaking in Arapaho. Father John recognized the tone: formal and declaratory, the tone the chiefs had used in the Old Time to address the village. He closed his eyes and let the words roll over him. How many times had he heard the elders speak? How many funerals? He understood a few words, a phrase here and there. He knew what Max was saying.

"Jevaneatha nethaunainau. God is with us. Jevaneatha Dawathaw henechauchaunane nanadehe vedaw nau ichjeva. His spirit fills everywhere on earth and above us. Jevaneatha nenenadonee naideed. He has lived always. Jevaneatha nenaideed detjanee. He will live forever. Ha, adnauhawanau Jevaneatha ichjeva ith ithinauauk. Yes, those who are good will be with God in heaven."

The elder paused. No one moved. An air of expectation engulfed the crowd as he nodded to the musicians seated around the drum near the foot of the graves. The drumming and singing began, the high-pitched voices mingling with the sound of a truck out on Seventeen-Mile Road. When the song ended, the elder cleared his throat and let his eyes roam over the faces turned to him. "We ask the Creator and the ancestors to welcome our sister and brother, Denise and T.J. Painted Horse," he said, his voice piercing the air like an arrow. "In the name of Jesus Christ. *Iesous Christos.*

He motioned to two men who stepped forward and stooped over the wheels that controlled the gray straps.

There was a squealing noise as the coffins began to descend, and someone in the crowd let out a sob. In a moment the coffins were out of sight. Nothing remained but the two oblong holes gaping in the earth. Immediately, three Arapaho men began shoveling the dirt piled a few feet away into the holes.

Max stretched out his arm, and Father John clasped the elder's hand in his own. In the firm grip, he could sense the strength and determination passed down through the generations, like the old stories. "We appreciate what you've been doing for the people," Max said. Then he turned to Father Damien and shook his hand. After the graves had been filled, the elder motioned to the crowd still fixed in place. Little by little people started forward, dropping flowers onto the mounds until they were covered with pink wild roses and yellow tansies and white asters. Then the people began peeling away. Bunched into little groups, they trudged around the other graves toward the parked vehicles.

Father John went to the family, still hovering about, reluctance etched in their faces. Denise's people first, shaking hands, patting shoulders. Then Vera, dabbing wads of tissue against her mouth, her eyes fixed on the rectangle of flowers that lay over her brother's grave. Father John told her again how sorry he was and promised to stop by for a visit soon.

Out on the road, the line of vehicles had started moving around the cemetery in a jerky, stop-and-go motion, plunging one by one out onto Seventeen-Mile Road. There was the sound of engines straining, and puffs of black smoke belched out of tailpipes. Still little groups of people lingered near the gravesites. Max Oldman was on the other side of the cemetery, bent over one of the other graves.

Father Damien stepped away from several members of T.J.'s family and walked over. "Looks like Senator Evans has decided against running for president after all," he said. "Too many things he'd have to explain, I guess. The senate's going to investigate his campaign anyway. Saw him on TV last night. He looks like a beaten man."

"He'll go on," Father John said, remembering what Vicky had said. He clasped the other priest's shoulder. "Don't worry, Damien. We always seem to get enough donations to keep the mission running. The little miracles keep happening."

Damien shook his head, the shadow of a smile playing at the corners of his mouth. Then he turned and hurried toward the line of people still making their way to the vehicles.

"Did you find the photographs?" Vicky's voice behind him. He'd spotted her earlier at the outside edge of the crowd with Adam Lone Eagle, and he'd had to look away. He hadn't seen her walk over.

He turned toward her now. It surprised him, how much he wanted to tell her what he'd worked out in the last few days, to take her into his confidence. They'd worked together on how many cases? Lawyer. Priest. They'd made a good partnership, and he'd always looked forward to holding up a hypothesis to the bright light of her mind. But things were different now, and he felt himself pulling inward. It was like crawling into a cave and pulling a blanket around himself against the cold.

He glanced across the cemetery at Max Oldman, who was standing with his hands clasped behind his back, staring down at a white cross trimmed with plastic flowers. And beyond, near the Jeep, Adam Lone Eagle. Waiting.

Finally, he said, "Not yet."

She looked out in the direction of the Jeep. "I have a new law partner. Adam and I are forming a firm together. We'll be moving into a larger office. I'll be busy . . ."

"I hope it works out for you, Vicky," he said hurriedly, aware that her gaze had shifted in the direction of Max Oldman, and in that instant, he realized that she had also worked it out.

They started off together, threading their way around the mounds, not saying anything. There was no need for words. Max had stopped at another grave when they walked up. Vicky moved to one side of the elder, and Father John took the other side. "Are you all right, grandfather?" he asked.

The elder studied him a moment. His light-colored eyes were suffused in sadness. Then he turned to Vicky. "You did right, granddaughter, sticking up for T.J. The fed could've railroaded that Indian right into prison, if you wasn't there protecting his rights. Maybe T.J. didn't do right by Denise, but he wasn't no murderer."

"Thank you, grandfather," Vicky said, her gaze on the ground a moment, respectful. But in the slope of her shoulders and the way that she finally raised her eyes to the sky, Father John could almost feel the invisible weight lifting from her.

"It was them damn photographs that killed both of 'em," Max said, pivoting about and heading down the row of graves. "This way," he called over his shoulder.

Vicky started after the elder, and Father John fell into step behind. A three-person cortege, he was thinking, reverent and silent, heads bowed, stepping between the mounds topped by wooden crosses and tangled garlands of plastic flowers. They had gone about fifty feet when Max stopped, his head bent toward another white cross. Chiseled into the horizontal bar were the words ELLEN OLDMAN, BELOVED WIFE AND MOTHER. GRANDDAUGHTER OF CHIEF SHARP NOSE. DIED OCTOBER 10, 1965.

"She was my mother. She was the daughter of Bashful Woman." Max took in a gulp of air. "Bashful Woman and Carston Evans. A little half-breed girl that Stands-Alone raised up with his own kids. He had ten, you know, so people sort of lost track. He treated them all the same."

The elder squared his shoulders and tilted his chin toward the sky for a long moment, and Father John had the sense that the old man was praying. Finally Max said, "Bashful Woman was where the deaths started."

Father John caught Vicky's eye for a moment before Max set off again, and they fell into line behind. Right turn, left turn, zigzagging around the mounds until Max found the one he wanted. Etched on the cross were the words: THOMAS BRAVE WOLF. SEPTEMBER 2, 1890–JUNE 6, 1921.

"One of Stands-Alone's boys," Max ran the back of

his hand over his mouth. "He was next to die. Thought he was smarter than his father. Didn't stop there, the deaths." He was walking again, this time Vicky stayed on his right and Father John moved in on the elder's left, bending his head to catch the old man's words. "Twelve years ago, Thomas's grandson, Lester, got himself shot. Found him down by the Wind River with a bullet in the back of his head, like he'd been executed. The FBI agents said he must've gotten mixed up with a bad crowd. They never got the killer."

Max halted next to another grave. On the crossbar, the words LESTER BRAVE WOLF, AUGUST 6, 1948–JULY 1, 1992." In the silence engulfing them, Father John again had the sense that the elder was saying another silent prayer. He offered a silent prayer of his own: "Dear God, have mercy on the souls of the people here. Grant them peace."

A few moments passed before Vicky said: "Please tell us about the deaths, grandfather." Her voice was low and respectful.

Max sucked in his breath and nodded toward her. "They was after justice," he said. "They wanted what was ours. They knew they wasn't ever gonna get the ranch back, so they wanted some compensation. They had proof of how Carston Evans got hold of Arapaho land."

"The Curtis photographs," Vicky said.

"Three photographs and the glass plates they come from. They showed what happened, how Evans shot her, cold-blooded, not a thought about the beautiful life he was taking. Just wanting the land, that's all. It was all there in the pictures, the story of grandmother's death. First Thomas, then Lester thought all they had to do was show the Evans family the proof and they'd give us something of what belonged to us." Max gave a snort of laughter. "Stands-Alone was the one with sense. He said, 'We ain't never getting the land. We got what's important. We got the child. Let it be.'"

"The child," Father John said, almost to himself. He glanced at Vicky, and in her eyes—the brown, knowing eyes of her people—he could almost see what must have happened, and he understood why Bashful's family hadn't taken revenge on Carston Evans. Stands-Alone had made a deal with the man. He could keep the ranch. Stands-Alone would take his sister's child, because the child belonged with the people.

"Long as Stands-Alone stayed alive, nothing happened," Max went on. "Soon as he was gone, his first son, Thomas, paid a visit on the Evans people. Next thing you know, somebody found Thomas out in his field shot in the head. After that, the rest of the clan said, 'We gotta let it be, like Stands-Alone told us.' So that's what happened, till Lester got to thinking he was smarter than everybody else. Evans was running for senator, Lester said, and no way was he gonna want people to know the truth about his grandfather and the ranch. Evans was gonna give us some money now, Lester said. I told him, don't be a hothead. Nothing good's gonna come from this. Next thing I hear, Lester's body is down on the riverbank."

Max turned slowly and faced Father John. "I never told the FBI agents, if that's what you want to know.

What was the FBI gonna do? Go to the brand new senator and say, you know anything about this Indian that got himself shot?"

"What about the photographs and the glass plates?"

"Funny thing, they disappeared."

"Disappeared?" A note of incredulity sounded in Vicky's voice.

"Before Lester went to see the Evans people, he brought the box of plates and pictures over to my place. For safe keeping, he tells me."

"You had the photographs and plates?" Vicky asked.

"After Lester got himself killed, I put the box out in the shed. Maybe someday the time was gonna be right for the truth to come out, but the time wasn't here yet. Then Denise started coming around, asking questions. Always wanting to know how things used to be. She come down straight from Bashful, so I decided she had the right to know about her great-grandmother. I gave her the box. You be the keeper of the past, I says to her."

He paused and shook his head. "Only mistake she made was showing the photographs to that husband of hers. The temptation got too big for T.J., just like it did for Lester and Thomas. Like a monster on their backs that they couldn't carry around no more, so they had to do something about it. Denise knew she'd made a mistake, so a couple days before she died, she comes driving into my place and gives me the box of photos and plates. She says they wasn't safe at her house anymore 'cause Evans was gonna get 'em, one way or another."

The elder turned and started toward the road and the brown pickup parked a few feet back from Father

John's pickup. Farther down the road was the Jeep, Adam Lone Eagle still leaning against the side, hands in his trouser pockets, his gaze not leaving Vicky.

"There's been enough deaths," Max said, evenly. "I went to the library and read a book about Curtis. You know what his family did? Smashed his glass plates. Forty-thousand glass plates smashed to smithereens. All them images of Indians was what took Curtis away year after year and hurt his family, and they hated the images. I figured the plates that Curtis left here been hurting the Sharp Nose family ever since."

When they reached the brown pickup, Father John held the driver's door open while Max climbed inside and settled behind the wheel. The elder dragged a key out of his jacket pocket and inserted it into the ignition. The engine sputtered, then turned over.

"After Denise got killed, I got to thinking that Curtis's people was right." Max kept his eyes straight ahead. "I burned the photographs, then I got out my hammer and smashed all three plates. Yesterday I took little pieces of glass out to Black Mountain and scattered 'em over the earth. They ain't gonna bring any more death." He turned his head up to Father John. His eyes seemed darker, more intense. "You coming to the giveaway?" he asked.

The giveaway—he'd almost forgotten. The family would give away all the new blankets, shawls, and dress goods that their relatives and friends had brought them before the funeral. It was the Arapaho Way.

"I'll be there," he said, closing the door. He stepped back, watching the old pickup pull out and start down the center of the road, pitching from side to side.

"It's over now," Vicky said, her voice small beside him.

"Yes," he said.

"Adam's waiting. I should be going."

When he didn't say anything, she started walking away, then stopped and looked back. "I miss you, John, you know."

He gave her a nod that he hoped conveyed what he was thinking—that he also missed her. He didn't take his eyes away as she hurried down the road and got into the Jeep. Another moment and the vehicle was heading around the drive after Max's pickup, Adam at the wheel.

He waited until the Jeep had turned onto Seventeen-Mile Road and disappeared behind the spray of gold and bronze cottonwood branches. Then he walked over to his own pickup, started the engine, and pulled into the tracks in the dirt road worn by the other vehicles. He would go to the giveaway. He would drink the coffee and eat the plate of roast beef and fry bread and gravy that someone was sure to give him, and he would visit with the family and friends and try to pull from his own heart some words of comfort. Words. He wanted to laugh at the idea. Such a small, fragile bulwark against the enormous sense of loss opening inside him.

He would do his job, he thought, and he would put her out of his mind. He would be the priest his people needed him to be, for as long as they needed him. He would try.

AUTHOR'S NOTE

Chief Joseph. Geronimo. Canon de Chelly. The Vanishing Race. Countless people, not only in the United States but around the world, recognize these photographs that capture the haunting beauty and spirit of the Old West. They are like old friends, imprinted in our consciousness, containing such clarity and detail that the subjects seem to exist in a timeless space of their own.

The photographs are only a few of the magnificent images of western American Indians made by the photographer Edward S. Curtis. From the late 1890s to the late 1920s, Curtis logged 40,000 miles across the West, consumed with the desire to photograph Indian traditions before those traditions had vanished. He traveled by train, boat, horseback, and on foot, packing his favorite Premo camera and cartons of supplies, eventually visiting eighty western tribes and capturing on dry glass plates a total of 40,000 images.

Between 1907 and 1930, Curtis published 272 twenty-volume sets of photographs and ethnographic texts. Each set was accompanied by a portfolio containing large photogravures printed from engraved copper plates. The sets were titled *The North American Indian.*

Volume VI in the series, published in 1911, contains nine photographs of Arapahos on the Wind River Reservation—a very small number considering that Curtis took dozens and sometimes hundreds of photographs of

318

other tribes. The few photographs of Arapahos suggest that he spent only a brief time on the reservation, but there are no historical records that might explain why that was the case.

Neither are there records to document when Curtis actually visited the reservation. Records do show, however, that between 1904 and 1909, he photographed numerous tribes on the northern plains, including the Sioux and Cheyenne, both closely allied with the Arapaho. And in the summer of 1907, he was again on the northern plains photographing the Sioux, Mandan, Arikara, Hidatsa, Apsarokee, and Atsina. It is likely that at some point within this time frame, Curtis traveled south to Wyoming's Wind River Reservation.

For the purposes of the story, I have chosen to place Curtis on the reservation in October 1907. I have also imagined the circumstances that would explain why his stay among the Arapahos had been so brief.

Other parts of the story, however, are based on documented facts, including the unintended and often horrendous consequences of the Indian allotment acts and the fact that one of Curtis's daughters elected to destroy her father's 40,000 glass plates.

Center Point Publishing
600 Brooks Road • PO Box 1
Thorndike ME 04986-0001 USA

(207) 568-3717

US & Canada:
1 800 929-9108